HIDDEN AMONG US

Garrett Hutson

Warfleigh Publishing first edition June 2018

Cover design by Steven Novak

For more information, or to book an event, please contact the author at www.garretthutson.com

ISBN 978-0-9982813-5-3 (paperback)
ISBN 978-0-9982813-4-6 (eBook)

For Paige, who always inspires me

1

Monday, February 20, 1939
New York

Martin Schuller's nerves made his body tingle as he stood at the corner watching the endless stream of vehicles passing, his chin huddled down in the upturned collar of his overcoat. He listened to the snippets of conversation from the crowd—most in English, some in German—and wondered if the man known as *Immergrün* were somewhere among them.

He'd be keeping to himself on the street, Martin thought. *Immergrün*—Evergreen—might be only a few feet away, but he'd be silent in public.

The neon lights of Madison Square Garden lit the street like midday, illuminating the snow flurries swirling around pedestrians and automobiles, each billowing clouds of steam in the cold February air. The overcast sky seemed to glow a dirty yellow, and it appeared low enough that someone standing on the roof of The Garden might reach up and touch it.

The stoplight facing him changed from red to green, and he led the crowd across 50th street toward The Garden, quickening his step as a bitter wind whipped down Eighth Avenue.

A long line of people snaked down the sidewalk from the marquee that announced the German American Bund rally. Martin took his place in line, and as it crept toward the entrance he scanned the crowd.

Their excited expressions filled him with disdain, but he kept his face expressionless. As distasteful as their politics might be, there was nothing illegal about it; and as citizens of a free society, they had the right to assemble and speak their minds—even if that meant denouncing the very freedom they took advantage of.

They were not his concern; his concern was the illegal activities of a few.

At a nearby corner, protesters stood with placards declaring "No Nazi Hate in New York," or "Bund is Un-American." They stood in silence, but glared at the people in the line.

One of them locked eyes with Martin. He was a tall, thin man, with jet black hair showing beneath the rim of his gray fedora, and dark eyes above a large nose. He fixed Martin with a look of such accusation that Martin had to look away. He felt sudden shame over his presence here, realizing it implicitly endorsed the agenda even though he was here on a mission.

None of them could know that, however.

He forced it down. He had a job to do, and this was the only way to do it.

A man a few feet in front of Martin shouted at the protesters in a thick Brooklyn accent. "Go back where you came from, yids! We don't want you here!"

Several of them stared at him, only their eyes betraying their anger.

The man motioned to the woman beside him to stay where she was, and he stomped toward the protesters. He was a short man, shorter than any of the men in the protest, but he was stocky and thick, and he got right up in front of one of the protesters and shoved a fist in his face.

"You want a piece of this, yid? You dare look at me? I'll give you a knuckle sandwich."

The Jewish protester continued to stare down at the angry man, but said nothing.

The short man shoved the protester, who stumbled back and nearly fell into the street before his companions grabbed his arms.

Other men left the line and joined the short man, who was waving his fist at the protesters. They all began to shout at once, screaming obscenities and anti-Semitic slurs. Shouts of agreement began to rise from the others around Martin in line.

"Give 'em hell, boys!" a man right behind Martin yelled. "Teach those yids a lesson!"

Out the main doors of The Garden emerged a dozen or more men in the dark pants and light gray shirts of a Nazi Stormtrooper, minus the swastika armbands that the German party had forbidden from use by the German American Bund. They surrounded the protesters, shouting and shoving.

It was known that Stormtroopers policed the Bund's many campgrounds around the country, but Martin was still surprised to see them appear in the open here in New York.

One of the protesters shoved a Stormtrooper back, and fists began to fly. Passersby on the sidewalk joined in the growing melee, punching and kicking at the Stormtroopers, yelling "Go back to Germany, you Nazis!"

Martin's insides went cold at the sight. *This is what we've come to as a country?*

The bright flash of a camera bulb illuminated everything.

Front page news, Martin thought as he tucked his chin further down inside the collar of his overcoat, and pulled his hat lower. Even with a fake mustache and glasses, he didn't want his face in the papers, not in these circumstances. He stared ahead at the entrance, mercifully not far now.

Police whistles filled the air from behind him a moment later, and cops in long blue overcoats, batons in hand, surrounded the brawl. They grabbed men at random and threw them to the ground.

Martin turned away and shuffled inside.

The sudden shift from winter cold to the hot and stuffy interior of Madison Square Garden was a shock, and he unbuttoned the front of his overcoat. The bigger shock was how full the arena was—the estimates of twenty thousand that he'd heard weren't far off.

He blended in well. His torn and stained overcoat, together with the tweed suit that was frayed at the cuffs and collar, and worn threadbare at the elbows, lent credibility to his cover as a down-on-his-luck laborer in the lingering Depression. And with his sandy blond hair and green eyes, he looked closer to the Nazi image than most of the people here.

Martin scanned the crowd—men and women, old and young, beaming with excitement. He again fought the disgust that welled up unbidden, and focused on his task.

He headed for the far corner. The rendezvous point had been settled as the back left corner, ten feet from the emergency exit, behind the black curtain. He located it, and hung back a short distance, watching.

Rows of American flags lined the back of the stage, and a fifty-foot portrait of George Washington hung behind the center podium. Martin saw a hand-painted banner hanging from the second level, declaring "Stop Jewish Domination of Christian Americans."

Martin ignored the inflammatory rhetoric, and scanned the crowd, face by face. One of them was a newly-arrived German spy. And one of them was a long-sought spy master.

The U.S. government, on principle, did not send spies into foreign lands; foreign governments, however, did not return the favor to the United States—creating the need for men such as Martin to identify and apprehend foreign agents on American soil.

The Department of State's counterintelligence bureau sought out anyone using, or attempting to acquire, a fake U.S. passport—with particular focus on infiltrators from the Soviet Union and Germany. Martin worked for State as a senior analyst and sometime undercover operative.

He saw his colleague Joe Hansen standing nearby in the uniform of a Madison Square Garden usher, hands clasped behind the small of his back, staring out over the heads of the crowd. His eyes found Martin's for a second, and looked away.

Good, he's spotted me. Martin checked that off his mental list.

He noticed a slightly-built young man with neatly-combed dark brown hair, probably no taller than five-foot-seven, looking around in an agitated way.

These *Abwehr* agents were so damned obvious. Almost too easy.

Martin pulled the pipe from the inside pocket of his overcoat and stuck it in his mouth. He didn't fill it or light it, but held it in his mouth as he moved to the rendezvous spot.

That was the signal. If his instincts were correct, the short thin little man was *Immergrün*.

A speaker had taken the podium—not Fritz Kuhn, the keynote speaker, but one of his underlings, a younger redhead—and was delivering a tirade in German-accented English against the "socialist traitor Rosenfeld," the Bund's favorite moniker for President Roosevelt.

The slightly-built man approached Martin, cautious and hesitant. He kept looking around, his motions jerky, and Martin resisted the urge to roll his eyes.

When the man finally stood next to Martin and turned to face the front, he waited in silence for several seconds, as if he were afraid he'd made a mistake.

Get on with it, Martin thought. *Say it, God damn it.*

"Have you got any Prince Albert tobacco?" the little man finally said, in German.

That was his signal.

"No, I'm all out," Martin replied, also in German. "But there is a tobacco shop on 59th Street that sells it."

That was his preset reply, but the young man turned to him with surprise, his deep blue eyes wide and his mouth slightly open.

"Are you Swiss?" he asked.

Martin was used to that question from native speakers—he'd heard it countless times during his two-year stint as a Foreign Service Officer in Austria several years ago. His Pennsylvania Dutch accent sounded vaguely Swiss to most German speakers.

"Alsatian," he replied. The Alsatian dialect and accent were close to the Swiss, sharing an ancient Alemannic origin. They were easily confused.

That seemed to satisfy the diminutive young man. He nodded and looked back toward the stage. "Yes, a great many of you Alsatians are still loyal to the Reich."

"I came to America after the war, rather than stay at home and be ruled by the French," Martin said, reciting part of his official cover biography.

"If I may—why did you not cross the Rhine and live in Germany?"

The young man actually looked troubled by this. It made Martin smile.

"There was work in America," he said. "With the idiots at Weimar, there was no work in Germany."

That earned Martin the intended reaction. The young man grinned and nodded vigorously. "Yes, yes indeed."

An unnatural silence fell over them, and the young man's posture grew stiff, as if he were uncomfortable with how easily he had let his guard down, rather than sticking strictly to the pre-arranged script. He stared at the podium on the stage, as if listening in rapt attention—but Martin could see his eyes shifting among the people crowded in front of them.

Martin waited, reminding himself to be patient. *Let him come to you, Martin.*

The man took a tiny side step closer. He turned his head just slightly toward Martin, and spoke out of the side of his mouth.

"You brought something from Mr. Ketterman, yes?"

"Yes," Martin said, and waited.

Stefan Ketterman, a printer in Yorkville on the Upper East Side of Manhattan, who had come to America from Dusseldorf as an infant forty years ago, had until recently been the most sought-after supplier of falsified U.S. passports in New York—that is, until Martin and his colleagues busted the operation. A deal was cut, and Ketterman now worked for them.

The young man hesitated, nervous. Martin noticed his hands trembling.

"The documents in your possession—they are for Jan Hoffman?"

"*John* Hoffman, but yes," Martin said, giving it the American pronunciation.

"I am he," the young man said.

"But we know you as...?" Martin asked, raising his eyebrows and staring at the little man.

"You know me as Evergreen," the young man whispered. "And you are Augustus Graeter?"

"I am he," Martin said, pleased that Ketterman had given the correct name.

Glancing at Joe Hansen standing about twenty feet away, who nodded and took a step their direction, Martin reached into his overcoat and began to remove the false passport.

Strong arms grabbed him from behind, and a gruff voice whispered in his ear. "Don't move another muscle, bub. FBI—you're under arrest."

Martin glanced at *Immergrün*, and saw a man in a dark trench coat, a cigar clenched in his teeth, holding the young man's arms behind his back.

He looked toward where Hansen stood, saw his colleague's eyes widen for a second; but then Hansen moved farther away and stared forward, hands clasped behind his back.

Seconds later, Martin was tugged backward, through the emergency exit and into the cold of a snow-covered alley. Unseen hands patted him down. *Immergrün* was ushered out a moment later, accompanied by several men in dark trench coats, hats tugged low over their brows.

He heard a car door open behind him, and he was shoved unceremoniously into the back of a vehicle. Two men slid in on either side of him.

The car began to move the second their doors closed.

"What is the meaning of this?" he demanded.

"Don't play dumb with us, *mein herr*," one of them said, and Martin recognized the voice of the man who had initially grabbed him.

"I think there's been some mistake," Martin said, his face flushing with a rush of anger. All the weeks of planning and maneuvering, down the drain just like that. "I'm an American. I think you have me mistaken for someone else."

The man looked across Martin to his companion. "Their accents are getting better," he muttered, then sat back in his seat.

Martin began to panic as he realized the only identification he had on him was for Augustus Graeter, his undercover identity. There was nothing unusual about this—it was necessary, in fact—but at this moment it was a big problem.

Don't say anything more until we get to their headquarters, he told himself. Trying to defend himself now would only hurt him. He'd straighten it all out when they got to the local FBI office.

They drove downtown in silence. The car pulled into an underground parking garage, and the driver lowered his window to show identification to the guard, letting in a blast of frigid air. The guard raised the gate, and they proceeded into the garage.

The car stopped in front of a set of doors. The men on either side of him got out of the car, and ushered him inside.

As they went through the glass doors toward the elevators, Martin looked back and saw two other cars idling behind the car he had just left, but their doors remained closed.

Hutson

2

"I've told you already, my real name is Martin Schuller, I'm an American, and I work for the U.S. Department of State. You interrupted an official operation tonight—a very *important* operation—and I'm sure State will file an official complaint with Director Hoover before morning."

"Tell me again why you don't have any identification to prove this," the FBI agent who had been questioning him for the last twenty minutes asked.

Martin was losing his patience. "Do you normally carry your real identification when you go undercover, Special Agent Sloan?"

"I don't do undercover work," Sloan said, standing. He was about forty, tall and thin, wore a dark blue suit, had brown hair parted on the left and brillantined, and smoked hand-rolled cigarettes.

"If you'll just call the telephone number I gave you, my supervisor at State will verify my identity, and you can let me go."

"We're getting to that," Sloan said, not sounding as if it were a high priority. "Do you mind telling me why the State Department would be conducting 'a very important operation' at the Bund rally in the Garden?"

"I'm sure for the exact same reason your men were there, Special Agent Sloan—to apprehend an *Abwehr* agent. Though I have no doubt our motivations were different."

Sloan looked amused. "Yes, no doubt." He paced the room for a moment, took a drag on his cigarette, allowing ash to fall to the floor.

Martin wondered if it was possible that the FBI agent still didn't believe him.

"I'm just curious why the *State Department* would be intruding into law enforcement. That's our jurisdiction. You fellas at State are diplomats, arntcha?"

Martin took a breath and fought back the defensiveness rising inside him.

"We have jurisdiction over the issuance of United States passports and visas—and the enforcement of laws against the unlawful forging of such documents."

"Uh huh," Sloan said, and moved closer. He leaned down toward Martin. "Who is '*Der Skiläufer*?'" he asked, butchering the German pronunciation.

Martin was unable to keep the surprise from his face; he could see from the amused twinkle in his eyes that Sloan had noticed.

"We don't know."

That was technically true—they had seen the code name in a handful of decoded German communiqués, and deduced it was someone already in the United States, but they had uncovered no leads to who that might be.

None except *Immergrün*, whom they had learned was supposed to meet with *Der Skiläufer*—the Skier—for further instructions.

Sloan shook his head, and leaned down close to Martin's face. "Are you *Der Skiläufer*, Mr. Graeter?"

"My name is Schuller."

"That's right," Sloan said, and straightened back up. "And you're an agent for the State Department. An *undercover* agent. For State."

Sloan's amused half-smile made Martin seethe. They would find out soon enough it was all true—if they bothered to check up on it. He realized he might be here all night.

Hansen's probably already notified the chief, he reminded himself. *Relax, they'll probably be here within an hour.*

12

"Why don't you sit here a while and rethink your story, Mr. Graeter," Sloan said, walking toward the door. "I'll be back in a while, and we'll chat some more."

Martin sat still after Sloan left. The room had no clock, so he wasn't sure how long he waited, but he stayed patient.

Eventually, the door opened and an older man walked in.

"Our apologies, Mr. Schuller—you're free to go," the man said.

Martin nodded and stood. "Thank you, Mr..."

"I'm Special Agent in Charge McGuire," the man said, though Martin noticed he did not extend his hand. "Your colleague Mr. Hansen vouched for you, so we made a couple of calls and verified both of your identities. Our apologies again for the mix-up—just see that you don't get caught up in one of our investigations again, eh?"

Martin didn't reply, and McGuire showed him out without another word.

Hansen was seated at a desk in the large office, drinking coffee from a porcelain mug, and he stood when he saw Martin. He'd changed back into his own clothes—a brown suit over a white dress shirt.

"Sorry, Martin," he said in a low voice. "I didn't see 'em coming. They swooped in real quick."

"It's not your fault, Joe. You talked to the chief?"

"Yep. He was madder than a hornet, let me tell you—said he'd call J. Edgar Hoover himself if he had to."

"He didn't, did he?" Martin said, chuckling at the thought.

"Nope, didn't have to. The Special Agent in Charge here told him he'd take care of it. And here you are, so he must have done like he said."

Something told Martin that Director Hoover might still hear about it, one way or another.

At the front desk, he signed a paper and was given back his overcoat, wallet with false identification, fake mustache, and glasses.

13

He noticed the fake passport that Ketterman made for *Immergrün* was missing.

The FBI agent at the desk shrugged when Martin asked about the missing passport. "This is all that's here."

Martin hesitated, but let it go. It was evidence against *Immergrün*, and the FBI held him.

He and Hansen stepped out into the cold night, and Martin turned up the collar of his overcoat against the biting north wind.

"I take it we're heading back down to Washington tonight?"

Hansen nodded. "We're to go directly to Penn Station and get on the next train."

That was what Martin expected. He was no stranger to having to clear out in a hurry. The only thing back in his room at the boarding house on East 88th Street was a spare set of "Augustus Graeter's" clothes, and he didn't need those any more. There was also a pencil and half a pad of notebook paper—all blank—but that was no loss, either.

It was always good to get home after a week or two on a mission, but usually that feeling was accompanied by a successful conclusion. The success of tonight's operation was tempered by the stolen glory of watching the FBI nab his target. Martin wasn't sure what kind of reception he'd get from his boss tomorrow.

Or what kind of reception he'd get at home.

They managed to catch the last train for Washington at ten-thirty, and sat up in the club car. Neither of them was very talkative, and after a while Martin leaned back, pulled his hat down over his eyes, and tried to sleep.

He dozed fitfully, never falling deep asleep. At one point he raised his hat and looked around; the club car's lights had dimmed, and Hansen slept across the table from him, head leaning against the wall and mouth open, a thin trail of drool dangling from the corner.

Martin lowered his hat back and tried to sleep, with limited success. His mind kept replaying the scene at Madison Square Garden, and kept grasping for things he could have done differently.

No solution presented itself after a seemingly endless loop in his brain. He was jolted awake by the sound of brakes squealing and steam releasing. He looked out the window, and saw the familiar sign for Union Station.

Hansen stretched and yawned, and Martin motioned for the doors. They stepped onto the platform as soon as the train came to a stop and hurried toward the exit. The clock on the wall said it was quarter after two in the morning. They hurried through the grand hall, mostly empty at this hour, and out the large front doors.

They found a taxi cab sitting idle on the corner of Massachusetts Avenue and E Street NW. The driver was asleep, and Martin rapped his knuckles on the window to wake him up.

"Sorry gents," the driver said, getting out and opening the back door. "Where to?"

"Take him home first," Hansen said, pointing his thumb at Martin. "He's married."

"Lucky you," the cab driver said to Martin.

The cab let him off ten minutes later in front of a red brick building on 17th Street NW. Martin handed the driver a couple of dollars, said goodnight to Hansen, and hurried up the front walk and the three concrete steps to the heavy front doors with wrought iron fixtures. Once inside, he rushed up the stairs to the third floor, retrieving the spare key from its hiding place. He opened the door as quietly as possible.

The apartment was dark, but he didn't need light to hang his overcoat and hat on the coat rack. He slipped out of his shoes, and carried them down the hall to make as little noise as possible.

The kids' door was closed, but he eased it open and peeked inside at three little heads on their pillows. He smiled to himself, and quietly pulled the door closed again.

Becky stirred, and then bolted upright as he set his shoes on the floor next to the bed.

"It's just me," he whispered.

She didn't say a word. There was just enough light from the window that he could see her head turned toward him; and though he couldn't see her face, he could imagine the hostile expression it wore at that moment.

"We got in on the last train," he whispered, leaning over the bed to kiss her cheek.

She still didn't say anything, so he concentrated on removing his tie, then unbuttoning his shirt. He knew where the pegs were in the closet, so he didn't need to turn on the lamp to get undressed, hanging his shirt, slacks, and tie in their respective places.

Too tired and irritable to go fishing through his dresser for his pajamas, he slipped into bed in his boxer shorts. In the near darkness, he could make out Becky's figure, still sitting up, and he was pretty sure her arms were crossed. He leaned over and kissed her cheek.

"Happy belated birthday," she said as he turned over and fluffed the pillow beneath his cheek.

She sounded angry. He sighed.

"Thank you. You know that's not important to me."

"It's important to your kids, Martin," she said, her voice rising. He cringed and thought of the three kids asleep on the other side of the wall. "They made a cake for you."

"Didn't you tell them I was out of town?"

"Of course I did. And I told them I didn't know when you'd be home—as usual."

There was venom in those last words, and he felt his pulse quicken in anger.

16

"You know there are reasons."

"That doesn't make it any easier to explain to your kids why you aren't here to thank them for the nice birthday cake they made you. They iced it themselves, even—Marty helped Jackie and Stevie with everything. It was really cute. I wish you could have seen their faces when they realized you wouldn't be home."

Martin's insides tightened, a combination of sadness and anger. He forced his breathing to slow, and his voice to stay calm. "We'll talk about it in the morning."

"Whatever you say, *dear*." Her voice was ice cold, and she flopped over onto her side, her back to Martin.

Martin's temples pulsed, no matter how much he tried to calm down. There was no reason to think the morning's conversation would go any differently than the dozen others they'd had over the last couple of years. He knew her position, and she knew his.

And neither of them was willing to budge an inch.

Hutson

3

Tuesday, February 21

Martin awoke to the smell of frying bacon. He glanced at the clock on the nightstand, and saw that it was just after seven o'clock. Pale winter sunlight peeked around the corners of the window blinds. He was surprised Becky had let him sleep that late.

He got up and put on his robe, then walked to the kitchen. He could hear the kids chattering before he got there, and as he walked through the doorway they shouted almost in unison, "Daddy!"

"Hey there, kiddos," he said with a grin as they ran up and threw their arms around his legs. He rumpled their hair and patted their heads.

"Let Daddy sit down," Becky said, cracking two eggs into the frying pan next to the bacon. "Jackie, Stevie—finish your cream of wheat. Marty, don't eat your brother and sister's breakfast."

"Good morning," he said to Becky, kissing her cheek. She was dressed for housework, in black slacks, red blouse, and flat shoes. Her light brown hair was pulled back in a ponytail.

She gave him a weak smile that didn't extend to her eyes. "Good morning. I knew the bacon would get you out of bed."

"We ate all your birthday cake, Daddy," four-year-old Stevie said with an impish grin, then put a hand in front of his mouth and giggled.

Martin played shocked. *"All* of it?"

Stevie giggled harder, and was joined by his sister, five-year-old Jackie.

"You are in big trouble!" Martin said, reaching over to tickle Stevie's tummy, sending him into convulsions of laughter.

"Mommy said we could," said Marty, the oldest at seven and a half, and a spitting image of his father. He didn't look up from the Sunday funny papers. He was dressed for school, in a light brown sweater over a white collared shirt, and dark brown corduroy pants.

"So...stop...tickling...me!" Stevie said through his laughter. "Tickle Mommy!"

"Don't you dare," Becky said, pointing a greasy spatula Martin's direction. She was smiling, but the look in her eyes said it was for the kids' benefit and she wasn't amused. "Stevie, stop playing around and eat your breakfast."

Martin winked at his youngest son as he took the seat next to him, his back now to his wife. She came around his side a few seconds later, and set a steaming cup of black coffee in front of him without a word.

"How old are you now, Daddy?" Jackie asked. She was dressed for kindergarten, in a dark blue dress and white cardigan sweater. Thick white woolen stockings and shiny black patent leather shoes adorned legs that didn't reach the floor, and swung back and forth beneath her chair. She had her mother's curly brown hair and big blue eyes, which now stared at him wide-eyed.

"Thirty-one," Martin said, and reached out to touch her button nose.

Her face screwed up. "Wow, that's a lot."

"It's the same as Mommy," Marty said. "Remember, dummy?"

Jackie stuck her tongue out at him.

"Marty, don't call your sister names," Becky said, having appeared at Martin's side. She set a plate in front of him, tilted the frying pan in her other hand, and two fried eggs over easy slid onto the plate. She forked up a couple strips of bacon and set them next to his eggs.

"Where did you go on your trip, Daddy?" Marty asked, ignoring his mother's admonition.

Martin couldn't say, as usual. "Well, I'll give you a hint—there was deep snow on the ground there."

Marty thought for a moment. "Must be Canada. My teacher said they have lots more snow than we do."

"Doesn't look like we have any snow here at all today," Martin said.

"It melted last week," Marty said with a shrug.

"Did you have a snowball fight in Canada, Daddy?" Jackie asked.

Martin laughed. "It would have been a lot more fun if I had."

Becky took a seat next to him, a fresh cup of coffee steaming between her hands. "Why don't you run out and listen to the radio for a bit, and let your father and me talk for a while."

"But they didn't finish their cream of wheat like you said!" Marty protested, looking genuinely scandalized as he pointed at his sister's half-full bowl.

"Do as I say," Becky said, her face and voice stern.

"We'll catch up in a little while, sport," Martin said to his eldest son, giving him a quick wink. He play-swatted Stevie on the bottom as the youngest scrambled out the swinging door behind his brother and sister, making him giggle again.

"So where was it this time? New York again? Philadelphia? Or Milwaukee this time? Or can't you tell me, either?"

He wasn't really supposed to, but he hated keeping secrets from her after the mission was already over, and there was no more danger of his cover being blown.

"I always tell you," he said between bites of fried egg. "New York. Just remember you can't say anything."

She let out an exasperated sigh. "I know that drill backward and forward by now, don't you think?"

He didn't take the bait, and chewed on a bite of bacon.

"You were gone more than two weeks this time," she said.

21

"Fifteen days."

"It was the longest yet."

"I couldn't help it, Becky," he said, struggling to keep his patience. "There was a lot involved in this job."

She got up and began collecting the children's bowls and spoons. "Do you ever think about what it's like to sit here, knowing nothing, not even when you're going to be back?" she asked, marching to the sink.

How many times are we going to have this exact same conversation? "What do you expect me to do about it?"

As soon as he asked that question, he cringed. Why did he ask that?

"You know what I want."

He did. And he'd told her more times than he could remember that it would make him miserable.

"I spoke to my father a few days ago. He said the offer is always open; all you have to do is ask."

"No, thank you." His voice was harsher than he'd intended, but he was getting tired of having to defend his position.

"This was not the life I envisioned for us," she said, quieter. She stood at the sink with her back to him.

"We talked about it before I ever took the position," he said, letting his irritation show. "We talked about the absences, the secrecy— everything. There were no surprises. We agreed it was an important promotion, important work. You agreed to *everything*."

She spun around, eyes flashing—but then the fire seemed to go out of them, and she deflated in front of him. "I'm tired, Martin—really tired. Talking about it beforehand and really comprehending what it would be like are two very different things. I didn't know it would be this hard. I thought I could do it, but it's lonely, Martin. Really lonely."

He shook his head. "Don't blame me, it's not my fault. I told you to make friends. You've had five and a half years to make friends here—

five and a half *years* since we came back to Washington. It is *not* my fault if you think you're too good to associate with Washington folk."

He'd gone too far, and he knew it.

Her face flushed crimson, and her fists balled at her sides. "So it's all *my* fault? *My* fault, Martin? How am I supposed to make friends with any ladies I meet when I can't even tell them what my husband does for work?"

His anger deepened. "You are hardly the only woman in Washington who's not allowed to talk about her husband's work."

He forked up the last of his eggs, then flung his chair back and dumped his plate in the sink. He stood in front of her, glaring down at her face. "How many women in this town do you think don't even *know* what their husbands do? Huh? Hundreds at least, maybe thousands. At least you know what I do."

"Oh, don't exaggerate."

"How do you know it's an exaggeration?"

She threw her hands up and turned around. She nudged him away with her hip, then turned on the water and dropped the plug in the drain.

"Life was simpler when you were just an analyst," she muttered.

He took a deep breath. "I'm still an analyst—with additional duties from time to time."

"That we can't talk about—or even *know* about until they're finished. And in the interim, we can't even know *when* they're going to be finished, not until you walk through the door."

He leaned against the counter and watched her washing the dishes.

Maybe it wasn't fair, but how was he at fault for that? They'd talked about it, they'd agreed—three and a half years ago, when the Department expanded its undercover counterintelligence efforts. He'd wanted to jump on the opportunity the minute it was offered, but he'd taken the time to talk it over with his wife first, and to get her agreement.

Sure, maybe he'd pushed her hard to agree, but she *had* agreed. And now it wasn't fair for her to blame him for what it was like.

As she finished drying the last dish and setting it in the cabinet, he put his hands on her shoulders, but she shrugged them away and walked out of the kitchen.

4

Martin got into the office early that Tuesday.

He dressed in a hurry after his fight with Becky, in his good gray suit that she'd had cleaned while he was away. He left a few minutes later, patting his kids on the heads on his way out.

The Executive Office Building was a little less than a mile south of his apartment, straight down 17th Street NW, and except in the worst weather he usually walked.

The pale February morning light glinted off the frost on the sidewalks and bare trees, giving the world an eerie quality before most of the morning commuters began to fill the streets.

It was usually his favorite part of the day, the twenty-five minutes he spent walking alone to and from the office. The quiet solitude, alone with his thoughts, refreshed him. It was a refuge, a respite.

Today, though, he was in a hurry, with work on his mind.

Only a couple of girls in the typing pool were already at work, the clacking of their typewriters echoing in the large, mostly empty room he crossed toward his group's office. The door labelled "Office of the Chief Special Agent" was still locked, but he fished the key out of his suit pocket and let himself in. He turned on the lights and walked to his desk.

He had a report to draft, and he wanted it finished before the boss arrived at eight o'clock.

Hansen arrived at quarter to eight. "I talked with Sam on the way in," he said. "He saw the chief having breakfast over at Fowler's, and he said he was not happy at all."

"That's what I was planning for," Martin said. "You, too, apparently. When was the last time you got to the office before eight o'clock?"

"Touché."

The office secretary, Trudy, arrived at ten to eight. She was a tall thin young woman in her mid-twenties, with black hair fashioned into finger curls along the side of her head and pinned up in the back. She wore a white blouse with ruffles in the front, and a black skirt that came down just below her knees.

"Wow, lots of early birds out this morning," Hansen said. "Actually, I'm glad you're here early—Mr. Schuller and I could use some coffee."

Trudy gave him a look. "The chief called me at home, woke me up, and told me to come in early. Since you're both here already, I figure you gentlemen must have done something bad up there in New York." She took the cover off her typewriter. "You'd better do something to put the chief in a better mood PDQ, or I'm going to bear the brunt of it all day."

She walked over to the big silver coffee pot, took off the lid, and began scooping in coffee from a can.

"We'll take care of it, Trudy," Martin said.

The boss swept in ten minutes later, flinging his overcoat onto the back of Trudy's chair as he rushed past.

"Good morning, Chief," Hansen said, faking a big smile.

"You two, in my office."

Martin picked up his report and followed Hansen into the boss's office.

"Close the door, Schuller."

Martin complied.

"This Bund thing is blowing up in our faces as we speak," the chief said, scowling at them. "J. Edgar Hoover himself called the Secretary at his *house* this morning, complained of us 'trespassing on his turf,' as he put it. Said *we* ruined *their* operation. Threatened to go to the President, even. Our undercover operation has been a tightly-kept secret for *three years!* And now the damned FBI Special Intelligence Service knows about it. So I had to take a call from the Secretary first thing this morning, and assure him that we followed protocol to the letter."

His eyes narrowed further, and he leaned forward and jabbed a finger in their direction. "And you'd better tell me this morning that we followed protocol to the letter, or I'll have you working the slush piles for the rest of your natural lives."

"We followed protocol, Chief," Martin said, and handed him his preliminary report.

The chief leaned back in his chair, reading, and grunting from time to time. At the end, he flung it onto his desk and shook his head.

"According to this, we didn't do a damn thing wrong. We might've guessed the FBI would be all over this, though—they're still smarting from their loss of Griebl."

Martin heard the chief's reprimand loud and clear. What bothered him most was that he couldn't disagree. He *should* have guessed the FBI would be in the thick of things after last year.

The previous spring, the FBI arrested seven German agents in New York, including Dr. Ignatz Griebl, who was suspected to be the ringleader of an extensive spy ring. As a naturalized citizen, Dr. Griebl was released from custody pending indictment by a grand jury. Instead of showing up for his hearing, Griebl boarded a steamship bound for Europe and disappeared.

The FBI had fumed over the loss ever since. Rumor had it there were several German sleeper agents still at large, who could not be identified now that their leader had been allowed to fly the coop.

The chief drummed his fingers on his desk in irritation. "Because of their interference, we still don't know who The Skier is, and the FBI's got Evergreen and we don't." He looked Martin directly in the eye. "You vouch for the accuracy of this report, Schuller?"

"Absolutely, sir."

"Good," the boss said. "I'll encourage the Secretary to stand his ground with Director Hoover. With any luck, this will all blow over by midweek." His tone didn't suggest confidence that it would. "We'll talk more about the operation later." He picked up a file from his desk, and motioned them out without looking back up.

"That wasn't too bad," Hansen whispered to Martin after they walked back into the main office.

Martin just shrugged.

"Trudy! Coffee!" the boss shouted from his desk.

Trudy glared at Martin and Hansen as she rushed to the percolator and poured a cup.

"Sorry, Trudy," Martin said quietly as they passed her on their way back to their desks. She ignored him as she hurried into the boss's office with the steaming cup.

Martin sat back at his desk, unlocked a drawer, and began going through all of the intelligence they'd analyzed before this latest undercover job.

It wasn't clear if this *Skiläufer* was supposed to meet *Immergrün* at the Bund rally, or elsewhere in the city. For all Martin knew, he'd laid eyes on the man at some point.

They didn't even know if he was in New York—in fact, Martin reasoned, if *Der Skiläufer* had been in the country long enough, he might have gravitated toward the Midwest, with its massive German-American communities for cover, and possible source of support.

The mail boy came into their office at eight-thirty, pushing a cart.

"Copies from the diplomatic packets from Germany," he said, laying several thick envelopes on Trudy's desk. He was a tall and skinny boy, about nineteen or twenty, in brown wool slacks and a brown argyle sweater over a white collared shirt. Martin sometimes wondered how someone so young had cleared the security screens for handling classified documents, even in sealed envelopes.

Every week, there was a delivery of intelligence documents that had been sent from their diplomatic missions in Germany—most from the embassy in Berlin, but others from the consulates in Hamburg, Munich, Vienna, and Frankfurt. Trudy sorted them, and assigned them to the half-dozen intelligence analysts in the office.

It still rankled Martin to think of the old U.S. embassy in Vienna as a consulate in Germany. That reality was almost a year old, but he doubted he'd ever get used to it. He'd worked at the embassy in Vienna for two years as a consular officer in the Foreign Service. He loved Austria, and the thought of it under Nazi rule made his skin crawl.

Becky had loved Austria, too. Little Marty was an infant when they arrived in the fall of 1931, and everything seemed like a great adventure. Looking back, those were the happiest years of their marriage. They travelled all over central Europe—Hungary, Czechoslovakia, Switzerland, and Germany.

They visited Germany on several occasions—both before and after the Nazis took over in January 1933—and the changes there had been swift and obvious. They'd both worried that Martin would be assigned to one of the missions there when his two-year assignment in Vienna ended; both hoped for an assignment in Switzerland instead. Much to his surprise, Martin was offered a position back in Washington in the fall of 1933, as an Intelligence Analyst.

He'd enjoyed the work, in spite of the tedium involved. He loved looking for clues and patterns in the raw data.

For her part, Becky had seemed happy to be back in the U.S.—she was seven months pregnant with their second child when they returned—but she hated Washington as much the second time around

29

as she had when they were first married. She complained about Washington even before his promotion to agent in October 1935.

Martin sometimes wondered if they would have been happier staying in Europe. If he'd turned down the Intelligence job and instead taken an assignment in Germany or Switzerland, would Becky be happier now? He somehow doubted it. She wanted to return home to Philadelphia more than anything, he knew.

And that was the root of their problems—he was happy here in Washington, happy with his work, happy with their life, and didn't want to change any of it. And she was unhappy with all of it.

The boss called Martin and Hansen into his office later that morning.

"Overall—aside from our success with the printer Ketterman—this job was a disaster."

"It wasn't a total loss, Chief," Martin said. "Since I was dragged out by the FBI along with Evergreen, we can be reasonably certain my cover as Augustus Graeter has not been compromised—if anything, it's been enhanced. The next time the *Abwehr* sends an agent, I can resume that identity without suspicion. We can add that to the cover, that Graeter was persecuted by the FBI for his 'loyalty to the cause.'"

The chief considered this a moment. "You're probably right. But that could be months. In the meantime, the FBI gets to interrogate Evergreen, and we likely won't get an opportunity."

Martin didn't argue. "My feeling is that *Der Skiläufer* has built a cell, or wants to build a cell, and the Nazis will continue to send agents for that purpose."

"But that's still conjecture," the boss said.

"That's true."

"So let's go over what happened with this job, step by step."

**

30

After spending more than an hour going over every detail of the operation, all fifteen days' worth, the boss seemed only slightly less peeved. "Damn FBI," he muttered at one point.

When they'd finished, he closed the file and shoved it aside. "Let's not dwell on this, shall we? Get back to work, and we'll get them next time."

"Thank you, Chief," Martin said, and was echoed by Hansen.

"Late lunch off the cart?" Hansen asked. "Or do you want to run out and grab a bite at the tavern?"

Martin shook his head. "I want to get back into the routine. I'll get a sandwich off the cart. Want me to bring you something?"

"That's alright, I'm going to run out and get something. Catch up with you later."

Part of Martin felt bad about not going along with his younger colleague. But on days after he returned from a stint undercover, he mostly wanted to catch up on his regular work.

He knew Hansen envied the amount of time Martin spent in the field—it was usually only after Martin secured a rendezvous with a target that Hansen was sent in to help nab the Nazi spook. To him, sticking around the office was dull and unexciting—to Martin, it was a welcome return to normalcy.

He found the lunch cart one floor down. A pair of office girls stood in the front of the line, ordering sandwiches from the middle-aged lady operating the cart. Behind them stood a trio of gossiping effeminate boys, the so-called "faeries" from the clerical pool, not particularly secretive about their alternative lifestyle.

Martin always cringed a little bit when he'd find himself in an interaction with the "fine sisters" as they called themselves, not terribly fond of their mannerisms; but he also learned a thing or two by eavesdropping on their gossip, though he would never admit that.

When he reached the cart, he got a liverwurst sandwich and an apple and carried them back to his desk. He always took the stairs one flight rather than waiting for the elevator, and he emerged onto his floor at the far end of the typing pool, by the curtained off area under a sign that read "Colored Typists."

It seemed silly to Martin that black typists and clerks were hidden away from white office workers—a vestige of the days when Washington was still a small southern town. It was hardly that anymore, and hadn't been for a quarter-century. If the obvious presence of the "faerie boys" didn't disturb the sensibilities of most of the staff at State, Martin didn't understand why being in proximity with a black typist should.

To Martin, it seemed a little too reminiscent of the way the Nazis now kept the Jews hidden from public life, away from "real Germans."

Trudy had put a stack of documents in his inbox from this morning's delivery, and he perused them while he ate.

It consisted of mostly routine reports of the movements and communications of various Nazi officials, and some interesting tidbits about communications between Berlin and various far-right political groups in Hungary and Romania. Nothing mentioning *Immergrün* or *Der Skiläufer*, or any of the dozen or so other code-named *Abwehr* agents that they'd been tracking.

Still, Martin jotted down some notes, things to watch for in the coming weeks, and things to double check in his files.

He immersed himself in his work, and the feeling of normalcy returned.

5

Wednesday, February 22, 1939

The man known as *Der Skiläufer* paced the room in irritation. A small lamp on the desk provided the only illumination. A little gold clock next to it chimed the three-quarter hour. He went to the window, pulled back the heavy velvet curtain, and looked out.

It was a clear, cold night, and a crescent moon provided a small amount of silvery light that shone off the snow on the hills.

At least that much had gone his way—a clear night made for better transmissions.

Immergrün had been expected yesterday, but he failed to show up. When he did not arrive by noon today, *Der Skiläufer* had been forced to make phone calls.

The first call had been to his man in New York, who had arranged the safe house and the false papers. He reported that *Immergrün* left the safe house on Monday evening as planned, and had been escorted by a trusted courier to Madison Square Garden to meet the printer's man.

Der Skiläufer had expected that much—his man in New York would have contacted him already if something had gone wrong before the rally, unless he himself had been arrested. That was one small relief, anyway.

But that forced him to make additional calls, to the loyalists in New York that he knew to have attended the Bund rally. None of them knew his real identity, but it still made him nervous to speak on the phone with them. If one or more of them had been turned—become double-agents for the government—his call could be traced.

He kept the calls brief, to avoid that possibility.

The third one he called reported seeing *Immergrün* and the printer's agent—a man named Graeter, about whom they knew little—being nabbed by a bunch of men in trench coats. Rumor said it was an FBI sting.

Der Skiläufer had cursed and slammed down the phone receiver. Now he had to report the arrests to Berlin.

His fingers drummed on the desk. This would set him back months. Though he'd heard there was a nationalist in Philadelphia who offered to carry secret documents to the German ambassador in Washington, *Der Skiläufer* was wary. An American or permanent resident making frequent visits to the German Embassy would draw FBI scrutiny—and that was a risk *Der Skiläufer* was not prepared to take.

Not after last year's near-miss.

No, he needed a German national to do it. He needed a trained *Abwehr* agent.

At five minutes before midnight, he left the room, a book in hand. It was a large tome in German, by the nineteenth-century nationalist philosopher Johann Gottlieb Fichte. He walked down a long hall to a door, unlocking it with a brass key from his pocket.

A narrow stairway rose in front of him, and cold air chilled him as he climbed into the attic.

The attic was dark, save for a tiny bit of reflected moonlight that came through the small round glass windows at either end. At the top of the stairs, he reached out and pulled a chain; a single bare lightbulb illuminated the room. A key from his pocket unlocked a trunk sitting on a table in a corner. The radio set sat inside, a collection of wires and switches and knobs.

It was two minutes before midnight, according to his watch, so he switched on the power, and listened to the soft hum and whine of the radio transmitter coils warming up. Today had been the twenty-second, so he turned to page twenty-two of the book.

At precisely midnight, he typed out his code name, *Der Skiläufer,* in Morse code. Then he waited.

Ten seconds later, the radio received the beeps and dashes identifying a U-boat out in the Atlantic. He replied with a series of Vs, to verify signal strength, and allow them to tune in. They replied 'GV'— the first letters of the German words for "Go Ahead."

It was Wednesday, the fourth day of the week, so every letter of his message would be replaced by the fourth letter after it in the alphabet—A became E, B became F, and so on.

He tapped out the first line of page twenty-two in the book, in code; this was to verify his identity, and prove that he was not someone else who had captured his radio transmitter. He waited, and about twenty seconds later, the U-boat sent the message "Verified," in the same code.

He began tapping out his message in German, in the code.

> *Evergreen apprehended by Federal agents two days ago. Contact not made.*
> *Replacement needed at earliest available date. Better training requested. The Skier, over.*

He took a certain satisfaction in criticizing the inadequate training the *Abwehr* provided to its agents sent to this country. He knew part of the reason was that the *Abwehr*—German military intelligence—did not risk its regular agents on a country with which Germany's interests were primarily political rather than military.

For *Der Skiläufer*'s purposes, ideologically loyal Nazis were required, and these were rare in the military establishment. Therefore, the *Abwehr* had to recruit and train from outside of itself for the missions to the United States, and the training they provided was haphazard and rushed.

He refused to blame himself for that. The *Abwehr* alone was responsible for the quality of its recruits, and the quality of their training regimen. At some point—he hoped—the High Command would question their repeated failures in this theater. Until then, all he could do was send negative commentary and hope that someone in Berlin was paying attention to it.

A moment after he finished his transmission, the radio beeped out the words, "Message received" in German, without code.

There was no further communication.

He switched off the radio, turned off the light, and marched back downstairs.

6

Wednesday, March 15, 1939

Martin sat at the table in the kitchen with the newspaper. The headline shouted in big, bold letters:

NAZIS INVADE CZECHOSLOVAKIA

Slovakia Declares Independence; Bohemia & Moravia German 'Protectorate'

The Wehrmacht had plowed across the entirety of Bohemia and Moravia in a single morning; Czech resistance had collapsed almost immediately. Martin shook his head as he read.

It had been inevitable, he knew. After the Sudetenland had been partitioned from Czechoslovakia last fall and given to Germany, everyone in the intelligence community had agreed it was only a matter of time.

Still, it angered him. Prague was a beautiful city, with wonderful, friendly people. He and Becky had visited there several times. The Czechs had been so happy to finally have their own country after centuries of Austrian rule. Now that had been stolen from them in one day.

Becky looked over his shoulder as she cleared the kids' breakfast bowls from the table. "It's so sad. Those poor people."

Martin nodded with a grunt. "Hitler's a megalomaniac," he grumbled. "He wants to rebuild the old Austrian empire, under unified German rule."

"Do you know anyone at our embassy in Prague?"

Martin shrugged. "Not really. I know some by reputation, that's all."

She left him to read the full-page article in silence.

After a full column and a half about the invasion and the declaration of the new German "Protectorate of Bohemia and Moravia," the article dove into details about last fall's Munich Agreement, and the resultant German annexation of the Sudetenland.

In true neutral American journalistic fashion, it described the Sudetenland as "...a ring of mountainous territory on the edges of Bohemia, stretching along the German and Austrian borders. A traditionally German area, at the time of annexation, the Sudetenland was home to 3,200,000 ethnic German inhabitants, and approximately 750,000 Czechs."

Practically making Hitler's case for him, Martin thought, recalling how the newspapers last fall had equivocated in similar fashion over the Munich Agreement. Was it any wonder the American people had viewed the events in Europe with ambivalence?

At least there was a mention that 115,000 Sudeten Czechs and 30,000 Sudeten Germans had fled the Sudetenland after the Munich Agreement. This detail was followed by a dry observation: "It is not known what fate will face those who fled the Germans in November, now that German occupation has spread to the entirety of Bohemia and Moravia."

Martin had little doubt. Those who had fled before were probably intellectuals, left-leaning political activists, or Jews—all targets of the Nazi regime.

He finished the article, folded the newspaper, and put it under his arm.

"It's going to be a busy day at the office because of this," he said.

"Did you have any indication this was coming?" Becky asked.

"Nothing definite. But we knew it was only a matter of time. The Czechs haven't had time to rebuild border defenses after losing the Sudetenland, so they were exposed. And like I said, Hitler's a megalomaniac." He shook his head. "With the way he's been ranting about Danzig since the first of the year, it seemed his focus had shifted to Poland. Maybe that was deliberate. Or maybe he's just a madman."

He kissed her on the cheek and hurried out the door.

It was a cool morning as he hurried down 17th Street NW toward the Old Executive Office Building, and the clear blue sky hinted at a mild spring day to come. He regretted that they would probably be too busy to go out for lunch.

He ran into Joe Hansen while cramming onto the crowded elevator.

"It's gonna be a busy one today," Hansen said out of the corner of his mouth as they exited onto their floor and began to cross the typing pool. "How many times do you think some higher-up is going to ask what we knew?"

"Too many," Martin said.

It was ten minutes before eight o'clock when they found the office door already unlocked, and Trudy busy at her desk.

"Coffee's already made," she said without looking up from her typewriter.

They saw the chief already at work in his office as they passed on their way to their desks. Martin wasn't surprised.

"You suppose we'll have to work over the weekend because of this mess in Czechoslovakia?" Hansen asked.

"I could only hope," Martin said.

At Hansen's questioning look, he explained, "We have to go to Philadelphia this weekend, for some charity event for Becky's mother. A white tie gala, so I have to rent tails and a bowtie." He shook his head, and added with an eye roll, "Daughters of the American Revolution."

"That doesn't sound so bad to me," Hansen said. "I'm sure you'll have good food."

Martin ignored him. "It's for a good cause, at least—a new pediatric wing for one of the hospitals up there."

"Enjoy the night out. You don't get many of those, you old married man."

Martin chuckled as he sat down to work.

Saturday, March 18

Martin stood in front of the floor-length mirror in one of the many guest bedrooms of his in-laws' enormous Philadelphia townhouse, trying for the fourth time to knot the white bowtie. He'd never gotten the hang of bowties, and hated wearing one because of that. He didn't care if it was a self-reinforcing cycle.

The black jacket and pants he'd rented fit well enough, but the jacket was straight and untailored, so he knew it wouldn't look quite as nice as the other men's jackets at the gala. He told himself that he didn't care.

He did care about the knot of the damn bowtie, however, and it refused to cooperate. He tugged it out from the starched collar of the rented white shirt with an irritated jerk of his hand, and mumbled curses to the blasted thing under his breath.

"Here, let me do it," Becky said, coming up behind him. She put her hands on his shoulders and turned him toward her, taking the ends of the bowtie and threading them through his collar, then deftly tying them.

She looked stunning in a floor-length ball gown of shimmering gold silk with a neckline that revealed just enough cleavage, and half sleeves that met the elbow-length white gloves. Her cinnamon-colored hair was curled and bound up at the back of her head, revealing her long neck. Her eyes were level with his, thanks to three-inch heels.

"There, all finished," she said, taking a step back and admiring her handiwork. He leaned toward her to kiss the side of her neck, but she pulled back. "My parents could knock at any moment."

He stifled a sigh, and turned back toward the mirror. The bowtie was the most put-together part of his appearance. He took a comb and straightened the part on the left side of his blond hair, and decided this was as good as it was going to get.

"We should get going," Becky said, picking up a small gold sequined purse that matched her gown. "My parents will be waiting."

"You go ahead, I'm going to say goodnight to the kids."

He held the door open for her, ignoring the irritated look she gave him, and closed it behind them. As she went down the stairs, he turned the opposite direction and went down the hall to the other guest rooms. He knocked on the first door, then opened it and went in.

"Hey buddy," he said to his eldest son as he walked in.

Marty lay on the large bed, propped up on a pillow, a Hardy Boys book open in his lap—*The Mystery of Cabin Island*. He looked up, and his eyes widened in surprise.

"Hi Dad—you look really sharp."

"Thanks, sport. Don't get used to it."

He walked over and rumpled his son's hair, then leaned down and kissed the top of his head. "Be good, and don't cause any trouble for Mrs. Kennedy." His in-laws' housekeeper had been with their family for thirty years, and she was getting arthritic in her old age.

"I will," Marty said, and turned back to his book.

"Good night," Martin said, closing the door.

The next room was shared by his two younger children, who sat on the floor with a French Bulldog named Rex, about forty wooden blocks spread out in front of them—twenty-six of them with letters, ten with numbers, and a few assorted punctuation marks.

41

"Hey there, kiddos," he said, tickling each of them in turn as they giggled. Then he kissed their heads, admonished them to be good for Mrs. Kennedy, and wished them good night.

As he descended the stairs, he saw Becky and his in-laws standing in the middle of the hall, an enormous room with black and white marble floor, and a grand crystal chandelier hanging from the twenty-foot ceiling. He took Becky's hand and kissed her cheek.

His mother-in-law smiled at him. "You look very nice this evening, Martin."

He knew she was just being polite, but he smiled back and nodded at her. "Thank you, Mother Walsh."

His father-in-law shook his hand. "Care for a cigar for the ride?" He held out a large Cuban.

Martin hated smoking, and it didn't matter if it was a pipe, cigar, or cigarette. "No, thank you, sir."

"Suit yourself, I'm having one." Walsh motioned for the butler, who approached and clipped off the end of the cigar, then held the match while his employer inhaled.

He puffed out a cloud of smoke in Martin's general direction.

William Grant Walsh, Esquire, was not the type of man to concern himself with his son-in-law's preferences.

"Ladies, if you're ready," he said, motioning toward the door, then placed his hand on his wife's back to guide her out. "The Rolls is waiting."

The Rolls tonight, instead of the Duesenberg. Martin couldn't help the sarcastic thought.

A black Rolls Royce limousine sat idling at the curb in front of the townhouse, and the middle-aged black chauffeur hurried to open the back door. Mrs. Walsh got in first, followed by her daughter, then her husband, and Martin last.

"How are you this evening, Peter?" Martin asked the chauffeur when it was his turn to enter the car.

42

A hint of smile came to the corners of the chauffeur's mouth. "I'm just fine, thank you, sir."

Martin patted his arm as he stooped his head and climbed into the back of the limousine. He could see the hint of a scowl briefly cross his father-in-law's face, and he had to stop himself from grinning.

The gigantic ballroom was packed with well-heeled guests. Martin took Becky's arm as they made the rounds with her parents. She was a natural at these sorts of things, smiling and engaging in conversation, but he felt as uncomfortable and awkward as a monkey in a suit.

A parade of businessmen, lawyers, doctors, and their wives passed in an endless blur. Becky seemed to intuitively remember their various connections—possibly she'd known some of them since she was a girl— but after more than a hundred new names and faces, Martin was hopelessly lost.

But he never really cared all that much about these swanky, self-important "friends" of his in-laws.

A waiter passed with a tray of champagne flutes, and Martin grabbed two, hopeful a slight buzz might make the evening more tolerable. He handed one to his wife, and clinked their glasses together. "Cheers."

She smiled and took a sip. He took more than a sip.

His in-laws had moved over to a group of their fellow senior citizens, who were listening in rapt attention to a rotund and balding man, his thin hair unnaturally black and slicked back—leaving them momentarily alone.

Martin took a deep breath. "How much did you promise from us, again?"

"Just fifty dollars."

Martin exhaled hard. That was a lot of money—almost two days' salary.

Becky seemed to read his mind. "It was the minimum donation. You know I couldn't refuse Mother's request—she would have been mortified. Besides, you said yourself—it *is* a good cause."

"I know."

She smiled at him and touched his arm. "I know how much you hate these things," she said. "Thank you for not complaining and making the evening miserable for me."

Instead, I'm the one who gets to be miserable, he thought. But he just smiled and said, "You're welcome."

His father-in-law motioned them over, and Martin sighed as he took Becky's arm and walked toward them.

"Rebecca, Martin—I'd like to introduce Congressman Barbour. Congressman, may I present my daughter and son-in-law, Mr. and Mrs. Martin Schuller."

"How do you do?" the congressman said, taking Becky's hand first, and then shaking Martin's.

"This is my son-in-law who works for the State Department," William Walsh said, a strange sort of gleam in his eye.

Martin was immediately suspicious.

"Ah yes, I've heard much about you, Mr. Schuller," the congressman said. "How are they treating you over there at State?"

"Very well, sir."

"I understand you're well versed in research and analysis," the congressman said. "Ever consider switching to the Legislative branch? I could find a position on my staff for someone with your skills."

There it was. If they couldn't lure him to Philadelphia with an office job at William Walsh's law firm, then they would make him a "better" offer in Washington.

He was about to refuse outright, when he noticed the warning look in Becky's eyes. Part of him still wanted to refuse, but at the last second he equivocated.

"I would need to know more about what you're looking for, Congressman," Martin said, hating the sound of the words as they came out of his mouth.

The congressman pulled a card from his jacket.

"Call my office on Monday, make an appointment. Perhaps we could sit down for lunch?"

Lunch with a congressman—whose time was precious these days—was a rare commodity. William Walsh must have pulled a lot of strings. Or been owed a lot of favors. Martin wondered which.

"I will do that, sir," he heard himself saying, and he cringed on the inside.

He glanced at Becky, and saw that she was beaming.

The congressman had already turned to the older gentleman standing next to him, and was discussing that gentleman's business. William Walsh stood with them. Becky and her mother moved a few feet away, in a circle of ladies who glittered with diamonds.

Martin found himself momentarily alone, and he took a large swig of his champagne.

"That's quite an offer you received, Mr. Schuller," he heard a voice say behind him and to his right, and he turned to see a dapper and dashing man only a few years older than himself, tall and thin, with a wave of thick black hair, strikingly blue eyes, and a pencil-thin mustache. For half a second Martin wondered if he were standing in front of Errol Flynn.

The resemblance was only superficial, Martin realized almost right away. The man looked familiar otherwise, but Martin couldn't be sure if they'd met or not.

The man seemed to sense his uncertainty, and laughed in a self-deprecating sort of way that somehow seemed both natural and purposeful at the same time.

"I see that I have the advantage. Maximilian Showalter," he said, extending his hand and giving Martin a dazzling smile. "We were introduced earlier, but it was in the middle of about a dozen other people to whom you were being introduced for the first time, so I do not blame you in the least for forgetting."

"My apologies," Martin said, genuinely embarrassed. He normally had an excellent memory for faces, and usually for names as well, but the night's introductions seemed to have become a bit of a blur.

"Not at all," Showalter said, still with that dazzling smile. "I have known Congressman Barbour for years, and he does not make idle offers. If he asked you to call his office, he meant it."

Something clicked in Martin's mind. "The Showalter Glassworks, in Easton," he said.

"That's right," Showalter said. "Congressman Barbour has been one of our more steadfast friends in Washington over the years, and we are proud to give him our support in return."

Martin wondered just how the congressman had been a "steadfast friend" to the Showalter Glassworks.

Showalter supplied the answer unbidden. "You may have seen in the newspapers several weeks ago that our new plastics division was awarded a contract to manufacture airplane windshields for the Army Air Corps. Of course I can't disclose details—parts of the contract are classified—but as a result we have been able to hire several hundred workers in our plastics division; proving that industry, and not government hand-outs, are what will end this Great Depression our country has foundered in."

Looking around the room at the guests in attendance, Martin had no doubt there were few fans of the New Deal in this ballroom.

"Do you know much about plastics, Mr. Schuller?"

"Only a little," Martin confessed.

"We live in an amazing time, Mr. Schuller," Showalter said, exuding enthusiasm. "Plastics are revolutionizing manufacturing. They are lighter, and yet more durable, than glass; resistant to shattering, which is important in the cockpits of fighter planes and bombers. They won't replace glass for everything—plastics are not very heat resistant, for example—but at twenty thousand feet in the air, heat is hardly a concern."

"That's very interesting," Martin agreed. He supposed it probably was interesting, though his discomfort with the small-talk made it less so at the moment.

"Indeed. Well, I could go on about business all night, but that wouldn't be very polite of me, in this setting. Perhaps we'll have the opportunity to discuss it in more depth the next time I call on Congressman Barbour in Washington."

It wasn't phrased as a question, but the single raised eyebrow suggested Showalter was looking for confirmation.

Martin was noncommittal. "Perhaps we will."

Showalter nodded with a brief chuckle. "Did I hear that you are Mr. William Walsh's son-in-law?" he asked.

"That's right."

"We've done some business with the firm of Walsh and Huddleston over the years. I've met him on several occasions, both business and social." He motioned around the room with his half-full champagne flute.

That didn't surprise Martin. His father-in-law seemed to be connected in some way to everyone in the room.

"If you should go to work for Congressman Barbour, I'm sure we'll have plenty of opportunities to get to know each other. We recently had the congressman and his family, along with some of his senior staff, on a little retreat at our place up in the Poconos. A very enjoyable week."

Martin started to feel that he was getting a bit of a hard sell; he shifted his feet and drained his champagne, uncomfortable.

Showalter regarded him with an unreadable expression. Martin knew he was expected to say something in response.

"That sounds very nice."

"Yes, well—if you'll excuse me, I have to find my wife before dinner. It was a pleasure to meet you, Mr. Schuller. Until next time."

He shook Martin's hand and slipped away.

Martin turned back to the group, and found himself in the middle of a tense political conversation. He looked for an opportunity to step away, but he saw his father-in-law watching him, so he looked around for a nearby waiter to signal for another glass.

"Dr. Atherton, you can't seriously think that Keynesian economics—government spending—can do more for the economy than the free market," a distinguished-looking middle aged man was saying to a shorter, older man across the circle.

"Of course I do," Dr. Atherton replied, looking both annoyed and at the same time happy to be contrarian.

This could be interesting, Martin realized. The other man—*Oh God, what was his name? Ballard? Yes, that was it, Ballard, an Executive Vice President of something or other at Baldwin Locomotive*—scowled at Dr. Atherton.

"Six years ago, twenty-five percent of this country's workers were without jobs, and after six years—*six years*—of Keynesian economics in the form of New Deal spending programs, seventeen percent are *still* out of work. That hardly sounds like progress to me. At that rate, we'll be out of the Depression by, oh, 1951."

The other men around the circle laughed. Dr. Atherton wore a strange sort of smile.

"To be completely accurate, Mr. Ballard, it *is* progress to go from twenty-five percent to seventeen percent unemployment," he said. "Perhaps we would have made more progress if we had taken the Keynesian approach further, as the Germans did."

There were stunned expressions all around, and several seconds of silence. Martin glanced at his father-in-law, and saw him close his eyes and take a deep breath.

"The German government has nationalized whole industries!" Ballard said, red-faced. "For declared anti-communists, the Nazis are awfully fond of state control of industry."

"Only certain critical industries—and you missed an important detail, Mr. Ballard," Dr. Atherton said, finger raised. "The German government fully compensated the former owners. The Bolsheviks in Russia did not."

"Immaterial!" Ballard argued. "It's still a socialist model, and socialism never works."

A smug smile crept across Atherton's mouth. "If that is so, then why have the Germans gone from thirty percent unemployment to full employment, in the same six years that we have gone from twenty-five to seventeen percent?"

"That's not entirely true," Martin said, before he could stop himself.

Several sets of curious eyes turned his direction, and Martin felt his heart begin to race from the sudden attention.

"What is not entirely true?" Atherton asked, a deep scowl furrowing his wrinkled brow.

"The Germans don't actually have full employment," Martin said.

"Poppy cock! All of the reports say they do."

"That's because their employment figures only count German citizens," Martin replied, trying to keep the nerves from his voice. "They don't count an unemployed worker if he's a Jew, for example, or a foreign national married to a German citizen, or a colonial—" he hesitated before adding, "—or a single woman, for that matter, citizen or not. They only count the men."

"My son-in-law works at the State Department," William Walsh said.

"Ah!" several of the men said, approving.

Atherton looked annoyed, his face turning red. "Well—why should they count non-Germans? Perhaps if we didn't count our unemployed immigrants, and counted only real Americans, our figures would be better."

"We have always employed immigrant labor at our factories," Ballard said.

"So have we," another said.

Atherton's voice was icy as he replied. "Perhaps if you didn't, there wouldn't be so many unemployed Americans."

Ballard ignored Atherton, and turned to the man next to him. "We should play a round of golf next weekend. The club will open the course next week." He put his hand on the man's shoulder and they started to turn away.

"I believe your country club removed the restriction on Catholics a couple of years ago, didn't it, Mr. Ballard?" Dr. Atherton called after him.

Ballard stopped mid turn, and shifted his gaze back over his shoulder at Dr. Atherton. "Yes, it did. Declining membership—caused, no doubt, by the Depression—made the ridiculousness of that silly restriction obvious to the board."

"So how do they keep out the undesirable ethnicities, if I may ask?" Atherton said, one eyebrow arched. "French or German Catholics might be acceptable, one would suppose—but how would you avoid the Polacks and I-talians?"

Ballard gave Atherton a dubious look. "I doubt we would have many applicants of that variety. Now if you'll excuse us?"

Ballard and his companion walked away.

Martin noticed with irritation that his father-in-law had already slipped away with a couple of others, leaving him alone in the group as it broke up. He saw Dr. Atherton looking his direction.

"I was in Germany last spring, Mr. Schuller," Atherton said. "My wife and I took a tour of the continent after my retirement. I was very impressed with the optimistic spirit we saw in Germany, all over the country. And no one there was lacking for work, unlike here."

Martin said nothing, gave him an awkward nod, and hurried off to find his wife.

They were seated a short time later at large round tables with ten place settings. Martin and Becky sat with her parents; and with William Walsh's law partner, Roderick Huddleston III, Esquire, and his wife. A pair of doctors from the hospital and their wives rounded out their table. Thankfully, none of them were Dr. Atherton.

As Hansen had predicted, the food was exquisite, in seven courses. Martin barely participated in the conversation, and had to struggle to appear interested in the subjects. The dinner seemed to drag on forever, though the clock indicated it was less than two hours.

He had to stop himself from indulging in more than two glasses of wine, fearing to say something that might make him look foolish.

Becky, as always, was able to navigate the conversation effortlessly, engaging in one subject after another with everyone at the table.

He had always admired that about her. It was one of the main things that attracted him to her at the University of Pennsylvania all those years ago, even more than her physical beauty. The fact that someone like her found someone like him—a grocer's son from Reading— interesting enough to talk to...well, he had been mesmerized. Never shy, Martin had nonetheless found himself unable to form the words to ask her on a date; and yet, somehow it was she who put those words in his mouth, using her charm and skill at conversation to move him to that action.

It hadn't felt like a manipulation, and yet in retrospect he supposed it had been. So many times over the intervening years he had rebelled at her attempted manipulations, which had earned her anger and scorn.

Watching her now at this table, with her easy charm and grace, he was as taken with her as ever.

He knew without a doubt that she was behind her father introducing him to Congressman Barbour, and the fact that the congressman knew he worked at State; but at this moment, watching her beautiful smile charm the table, he didn't mind so much.

And he also knew without a doubt that he would call on the congressman in Washington on Monday.

7

Monday, March 20, 1939

"Congressman Barbour is a Republican, you know," Hansen said.

"I know," Martin said.

"He's one of the biggest crybabies in Congress, throwing temper tantrums about the New Deal. He thinks the free market should be allowed to just correct itself. You can't be seriously considering his offer."

Martin shrugged. He'd expected this kind of reaction from Hansen, the office's resident liberal Democrat.

"I'm just going to hear him out, see what he has to say."

"But you love this work. Why would you want to give it up?"

That was true. Martin loved the undercover work, enough to endure Becky's increasing complaints about it over the last few years. And he loved his mission, keeping the country safe from infiltration by German agents. He didn't want to give any of it up.

But he'd promised Becky as late as this morning that he would give the congressman a call and set up a meeting with him.

"We'll see, OK? Now, let's get back to work—we've still got this cell leader out there somewhere, *Der Skiläufer*, and we can't slack."

Hansen nodded and looked back at the papers on his desk. After a moment, he looked up again, his head cocked to the side.

"Have you ever considered whether *Der Skiläufer* is just a ruse? False information meant to send us on a wild goose chase?"

"What would the Germans gain by doing that?"

"I don't know," Hansen said, shrugging. "They pulled stunts like that with the British; the French, too."

"But they consider the British and French likely enemies," Martin said. "They're less concerned about the U.S. trying to stop their ambitions in Europe. Look at the agents the *Abwehr* has sent here the last few years—their missions have been political, to aid pro-Nazi groups."

"That's true." Hansen nodded. "And there's nothing illegal about that—until they use fake passports."

"Which is why I think there's a possibility *Der Skiläufer* is in the country legally, perhaps even a naturalized citizen," Martin said. "We still need to lean on every counterfeiter we can, but we've got to keep in mind he may not have needed to use one."

"That would make him a whole lot harder to find."

"Until the next *Abwehr* agent comes looking for him," Martin said.

"I'm glad you called, Mr. Schuller," Congressman Barbour said after his secretary escorted Martin into the office at the U.S. Capitol Building.

Martin nodded and took the seat that was offered.

"Get you a glass of something?" the congressman said, motioning toward an array of decanters on a credenza. "I've got some fine scotches, or there's this nice little Cuban rum I picked up on my last visit to Havana."

"No, thank you, sir."

"Suit yourself. I'm having a scotch." The congressman took a tumbler, added a couple of ice cubes from a bucket, and poured a double shot. He turned and raised his glass toward Martin. "To your health, sir."

Martin nodded in acknowledgement.

"I understand from your father-in-law that you do research for the State Department."

"In a manner of speaking, sir," Martin said.

"Oh?"

"I'm an analyst with the counter-intelligence office at State."

The congressman nodded in appreciation, a strange sort of smile on his lips. "I see. That's very important work these days. Keeping us safe from the communists, are you?"

"The Nazis, actually, sir."

"Bah!" the congressman said with a dismissive wave of the hand. "The Nazis are no threat to the United States, no matter what Franklin Delano Roosevelt's propaganda machine might be saying to the American people. The communists, though—that's the *real* threat to our way of life. They won't rest until they've taken over every country, the United States included. Their politburo in Moscow sends thousands of covert agents all over the world, coordinating with communist parties in all the countries, plotting their 'workers' revolution.' I shudder to think how many Bolshevik spies we've got wandering around the U.S., fomenting revolution."

"We have a desk assigned to that threat, sir," Martin said.

"Is it bigger than the area you work for? Better staffed?"

Martin felt his gut clench, but he kept his face passive. "No sir, there are the same number of analysts on both the Soviet desk and the German desk."

The congressman shook his head in exaggerated fashion. "That shows you what Franklin Delano Roosevelt's *real* priorities are—keeping his socialist friends happy."

Martin had heard this sort of rhetoric before—most recently at the German-American Bund rally at Madison Square Garden, one month before. He kept his thoughts to himself.

"I take it you speak a little German, then?"

"Yes, sir."

"Study it in school?"

"Yes, sir—though I also grew up speaking German. Everyone in our family is bilingual."

"Immigrant family? Or Pennsylvania Dutch?"

"Pennsylvania Dutch, sir. Sixth generation."

The congressman gave him an appraising look. "Funny, you don't have the accent. You people finally starting to assimilate?"

Martin didn't reply, only made a little shrug. The line of questioning made him uncomfortable, though he refused to show it. His parents, in fact, had the classic Pennsylvania Dutch accent when they spoke English; but Martin and his siblings had attended public school, and lost the accent by the time they reached the second grade.

"Only took two hundred years," the congressman said, and took a drink. "So tell me, Mr. Schuller—why did you study German in school if you spoke it at home growing up?"

Martin's patience wore a little too thin. "Why did you study English in school if you spoke it at home growing up, sir?"

The congressman stared him hard in the eye for a second, and then his face broke into a grin and he laughed out loud. "Excellent point, Mr. Schuller. I like your style—I want you to come work for me. I need a man like you, who can analyze data, and who can read German. Germany's is one of the few strong economies in the world, and firms in my district need access to that market."

"Firms such as Showalter Glassworks?" Martin asked, thinking of his interaction Saturday evening with Maximilian Showalter.

"Yes, as a matter of fact, among others. Max Showalter must have cornered you at the gala Saturday night. I hope he didn't make you an offer you couldn't refuse."

"No, sir."

"Good, because I want you working for me."

Martin was stunned at how fast this had played out. "I don't know what to say, sir."

"Say you'll take the job. I'll pay you one hundred and seventy dollars a week."

Martin almost gasped, but stopped himself in time. That was fifty percent more than his current salary—and about six times what the average American made.

"It's a big decision, sir. I'll have to think about it."

The congressman stood, and Martin stood in response. "Talk it over with your wife, and come back and see me tomorrow."

That's an odd thing to say, Martin thought, but he just nodded and kept silent. As he put on his hat while leaving the congressman's office, he mused about how strange it was for a conservative like Congressman Barbour to suggest that any man consult his wife in making a business decision.

He saw Becky's fingerprints all over this.

"It's a wonderful opportunity, Martin!" Becky gushed when he filled her in on the details before dinner that evening. "And we could finally move back to Pennsylvania."

He didn't like the way this conversation was going, though he'd expected it.

"I'm not really interested in that kind of work."

Becky looked as if she'd been assaulted. "Why on Earth not?"

How could he explain so she would understand? "I do a lot of real good in my current job, Becky. I do real good for the country, for all of us. If I took the job with Congressman Barbour, I would only be doing good for a few rich businessmen, and cronies of the congressman."

He knew as soon as he saw her face that he shouldn't have said "rich" businessmen.

Or cronies.

"I see," she said, her voice biting. She turned back toward the oven, and stirred the pot of mashed potatoes.

"And what is that supposed to mean?" Martin hated having to ask that question.

"You think you're so noble," she said, her voice still hard as ice. "But you couldn't care less about your family."

He felt that in his chest, like a blow. "How can you say that? Of course I care."

She dropped the spoon hard on the counter and spun around. "Think about the life you could give our children with that kind of position. They'd have opportunities you never had. They could go to good schools, make good connections."

The carefully contained anger inside him boiled over.

"Do you know what your problem is, Becky?" he pointed a finger at her face. "You think you're better than everyone else, because your parents are rich, and you went to private schools and cotillions and all the other useless crap that came along with that rich life. And you know what? You and I ended up at the same university, and now we live the same life. You think I should be grateful to you for lifting me up to your father's level, but you know something? I don't need to be lifted up, by you or anyone else. I have a good job, doing good work, and making a good living doing it. This family wants for nothing. *Nothing*! So don't judge me because I don't want the fancy life your parents have."

She set the dishes on the table hard, and walked to the kitchen door.

"Kids! Dinner time!" she shouted.

After the kids came and sat down, she put food on their plates, and on Martin's plate, but left hers empty. She didn't sit.

"Aren't you eating dinner, Mommy?" Jackie asked.

"I'm not hungry," Becky said, and stormed out of the kitchen.

The kids all looked at Martin, and he gave them the best smile he could muster. "It's OK, kiddos. Eat your dinner. How was school today, Marty?"

8

Saturday, April 1, 1939

Martin stretched and half-jumped to snatch the ball from the air with his baseball mitt.

"That's better," he said to his eldest son as he switched the ball to his right hand and tossed it back to Marty. "But a little too high, still. Try it again."

It was a cool morning, and the narrow lawn between their building and the sidewalk still sat in shade. Martin wore his Saturday cardigan buttoned over a dress shirt and tie, and Marty wore a light jacket zipped up halfway. He lifted his chin to look at his father from under the rim of his blue and white baseball cap, wound his arm back, and threw the ball.

Martin still had to stretch his left arm to catch it, but not as much. "Getting better, kiddo. Just a little lower. Try again."

The rhythm of their game of catch calmed him. He'd been in a bad mood off-and-on since Tuesday, when the newspapers had reported from Spain that Generalisimo Franco's Nationalist Army had taken Madrid, the last stronghold of the Republican government's forces.

Then this morning, as the kids sat on the floor listening to their radio shows while he read the newspaper, the NBC newsman had interrupted to announce that Nationalist troops had "captured and disarmed" the last Republican troops, ending the three-year civil war in Spain.

That put him in a foul mood. It seemed fascism was winning everywhere. It was also a significant propaganda win for the Nazis, with their explicit military support for the Spanish Nationalists. Martin could imagine the smug expressions of men like Fritz Kuhn, head of the German American Bund—or that Dr. Atherton who had been so obnoxious a couple of weeks ago.

Unable to concentrate on the rest of his newspaper, he'd told Marty to get his ball and glove so they could practice before little league try-outs.

"Good throw!" he said as he caught one right in front of his shoulder. "Keep it up."

Marty grinned, showing the gaps from missing teeth.

They'd been tossing the ball for a half-hour, and the sun had just appeared above the roof of the three-story building when Becky came out the front door, purse clamped beneath her elbow, fastening her hat to her hair. Jackie and Stevie walked behind her hand-in-hand, each with a little book in their opposite hands.

"Marty, go put your baseball things away and grab your library books. And hurry up, young man—we need to leave in two minutes."

"We'll practice some more later, kiddo," Martin said, tossing the ball back as Marty hurried toward the building. He looked at Becky as she approached. "Didn't you just take the kids to the library a couple of days ago?"

"Wednesday," she said, and gave him a rueful smile that said she knew what he was thinking. "I can't keep that boy supplied with books. He checked out three, and read them all—one a day. And these are *chapter* books, Martin."

Martin nodded. It was true that Marty usually had his nose in a book after dinner every evening, even sitting with the rest of the family in the living room while they listened to the radio.

"It's no wonder he's reading a grade-level ahead."

Becky gave him another rueful smile. "*Two* grades ahead, now. We started checking out fourth-grade books a few weeks ago."

Jackie tugged the end of his cardigan. "Mrs. Baker says I'm the second-best reader in my class, Daddy!"

"She does?" Martin grinned at his daughter, and patted the back of her head. She was in kindergarten, so she could read a handful of simple sentences with three-letter words, such as "The cat sat by the hat."

"I think I'll go with you to the library," Martin said to his wife.

The surprised look on her face annoyed him, but not half as much as her incredulous tone when she said, "Really?"

He couldn't help the momentary scowl that crossed his face. "Of course. Why not?"

"For starters, you don't have your hat."

"It won't take me a minute to get it."

Becky looked down at her purse, and removed a pair of white gloves, her expression now blank. "I think it's good that you want to take part in your children's interests, Martin," she said as she put on the gloves, not looking at him.

He was about to respond to the barely-concealed reprimand when Marty came running out the front of the building, three books stacked in his hands.

"Walk, please," his mother admonished him.

"You said to hurry," Marty said with a shrug.

Martin couldn't help the smile that his son's retort brought to his lips, and he looked away before Becky could notice.

"I didn't tell you to act like a wild hooligan, now did I?" Becky scolded. "Walk like a gentleman, please."

Marty shrugged again, and stood beside Martin.

"Hey sport, run up and fetch my hat for me, will you?" Martin said, taking the books from Marty's hands. Marty grinned and ran back to the door.

Becky scowled at her husband. "You just told him to run after I told him not to."

"Just a figure of speech."

"And you expect your seven-year-old to not take it literally?"

Martin glanced at Jackie and Stevie, watching them. "It's not that big a deal," he said, quieter.

Becky looked down and fiddled with her purse. "You are always undermining me with the kids," she muttered.

Martin didn't see it as *undermining* her—not as such, anyway. He just tried to soften her over-strict dictates. He thought his parents had been too strict much of the time, but even they allowed their children to run around and be kids instead of miniature grown-ups.

Marty came bounding out of the building, Martin's hat in-hand, and Becky sighed. The boy handed the hat to his father, took back his books, and fell into step beside Martin, with Becky and the two younger children right behind them.

They walked two blocks to Massachusetts Avenue NW, and Becky stopped to open her purse.

"What are you doing?"

"I brought money for a cab."

"It's not that far," Martin said. "It's closer than my office, and I walk there. Don't waste money on a cab."

Becky gave him a dubious look. "Not far for *you*—but far for little feet."

"They'll be fine," Martin said. "The exercise and fresh air are good for them."

It was about three quarters of a mile to the library, and by the time they got there Martin carried Stevie, while Jackie shuffled along holding Becky's hand.

"Mommy? I wanna sit down," Jackie whined as they walked through the doors.

"We'll find a chair in a minute. Marty, take your sister's hand."

Becky gave Martin an 'I-told-you-so' look as she took Stevie from him, and steered the other kids toward the children's section. "Return Marty's books for me, would you, dear?"

It wasn't a request.

"Of course," Martin said, taking the books from his son and carrying them to one of the librarians at the desk.

"May I have your library card, sir?" the young librarian asked as she stamped the date onto the card inside the back covers. She was early twenties, with carefully curled brown hair and deep blue eyes.

"It's my wife's card—Mrs. Martin Schuller. She has the card with her, I'm sure."

"I can record the name, sir," she said, and began making the entries in the ledger.

As she worked, Martin looked around the large room, and his eyes rested on the Reference Desk some distance away. He noticed a librarian helping a patron to feed a microfilm spool through a reader. He peered at the lighted screen and saw what appeared to be pages of a newspaper scrolling up.

Microfilm was a relatively new technology, and he had read about how it was being used by libraries across the country to archive old newspapers and magazines, preserving the often fragile pages.

The young librarian in front of him finished her entries, looked up and smiled. "Will there be anything else, sir?"

An idea struck him. "Do you by any chance have the Philadelphia Inquirer among your newspapers at the Reference Desk?"

"I believe we do," the young librarian said, her tone light and cheerful. "You can ask Miss Woodson at the Reference Desk, and she'll help you."

He thanked her, glanced over at the children's section to see Becky and the kids busy looking through the shelves, and strode to the Reference Desk.

The reference librarian was an older woman, about fifty, with silver-streaked black hair pulled into a tight bun. Her lined face wore a severe expression. The name tag pinned to her black cardigan said "Miss Woodson."

"May I help you, sir?" she asked, efficient more than polite.

"I'm interested to find news stories in the Philadelphia Inquirer about a year ago, about a specific person—is that possible? Is there an index that can be checked?"

Miss Woodson's severe expression made her look as if she were judging his ignorance.

"To answer your first question, sir—yes, it is possible to find news stories in that newspaper about a specific person, provided those stories exist and were printed in that newspaper. To answer your second question—no, there is not an index of such things. You will have to look through the newspaper for all of the possible dates, and locate the news stories that way. If you tell me the dates you would like, I will see if we have those on microfilm."

Martin hesitated. "Well—I'm not entirely sure. It could be any time last winter or spring. That's why I'd hoped there was an index."

He could almost see the librarian sigh, though her expression remained unchanged.

"I'm afraid that could take you quite some time, sir," she said.

Martin tried a cheerful smile. "Then I guess I'd better get started."

Miss Woodson didn't look amused. "From what date would you like to begin?"

Martin's mind went to the night of the gala in Philadelphia two weeks before, and replayed the conversation in the limousine on the way back to his in-law's townhouse.

*

"That was very level-headed of you earlier, Martin," William Walsh had said. "The way you deflated that fool Atherton. Nicely done."

"Thank you, sir."

"You punctured his argument with facts. That kind of cool-headedness under pressure will serve you well."

No doubt he'd meant in future service to Congressman Barbour, but Martin ignored that.

"I'm not even sure what the devil he was doing there." Walsh waved a hand in the air dismissively, and looked out the window.

"I don't know how they could show their faces, under the circumstances," Mrs. Walsh chimed in.

Martin was intrigued. "He said he retired from the hospital."

William Walsh looked uncomfortable. "He was asked to retire."

Martin looked at his father-in-law with a raised eyebrow, the question unspoken.

"Dr. Atherton is an outspoken Eugenicist—and that point-of-view has fallen out of vogue the last fifteen or twenty years." Walsh hesitated, and then added, "Plus, there were incidents. Bad for the hospital's image."

Mrs. Walsh leaned closer to Martin, and continued, her voice conspiratorial. "Mr. Walsh represented the hospital in the settlement negotiations with the boy's parents—after Dr. Atherton was 'allowed' to retire."

A twinkle in her eye said that she enjoyed this little piece of gossip.

William Walsh turned back from the window with a scowl. "I can't discuss that of course—attorney-client privilege."

"Of course," Martin said, amused at his father-in-law's sudden discomfort.

"What were they even doing there in the first place?" William Walsh said, irritated.

"The DAR certainly didn't invite them," Mrs. Walsh said, drawing up into a rigid posture. She looked at Martin and explained, "The Athertons didn't arrive in America until 1792—more than a decade too late to have served in the Revolution."

Given her encyclopedic knowledge of the family histories of everyone in Philadelphia's Society circles, Martin had no doubt that was true.

"Perhaps Dr. Atherton or his wife are related to someone in the DAR?"

Mrs. Walsh shook her head. "No. She was a McAlpin, and her people came from Scotland in 1819. They have no connections in the DAR, either of them."

Martin had learned years ago that the elite families of Philadelphia ranked themselves first by date of immigration, and only second by wealth. There was a blue-blooded snobbery that no amount of money could buy.

When he'd first been introduced to Becky's parents ten years before, her mother asked him when his family came to America. He hadn't known exactly—sometime in the mid-eighteenth century was the best he could say. The next time he met them, Mrs. Walsh informed him that the Schullers had arrived in 1748—and that the Walsh family had landed in America in 1715.

He'd been assigned his place.

"Well, *someone* must have invited them," William Walsh was saying.

*

"Sir?" the reference librarian said. "From what date?"

At the gala, Atherton had said he and his wife had toured Europe last spring, after his retirement—but he hadn't said how long after his retirement.

"Let's start at the beginning of 1938."

"What are you looking at?" Becky asked as she walked up to him an hour later.

He glanced up from the January 19th edition illuminated on the screen, and saw her standing over him with a curious expression. The kids stood a few feet behind her, books in their hands.

"Something for work," he said, and turned his attention back to the screen.

"On a Saturday?"

"We don't have these at the office," he said, nodding at the microfilm viewer, though in truth he didn't know that for certain.

He heard her sigh. "How much longer will you be? The kids are getting tired."

He glanced at his watch. "Just let me finish up this roll—fifteen more minutes."

"I thought we were coming here as a *family*," she said, quieter so the kids wouldn't hear. "You said you were taking an interest in your kids' activities."

He looked up at her with a scowl. "I am," he said, defensive.

"Funny way of showing it, Martin," she said, folding her arms.

He exhaled hard. She didn't know what she was talking about, implying he didn't take an interest in the kids. He did. At least, he had *intended* to look at books with Marty. He hadn't intended to get caught up in sleuthing for Dr. Atherton's misdeeds—but once begun, he couldn't pull himself away.

"I'll be done shortly, and then I can read to them."

"We have to leave. It's time for Jackie's and Stevie's naps," Becky said, opening the clasp of her purse and taking out a few dollars. "I'm going to get a cab and take the kids home. You can stay as long as you'd like."

"No, wait—just give me a couple of minutes to finish this issue, and I'll stop."

She stared at him for several seconds. "Alright—we'll be on the steps outside the door. If you don't join us in five minutes, we're leaving in the next cab that comes by."

A grunt and a nod were his acknowledgment, as he resumed scanning headlines and photographs.

He came to the end of the issue a few minutes later, and hurried to unwind the film. He turned off the light on the film reader and rushed back to the Reference Desk, putting the film reel back in its box as he went. He muttered thanks to Miss Woodson, put on his hat, and hurried to the front door.

Becky was opening the back door of a cab as he came outside.

"Hold on! I'm coming," he called, getting her attention as she ushered the children into the cab. He ran down the steps.

"I started to think you were going to stay and finish your work," she said, tight-lipped.

He shook his head as he got in the cab after her. "No, I want to read them stories when they go down for their naps."

9

Monday, April 3, 1939

Martin got to the office right at the stroke of eight o'clock, and noticed he was the last one in. All of the other men on their team—except the chief—were gathered around Joe Hansen's desk, big goofy grins on their faces. One slapped Hansen on the shoulder as he snickered.

"What's going on, fellas?" Martin asked as he hung his hat on the rack by Trudy's desk.

Trudy kept her eyes glued to her typewriter.

"Joe's filling us in on his adventures on *Ninth* Street this weekend," Louis Buschman said, emphasizing and drawing out the street name.

Martin got the reference. Ninth Street NW was notorious for its burlesque halls, and Hansen—an unmarried twenty-six-year-old—occasionally made it known in the office that he went there many a Saturday night "for the entertainment." The other men in the office—all married—always gathered around to ask him a hundred and one questions about his night. Hansen rarely gave details, saying a gentleman shouldn't tell, but he'd give them just enough innuendo to feed their imaginations.

The conversations made Martin a touch uncomfortable. It wasn't that he disapproved of burlesque—he'd gone to a couple shows with buddies a decade ago when he was a college student—but the banter always seemed a bit adolescent to him somehow, and something about a bunch of married men hanging on every hinted description of a strip tease seemed base and unseemly.

Dear God, I'm turning into my father.

No, that wasn't true, he told himself; his father would consider the entire thing a sign of moral decay, an unquestionable sin, whereas Martin saw nothing wrong with someone like Hansen—as a young, single man—enjoying burlesque.

Mostly he thought it unprofessional, the kind of conversation that should be kept to the bar after work.

He grabbed a cup of coffee, and walked around to the other side of the chief's office, where the so-called "Soviet desk" was located.

"Hey Steve, got a minute?" he asked.

Steve Krasinski looked up from the pile of papers spread before him, some in Cyrillic letters, and smiled. "Oh, hey Martin. How are you? What brings you by?"

"You boys regularly look into Americans, don't you?" Martin asked, grabbing an empty chair and pulling it over to the side of Steve's desk.

"All the time. You fellas got another Lindbergh you wanna look into?"

"Not so famous," Martin said. "But similar views."

Charles Lindbergh, the famed aviator, had become notorious in recent years for his sympathetic opinions of Hitler—which was one of the reasons his family had snuck away to Europe in December 1935. State kept close track of the number of visits he made to Germany, and whom he met there.

"Speaking of Lindbergh, though—he's coming back later this month," Martin said. "The embassy in London says it's for good."

"You don't say."

"Yep. He's rented an estate on Long Island, and he's bringing his family back stateside. Army Air Corps has reactivated his commission, to evaluate new aircraft. That last part is still classified." Steve had security clearance—and Martin knew it would be in the newspapers soon enough.

"How about that?" Steve said, impressed. "So who's the American you're looking at now, and what do you need me to help with?"

Martin recounted his conversation with Dr. Atherton at the gala, and what he'd learned about him.

"An old eugenicist, huh?" Steve mused, leaning back and stroking his chin. He was a few years older than Martin, about thirty-five, the father of six children and the son of Polish immigrants—though at the time, Warsaw was part of Russia, so their papers had listed them as Russian. "And an admirer of the so-called 'German Miracle'—I'd say he's a pretty good candidate for that Nazi cell leader you fellas have been looking for."

Martin frowned. "Not likely. *Der Skiläufer* means 'the skier'—and Atherton seems too old for snow skiing."

Steve shrugged. "He might lead you to him, then—which is why you're asking for my advice on how to look into Americans, isn't it?"

"Possibly," Martin admitted. "Though he's not of German descent, so it's a long shot."

Steve scoffed. "Almost none of the Americans we investigate are Russian."

"But communism's whole aim is internationalism," Martin said. "Nazism is the opposite—it's a form of extreme nationalism—so *Der Skiläufer* would be reluctant to trust an American who wasn't German."

"Still sounds like a solid lead to me," Steve said, sitting forward and putting his hands on his desk. "Even if he's not in the cell you're looking for, this Atherton fellow probably moves in the same circles as the creeps who are. We find that a lot on our side."

Martin nodded. He couldn't disagree with the logic. His gut had told him this anyway.

"I'd check public records in Philadelphia for that lawsuit your father-in-law mentioned. I'd bet money the plaintiffs are Jewish, or maybe negroes," Steve said. "Keep looking for newspaper references, too. You don't have to do all of it yourself, you know—get a clerk to do the grunt work, wade through the stacks of papers and all the irrelevant crap, and bring you the reference locations for the potential hits."

"Thanks, Steve," Martin said, standing and patting his friend on the shoulder. He strode to Trudy's desk.

"Trudy, get me a clerk who can do some library research."

Tuesday, April 4

A clerk entered their office late the next afternoon, carrying a pair of manila folders at his side. "Research for Mr. Schuller," he said to Trudy, who pointed toward Martin's desk.

"I've got the research you requested, Mr. Schuller," the young man said, stopping in front of Martin's desk. Then he looked past Martin and grinned. "Oh, hello, Mr. Hansen."

"Hello, Ben."

Martin glanced back and thought he detected a touch of discomfort in Joe's posture and expression, though he was smiling back.

"Where would you like these, Mr. Schuller?" Ben asked, shifting the folders from his side to in front. He was in his early twenties, slender, with thick, wavy brown hair that swooped over his forehead from a part on the right side. He wore perfectly-pressed charcoal gray slacks and royal blue shirt with a gray necktie under a gray argyle sweater-vest.

Another Andy Hardy clone, Martin thought, though this one's hair was floppy rather than glossed with brilliantine. He indicated a clear spot on the corner of his desk. "What have we got?"

"The big one here is everything I found in the public records, including family members like you asked. The thin one is what I found in the newspapers ," Ben said, setting them down.

"Thanks—Ben, is it?" Martin said, flipping the boy a dime.

"Yes sir, Ben Fitzhugh." He caught the dime and pocketed it in one swift move. "Thank you, Mr. Schuller, sir." He nodded at Martin, then looked over him and grinned. "Nice to see you again, Mr. Hansen."

"You as well, Ben."

After the young clerk had left, Frank Hooper snickered and said, "You'd better watch out, Hansen—I think you've got an admirer."

Joe blushed a deep red, and even his ears turned red.

The snickers from the other men in the office turned to guffaws as Hooper cocked his head, bent his wrist, and lisped, "Nith to thee you again, Mithter Hanthen!"

"Knock it off, you goofs," Joe said, waving them off and staring down at the papers on his desk.

Martin shook his head and turned back to his work, a little bemused by the interaction. Ben Fitzhugh hadn't seemed that effeminate to him—certainly not like one of the "faerie boys" who gossiped in the halls. And even if he had been, they were harmless, and Martin was uncomfortable with the adolescent tone of the mocking.

"Looks like I've got my work cut out for me," he muttered to himself, flipping through the corner of the pages in the thicker folder. It would take him all day tomorrow to get through that, even if there were no delivery from the diplomatic pouches.

Wednesday, April 5

"Hey Sam, Joe—come over here a minute and let me talk something over," Martin said the next afternoon after he'd finished going through the files on Atherton.

"Whatcha got, Martin?" Sam Watts asked as he lifted his stocky frame from his seat and shuffled over to stand next to Hansen beside Martin's desk.

In his early 40s, Sam was one of the older members of the team, and the only World War veteran among them. He'd learned German in high school, so the army assigned him to interview POWs in France in

1918. After the war he'd gone to college to study German and history, intending to become a teacher, but one of his professors referred him to an acquaintance at the State Department, and he started working there in 1922.

When Martin joined the team in the fall of 1933, Sam had been a mentor. Two years later, when Martin was selected for one of the new part-time undercover roles, Sam was the first to congratulate him.

Martin summarized his findings on Atherton, finishing with the dramatic end to his career. "He was accused of systematically sterilizing Jewish and colored boys without parental consent, after creating fake IQ scores below seventy-five. The family who sued him last year produced two independent tests that revealed their son's IQ to be twenty points higher than that."

"Woops," Hansen said, shaking his head.

"They had a good lawyer who took on the case pro bono—a fellow named Bernard Gold—and on discovery he got ahold of hospital records with the names of almost a hundred other boys Atherton had sterilized over the last thirty years."

"And I bet they were all Jewish or colored," Sam said.

Martin grunted. "No—but about three quarters of them were. More than half of the others were ethnics of one variety or another—Italian, Serbian, Greek, you get the picture."

"What a bastard!" Hansen looked disgusted.

"It was never clear how much the hospital knew," Martin said, feeling his throat tighten. "But if I were a betting man, I'd put my money on them turning a willful blind eye all those years. They settled with four families for *eleven thousand* apiece."

Sam let out a long, low whistle.

"They wouldn't admit to any wrong-doing"—his father-in-law's handiwork, Martin knew—"but they paid big to keep it out of court. And Atherton was forced to retire."

74

"But," Sam said, raising a finger, "none of that ties him to the *Skiläufer*, unless you've got something more to tell us."

Martin shook his head. "That's why I wanted to run it by both of you. Anything else you can think of?"

"How about the striking similarity to the Nazi eugenics programs in Germany?" Hansen said.

Sam grunted and shook his head. "The Nazis aren't the only practitioners of that sort of thing."

Hansen scowled. "But coupled with his statements of support for other Nazi policies, it seems pretty damning."

"Both circumstantial," Sam argued. "There needs to be more to go on than just that."

"What was his political affiliation?" Hansen asked.

Martin shook his head. "Registered to vote as a Republican, but that's all there is."

"Hell, if that makes him guilty, then so am I," Sam said with a chuckle, looking right at Hansen as he said it.

Hansen, to his credit, didn't take the bait. There had been enough political conversation around the office to know that Sam Watts was what was referred to these days as a "Liberal Republican"—only sometimes opposed to the New Deal ("The FDIC was a great idea," Sam had said more than once), and usually agreeing with the Roosevelt administration on conservation and civil rights.

"And my parents as well," Martin said to Sam. In fact, Martin himself had voted Republican in the 1930 election, when he was twenty-two—but he'd voted for FDR from abroad in 1932, as the Depression neared its nadir. Since then, he'd lived in the District of Columbia, and didn't bother to vote in what were only local races. "Got any other ideas for me?"

"Has he been to Washington recently?" Hansen asked.

"Not that I can tell."

75

"I've got some sources I can check," the younger man said. He walked back to his desk, opened a drawer, and began flipping through an index.

Sam looked at Martin with a grin, and pointed at Hansen with his thumb. "The kid's got sources." He chuckled on the way back to his desk.

Hansen shut the drawer with a bang. "Meet me at the Stars and Stripes after work," he said as he hurried by Martin's desk. "I'll be there by five o'clock. If the chief asks, tell him I'm out checking on a lead." He grabbed his hat from the stand by Trudy's desk and hurried out the door.

Martin had nearly finished his beer by the time Hansen got to the bar a few minutes past five.

Hansen raised his hand as he took the stool next to Martin's. "The usual."

"Well? Did you find anything interesting on our friend Dr. Atherton?" Martin asked as the bartender opened a bottle of Löwenbräu and set it in front of Hansen.

"Nothing you could use, unfortunately," Hansen said, sounding more disappointed than Martin felt. "He came to Washington in September, and stayed a couple of nights over at the Willard—but that's about all I could get. No visitors called on him there, no unusual activity. Sorry, Martin."

"Forget it," Martin said. "I appreciate the effort. Hope you didn't go through too much trouble."

Hansen shrugged. "I went a few places, no trouble. I talked to some bellhops I know at a few of the hotels downtown, and a reporter friend of mine over at the Post. Just wish I'd found something—you *know* Atherton's mixed up in anti-Semitic and pro-Nazi shenanigans."

Martin shrugged. "It was probably wishful thinking." Hansen *could* be right, he knew—the young man's instincts were good. He'd have to mull it over for a while.

He drained the last of the beer in his bottle, grabbed his hat off the bar and stood. "I appreciate the effort, though. Good work, Joe."

"Can't stay long enough for one more?"

Martin shook his head and turned toward the door. "I've got to get home for dinner. See you tomorrow."

"How was your day, dear?" Becky asked when he got home.

He kissed her offered cheek. "Very productive. I may have had a bit of a breakthrough today on a case we've been working for a while."

"Anything you can tell me?" she asked, turning back to the stove. Her tone sounded vaguely interested, but just barely.

Could he tell her what he'd discovered about Dr. Milton Atherton? He supposed he probably could—everything he'd learned was in the public record, or in a newspaper. None of it was classified. But then, she'd wonder why he was looking at Atherton in the first place, and she was an intelligent woman who could draw connections that she probably shouldn't have the knowledge to be able to.

"No, I'm afraid not."

She didn't react, just stirred the pot on the stove and reset the lid, then turned to the counter and began chopping carrots.

"Dinner will be ready in about forty-five minutes," she said, not looking back at him. "Check on Marty and see how he's doing with his homework, will you, dear?"

"Sure." He hesitated, feeling like he wanted to say something to her, but couldn't think of anything. He nodded to himself and walked through the kitchen door.

Hutson

10

Friday, April 14, 1939

The man known as *Der Skiläufer* kept his hat on when he entered the Horn & Hardart Automat at 6th Avenue and 55th Street in midtown Manhattan. When he'd asked his man in New York to meet him for lunch at a crowded venue, he hadn't anticipated that would mean an automat filled with low-level office workers getting pre-made sandwiches from a machine for a nickel. Still, the din of conversation echoing around the chrome furnishings was perfect cover.

His man had chosen wisely.

He worried that his silk suit would stand out among the office clerks in their sweater vests over dress-shirts and neckties, but he noticed a handful of other men in suits scattered around the long room, so he put that out of his mind and scanned the crowd for his man.

Der Skiläufer saw him waving from a small booth in the middle of the room. He made his way through the crowd to him, bumping into a couple of young secretaries who were more interested in their own conversation than watching where they were going. He touched the rim of his hat and excused himself, but they seemed not to notice as they went by.

"Is this satisfactory, boss?" his man asked as *Der Skiläufer* sat down and removed his hat.

"Yes, quite satisfactory." In truth, the seat was uncomfortable, the red cushion over the chrome frame being only an inch thick.

"I got you a pastrami on rye. I believe that's your favorite, right?"

"Yes, thank you," *Der Skiläufer* said, knowing it would not be as good as a fresh pastrami sandwich from a deli. He looked forward to those whenever he came into the City during the week.

His first bite proved his assumption correct. Still, it was passably good. He looked across the narrow booth at his man, who ate a liverwurst sandwich with gusto.

"I have another task for you, part of our special project," *Der Skiläufer* said.

"I'm listening."

"I'm expecting another package from Germany, to be delivered to the City in about six weeks."

"So you'll need for me to take delivery," his man said, wiping his mouth with a paper napkin from a metal dispenser on the table.

"Yes, and see that it gets delivered to me safely this time." *Der Skiläufer*'s eyes narrowed as he stared at the stocky man across from him, and his voice was stern.

His man didn't react to the reprimand. "How long do I need to hold onto it?"

"No more than three days, same as before. Keep the package in a different location this time, in case the previous location has been compromised." He leaned forward so that he could lower his voice. "The FBI have been snooping around quite a bit lately—you'll need to be extra cautious. Is your courier still trustworthy?"

His man grinned, and his pale blue eyes seemed to twinkle. "As long as he gets his pay, he keeps his mouth shut. He don't tell secrets."

"Can you be certain he's not been compromised?"

His man laughed. "This is the *least* of his activities, I can tell you. If they were onto him, he'd already be locked up for ten to twenty, no question. He ain't telling nobody nothing."

Der Skiläufer nodded, satisfied. "What about the printer?"

His man shrugged, and took a drink from his bottle of Coke. "I'll find out."

"Be extra careful," *Der Skiläufer* said. "Someone betrayed Evergreen, and we don't know who it was."

His man made a face. "I doubt it was Ket—the printer," he said, stopping himself from saying the name aloud. "He's been doing this kind of work for years, long before we hired him the first time—and that's been over a year now."

Der Skiläufer took another bite of his sandwich, and chewed it slowly while he looked up in thought. "I'm sure you're right about that. I trust your judgment, but I would be remiss if I did not warn you that the temperature is rising. Remember the disaster last year."

His man's expression turned solemn. He remembered.

"I appreciate that, boss. I'll get that package to you this time."

"Good."

In February of the previous year, an agent code-named "Mr. Crown" made a stupid mistake that got him arrested by the FBI. As it turned out, he'd already been under FBI surveillance because of his correspondence with an *Abwehr* agent in Britain who was under MI-5 surveillance, a Mrs. Jessie Jordan. After his arrest for espionage, Crown betrayed several fellow sleeper agents in New York.

It caused a panic that *Der Skiläufer* was not eager to repeat. He had communicated on several occasions with Mr. Crown—whose real name was Gunther Rumrich, the American-born son of an Austrian father—using him as a conduit for sensitive information to Berlin, via Mrs. Jordan.

But thanks to his many precautions, Rumrich didn't know *Der Skiläufer's* true identity.

It had been a near miss, one that still haunted him.

Der Skiläufer rose, leaving one corner of his sandwich uneaten, and placed his hat back on his head. "I'll be in town through Sunday. If you need anything, leave a message for me at the Waldorf Astoria."

"You and the missus taking in a show or two while you're in town?" his man asked, rising and accompanying him to the door.

"Yes," *Der Skiläufer* said, his voice flat. He didn't need to tell his man that he and his wife had tickets to see the Rockettes at Radio City Music Hall tonight, down 6th Avenue at 51st Street; or that tomorrow night they were going to the Shubert Theater on 44th to see "The Philadelphia Story" starring Katharine Hepburn.

"Well, enjoy yourself, sir," his man said, holding the door open.

"Thank you," *Der Skiläufer* replied over the honks of car horns and the angry shouts of taxi drivers. "I'll let you know when I have a firm delivery date. Until then." He touched the rim of his hat and strode away down 6th Avenue.

11

Monday, April 17, 1939

The chief called the agents into his office first thing that morning.

"Newspapers reported yesterday that the FBI gave stacks of evidence they've collected on the German American Bund and its subdivisions to the Dies Committee," the chief announced, using the colloquial name for the House Un-American Activities Committee, which was chaired by Congressman Dies. "The Secretary's ordered us to prepare to do the same."

"We don't want to look less cooperative than the FBI, now do we?" Sam Watts muttered under his breath to Martin.

Martin agreed with the sentiment, but kept it to himself.

"This is a priority directive," the chief continued. "Any time that you're not devoting to an urgent intelligence matter should be redirected to this collection effort."

At the collective groans from the seven men crowded in his office, the chief raised his hands to silence them. "This is only for the short-term. If everyone works together and puts in a solid six or seven hours at this each day, we should have this done before the end of the week."

Martin cringed on the inside, not looking forward to a week of tedious clerical work. He and Joe Hansen exchanged a look on the way back to their desks, and the younger man shrugged and frowned.

Tuesday, April 18

Sam approached Martin's desk at eleven o'clock, a crooked grin on his lips.

"How would you like to get out of the office for the rest of the day, and take a little car trip with me to check out a tip? Chief said I could take someone with me. Are you in?"

Martin shoved aside the files of postal inspector reports he'd been looking through and leapt from his chair. He didn't have to be asked twice. "Where to?" he asked, grabbing his hat from the rack beside Trudy's desk.

He ignored the envious look on Hansen's face.

"Gettysburg," Sam said, holding the door and motioning Martin through ahead of him. "Got a call from a police detective. Seems a lady up there thinks her handyman might be a Nazi spy. She called the cops on Sunday afternoon, and they called the State Police, who passed it along to the FBI. Apparently they came out, and she's complaining to the detective that they didn't believe her."

Sam chuckled and shook his head. "She probably read the reports in the Philadelphia Inquirer all weekend about the German American Bund, and now she imagines a Nazi spy hiding behind a tree on every Main Street U.S.A." He shrugged. "Still, gotta check it out—sometimes these crazy paranoid small-town biddies will uncover something real. Besides, it gets us out of collecting reports to give to Congress for the rest of the day."

"I'd rather be in the field than going through old intelligence," Martin muttered.

"I knew you would."

Ten minutes later they were in Sam's black 1936 Dodge sedan, cruising north toward Maryland. Sam was a fast driver, and the Dodge engine rumbled as he pressed the gas pedal to the floor after leaving the District behind.

"I'll have us there in an hour and a half," Sam boasted.

His timing was spot on. They parked in front of the Gettysburg Police Station just after twelve-thirty.

"We're here to see Detective Ross," Sam said to the cop at the nearest desk. "He called this morning. I'm Agent Watts, and this is Agent Schuller."

"Feds? You're here about Widow Richter's 'spy?'" the cop said with a big grin.

Martin didn't like his sarcastic attitude, and fixed the man with a cold stare.

"We're here to see Detective Ross," Sam said, level.

The cop snickered, but looked away from Martin's stare. "This way."

The detective was a big-shouldered man in a brown tweed suit, late thirties, with a thick mane of auburn hair combed back without brilliantine. A cigarette smoldered in his lips, but he removed it and set it in a tin ashtray on his desk before rising.

"Thanks for coming," he said in a gravelly voice, shaking their hands in turn. "Care for a cigarette, either of you?"

Martin waved him off, but Sam accepted, and the detective struck a match for him.

"Tell us everything you know about the suspected German agent," Martin said as he and Sam took seats in front of Ross's desk.

"His name's Schnell. Otto Schnell. German fella, thick accent. Only been in town a couple of months. Probably hitched a ride on an empty freight car. Does handyman work for folks around town, odd jobs." Ross paused to take a long drag on his cigarette. "I wouldn't take this kind of thing seriously, usually, but Mrs. Richter's nobody's fool. She had reasons to be suspicious."

"And what were those?" Sam asked, flicking ash into the palm of his hand.

"He's kind of a loner, keeps to himself, never talks much. He'd been in town two or three weeks before he rented a room, so probably sleeping in barns before he got a little cash."

Not unusual behavior for a hobo, Martin thought. *But this one has a thick accent.* He glanced sideways at Sam, but his companion's expression gave away nothing.

"What did he do to make Mrs. Richter believe he might be a spy?" Martin asked, a touch of irritation creeping into his voice. If the only thing that made Schnell suspect was that he was a loner from out of town with a funny accent, this would be a big waste of time.

Ross scowled. "I was just getting to that." He took a drag on his cigarette, and blew it in Martin's direction.

Martin stifled a cough, his throat constricting. He stared back at the detective, resisting the urge to blink away the sting from the smoke.

"Recently he's been seen with a couple of newcomers. German fellas, like him, just showed up in town last week, looking for work. Now, we don't get too many foreigners passing through here, so three of 'em together gets some attention."

Martin felt his irritation rising. Something about Ross's manner seemed arrogant as well as xenophobic.

"There is a large German-American community in this area, detective."

Martin drew a mental image of an adolescent Ross busting car headlights with a baseball bat and shouting anti-German epithets at the driver. He'd seen irrational hatred like that flare up during the World War, from people who had always been neighborly.

He took a strong dislike to Detective Ross.

Ross frowned. "Sure, we got us a whole bunch of German families in this area, but they've all been here for generations. Got deep roots in the community. Yeah, they got funny accents, but they speak real good English. This Otto Schnell and the others, they ain't like that. Folks say they've been acting strange—whispering, looking around, sneaking off.

Mrs. Richter happened to be near enough the other day to overhear a little before they saw her walking toward them, and they shut up real fast. She said they were speaking German, and she heard them say something about avoiding the police."

Ross stubbed the remnant of his cigarette in the ash tray and blew a stream of smoke out the side of his mouth.

Sam gave Martin a sideways look with a half-smile. "I can see how that would give her pause, Detective," he said without elaboration.

Patient like a spider, Martin thought with admiration. Sam didn't do undercover work, but he was damn fine at the rest of field work.

"She doesn't miss much, Mrs. Richter," Ross said. "She's not a gossip, she minds her own business, but she's got sharp eyes, and she sees most everything going on around this town. She's helped us out quite a few times.

"Anyway," he continued, leaning back in his seat and folding his hands behind his head. "She read in the newspaper this weekend about that Nazi organization in Philadelphia, the 'German Bund' or whatever it's called. There was a big write-up about how they spread propaganda over here for Hitler, and they got their own camp and rifle range over in Sellersville. They even have their own Hitler Youth."

The detective sat back up, his lips pursed in a look of distaste. "The Inquirer said they've got more than a thousand members in Philadelphia, and not but two of 'em American citizens. Mrs. Richter puts two and two together, and she came to see us yesterday. I think enough of Mrs. Richter that I called the State Police.

"They didn't come out themselves—but three FBI agents were here from Philadelphia first thing yesterday morning. They went out and interviewed her, but then they left without even looking for Schnell."

He paused to take a drink from a brown ceramic mug, but grimaced and set it back down. "Mrs. Richter came by the station to complain that they didn't take her seriously. I remembered reading several months back that the State Department warned anyone working for a foreign government that they had to register, so I called you up."

"We appreciate you thinking of us," Sam said. "We'll go talk to Mrs. Richter ourselves, if you'd be good enough to direct us there."

"Sure thing, as long as you promise to come back here when you're done," Ross said. "Those FBI fellas just left town without the common courtesy of checking in."

Big fish in a little pond, Martin thought. If leaving without checking in with him irritated Ross, Martin was tempted to do the same.

"You have our word," Sam said, shaking the detective's hand.

"You didn't seem too impressed with Detective Ross," Sam said after they walked out of the police station.

Martin shrugged, hesitating.

"Go on, what's your take?" Sam pressed.

Martin relented. "It seems to be pretty thin suspicion, don't you think?"

"How so?"

"Schnell and his cohorts might have been up to something criminal, given the furtive behavior, and that they wanted to avoid the police. But it seems the only reason to suspect them of being Nazi spies is their German origins."

"Sure, but aren't the spies we hope to catch always from Germany?" Sam said.

Martin couldn't argue with that. It didn't matter that the majority of German immigrants in the country were anti-Nazi. "It's not much to go on, that's all. But let's go check it out."

Sam stopped and faced him. "Listen, I understand your concern, and maybe Ross is a nativist jerk, who knows? But the bottom line is, he didn't say anything that isn't factually true. The Bund is full of German nationals, and the *Abwehr* agents blend right in among them. You know how these citizen tips go—sometimes it's a wild goose chase, but sometimes we catch a goose. We don't know until we check it out." He chuckled. "And besides, it gets us out of the office for a day, and out of drudge work."

Martin smiled and nodded.

"Let's grab some lunch, and then we'll go see what this widow Richter has for us."

Martin and Sam stopped at the diner down the block long enough to eat hamburgers and French fries, before taking Ross's directions. The farm was less than two miles from the center of town, out the Lincoln Highway, past the Lutheran Seminary on Seminary Ridge, and down Herr's Ridge Road.

Sam parked in front of an old stone house, two-story with a steep slate roof. Several brown cows grazed in the pastures between the house and a large round barn.

A boy of about ten, pale and gangly with thick black hair, tinkered with a broken bicycle chain in the gravel drive, and he looked up and stared at them with piercing blue eyes. An old hound dog beside him growled, hackles raised, and the boy put his hand on the dog's head.

"Quiet, Spike. Sit down." The dog sat.

"Your mother home, son?" Sam asked, smiling at the boy.

The boy didn't smile back, but he nodded toward the house without ever taking his eyes off them. "She's inside."

"Thank you," Sam said, still smiling, and touched the rim of his hat.

Martin nodded at the boy, but kept a respectful silence.

An older man in all black answered the door, about sixty, with white hair, his face freshly shaved. Martin was taken aback by the white clerical collar. His initial visceral reaction was suspicion and anger, but he didn't let it show. He remained outwardly professional.

"Yes? Good day. How can I help you, gentlemen?" the man asked in a Pennsylvania Dutch accent.

Martin let Sam do the initial talking. It was his investigation.

"We're here to speak with Mrs. Richter. Is she here?"

"Yes, one moment, please. Maria!"

"*Ja, Papa?*"

He spoke over his shoulder, switching to the Pennsylvania Dutch dialect, telling her that two Englishmen in fancy suits were here asking to speak with her.

"I didn't understand half of that," Sam muttered out the side of his mouth to Martin.

Martin chuckled. He'd understood perfectly. He'd grown up with it.

The Pennsylvania Dutch dialect was distinct from Standard German, and not easy for most Germans to understand, though the reverse was not true. Martin couldn't help but be amused that even though Sam spoke fluent German, he hadn't understood much of what the old minister said.

A young woman approached, wiping her hands on a dirty white apron. She wore a plain blue blouse and a dark skirt, and her light brown hair was pulled back in a bun.

"More police to ask about the handyman?" the old man asked her in the local dialect.

"Probably, but I won't know that until I speak with them." She looked at Martin and Sam, and addressed them in English. "Hello, I'm Mary Richter."

She spoke English without an accent. Martin realized she was only a few years older than he was, and like him and his siblings she had lost the Pennsylvania Dutch accent.

Sam introduced himself and Martin. "We're here to talk with you about the man you reported yesterday for suspicious activity, Otto Schnell."

"Are you from the FBI?" she asked. She'd straightened, raised her head a little taller.

"No ma'am," Martin answered. "We're from the State Department. We understand you spoke with the FBI yesterday."

Her demeanor relaxed only a little, and she nodded. "Yes. They were very efficient, but I don't think they took my observations seriously. I hope you gentlemen are not so quick to dismiss."

"May we come in?" Sam asked, giving Mrs. Richter a charming smile that she did not return.

"Yes, please do." She opened the door and stepped aside. "Over there, please."

The interior of the farm house was plain, the walls unpainted and unadorned. A few framed photographs sat on end tables, but everything else in the living room was utilitarian—a Singer sewing machine in the corner, wooden chairs, unpatterned upholstery on the couch and armchair.

A large and well-worn leather bible in German sat on the coffee table, and Martin observed it as one would observe a weapon sitting in plain sight. He chose a seat far from it.

The bookshelves on the far wall were filled with religious texts. The collected works of Martin Luther, in English and German editions, shared space with the Augsburg Confession and Lutheran catechism, also present in both languages, and volumes of Goethe and Shakespeare.

As Mrs. Richter took a seat opposite where he stood waiting, prim and proper with her hands flat on her knees and her legs crossed at the ankles, Martin wondered if twenty years earlier she had been the type to torment a girl in trouble.

Martin addressed Mrs. Richter in Pennsylvania Dutch as he sat, hoping it would put her at ease to know one of the agents was one of their own. "The minister who answered the door when we arrived, he is your father? I heard you call him 'Papa.'"

Mary Richter's eyes widened briefly, but Martin was pleased to see her visibly relax. She answered in the same dialect. "Yes, this is my father's house. My children and I came to live here after my husband died two years ago."

"I'm very sorry for the loss of your husband," Martin said, continuing in Pennsylvania Dutch. "Is your mother at home as well? We may wish to speak with her, if she also interacted with Mr. Schnell."

She shook her head. She glanced at Sam, who looked irritated, and answered in English, "No, my mother passed away last year."

"I'm very sorry to hear that," Sam replied with instant sympathy.

"Thank you, but it's not necessary."

He's good at this, Martin thought. He'd observed Sam in the field before, and he could turn on charm or empathy in a blink. That was a skill Martin wished he had.

"Why don't you tell us everything you told the FBI, and then my colleague and I will ask you some follow-up questions," Sam said.

Mary Richter repeated the story they'd heard that morning from Detective Ross, but with a few additional details. Nothing useful, in Martin's opinion.

"When was the last time Mr. Schnell worked for you?" Sam asked.

"Almost two weeks ago," Mrs. Richter answered. "He cleared away and burned the dead brush from the fence lines."

"Did he do anything while he worked for you that made you suspect him of illegal activity?" Martin asked.

She shook her head. "No. He minded his own business, and so did we. He worked, we fed him dinner in the afternoon, he worked more, and at the end of the day we paid him and he left."

"Did he say much during dinner?" Sam asked.

"We only talked about the work."

Typical, Martin thought. He knew the Pennsylvania Dutch tendency to privacy and reticence was driving Sam nuts, though. Seeing Sam hiding his irritation, Martin allowed himself a hint of smile.

"Just so I understand—you weren't suspicious of him until you observed him with the other two German men, saying they wanted to avoid the police. Is that correct?"

"Yes."

"And then on Sunday you read in the newspaper about the German American Bund, and the German spies that hide in its ranks, and so you did your patriotic duty and reported Mr. Schnell as a possible spy." Sam smiled at her. "Did I get all that right?"

She didn't return his smile, her expression remaining passive. "Yes, that's all correct."

"Is there anything else about Mr. Schnell you'd like to tell us?"

"If there is more you would like to know, I'll answer what I can."

For a second, Sam looked flustered. "Well...is there anything you told the FBI yesterday that you haven't told us?"

"No. They weren't really interested, though."

Martin asked, "Even though you weren't suspicious of Mr. Schnell while he worked for you, is there anything you can think of in hindsight that would be useful for us?"

Mary Richter looked up in thought for a few seconds. "No, there's nothing more."

Sam stood and put his hat on. "Thank you, Mrs. Richter. We'll look into it. The government depends upon citizens like you."

Martin followed Sam out the door, nodding to Mrs. Richter on his way out and touching the rim of his hat.

"You don't think there's anything to it, do you?" Martin asked after they'd gotten into Sam's car.

Sam chortled. "No—but we're going to track down Otto Schnell and have a chat. Just to close the file."

They found the road crew on the east end of Gettysburg, and the foreman pointed them at a man mixing cement in a big barrel. The woman in her fifties who had answered the door at the boarding house where Otto Schnell was said to be staying, had told them where he was working.

Schnell was short, five-foot-six or five-foot-seven at most, but he had the broad and muscular shoulders and thick arms of a much bigger man. He wore a faded blue shirt with the sleeves rolled up past the elbows, and he removed his tattered hat to wipe his brow with a red kerchief. His light blond hair was cropped short, almost a military-style crew cut, and his blue eyes peered at them through wire-rimmed glasses. He was a few years younger than Martin, probably late twenties.

Martin and Sam showed their badges.

"Otto Schnell?" Sam asked. When the young man nodded in silence, Sam said, "We'd like to have a word with you for a few minutes. Can we go over here where it's a little quieter?"

Schnell called to one of the other workers to come mix the cement, and he followed them to a nearby oak tree, where the tiny pale spring leaves didn't provide much shade yet.

"I am not a vagrant," Schnell said. "I have a room, and a job."

His accent was thick, but his English was good, Martin noticed.

Sam smiled to put him at ease. "We're not here to check you out for vagrancy. We just have a few questions. First, how long have you been in the United States, Mr. Schnell?"

"Almost five years."

"But you're new in Gettysburg."

A guarded look fell over Schnell's eyes. "Yes, eight or nine weeks."

"Before we go on, would you mind showing us your identification papers?" Sam asked.

Schnell pulled a small book of well-worn dark green leather from his back pocket. He handed it to Sam, who flipped it open, nodded, and passed it to Martin.

It was a German passport. Martin flipped it open, and noted the photo inside was a young version of the man standing before them. The issue date was December 1932—a month after the Nazis won a plurality in the elections, and a month before they took power. Martin suspected that wasn't a coincidence.

On the facing page was an exit visa, stamped June 1934. On the following page he found the immigration visa, issued by the U.S. Consulate in Hamburg, stamped July 2, 1934. Martin had issued enough of those visas himself when he was at the U.S. Embassy in Vienna to know it was legitimate.

If Schnell were a spy, the *Abwehr* had gone through an awful lot of trouble to get him legally emigrated. Not an easy task. Or a fast one.

The only entry stamps in the passport were issued at Southampton, England a week later; followed by a stamp from the Port of New York on July 19, 1934.

Martin handed the passport back to Schnell, who shoved it in his back pocket.

"Your passport expired more than a year ago," Martin said in German.

A momentary flash of surprise crossed Schnell's eyes, but he answered calmly in German. "I don't plan to ever go back, so it is not important."

"Are you from Hamburg?" Martin asked, still in German.

"Yes, I am Hamburger," Schnell said.

Martin wasn't an expert on accents in German, not enough to confirm a Hamburg accent specifically, but he could tell broadly that Schnell's was from the north. So that fit with his story.

"Have you got any identification that isn't expired?" Sam asked in English. "A driver's license, maybe?"

Schnell shook his head. "I do not drive."

Sam let it go. "Since you came to the U.S., where have you lived besides Gettysburg?"

The wary look returned. "Many places."

"Such as?"

Schnell shrugged. "New York, New Jersey, Pennsylvania. Many different towns."

"Who are the two German fellas you've been seen with lately?"

Martin noticed a touch of apprehension come to Schnell's eyes, and he wondered why.

"We are friends from Hamburg," Schnell said. "We all got out near the same time, and sometimes we find work together."

"Are they working here now?" Sam asked.

Schnell shook his head. "There wasn't enough work for them here. They went to Harrisburg a few days ago."

"What are their names?" Martin asked.

"Helmuth Oberhof, and Gottlieb Frei."

"Were they the two that Mary Richter heard you talking with a few days ago, when you said you had to avoid the police?" Sam's expression now was serious, and his eyes held Schnell's. "Is that why they skipped town? Because Mrs. Richter overheard you?"

Martin watched Schnell's mouth hang open for several seconds. Then he straightened up and took a step back from them.

"I need to go back to work."

"You need to answer our questions," Sam said, stern.

Schnell shook his head hard. "This is not Germany. You cannot make me talk to you. I know I have rights here."

Otto Schnell started to turn away, but Martin held up his hand. "Please, just a few more questions. Where did you learn English? You knew English before you came to this country, didn't you?"

Schnell hesitated, still half-turned. "Yes. I learned English at school."

"In Berlin?" Sam asked.

Schnell looked confused. "No, I studied in Hamburg."

Sam glanced at Martin with a wry look that seemed to say *I tried to trip him up*. Then he looked back at the young German man.

"Have you ever met Mr. Crown?"

Schnell seemed to think for a moment. "No, I don't think so."

"Perhaps you knew him as Gunther Rumrich."

Schnell shrugged. "No, I never heard that name."

"How about Dr. Griebl?"

He shook his head. "No."

"Gustav Guellich?"

Schnell continued to shake his head. "I am sorry, but I cannot help you. I do not know those men."

Martin watched Otto Schnell's eyes while Sam asked him about the German spies arrested in New York the year before. He saw no signs of recognition, or of deception. Sam caught his eye, and he shook his head almost imperceptibly.

"Thank you for your time, Mr. Schnell," Sam said, extending his hand. Schnell looked momentarily surprised, but shook their hands and returned to his cement mixing.

After they got in the car, Sam turned to face Martin. "Any reason you can think of that we should track down Helmuth Oberhof and Gottlieb Frei?"

Martin shook his head. "There's nothing here. But to be thorough, I'll write to the consulate in Hamburg tomorrow, ask them to verify that they issued immigration visas in '34 to all three. Schnell's is real, but we might as well ask about his along with the other two."

"I appreciate it. I'll check for arrest records with the state police in New York, New Jersey, and Pennsylvania." Sam put the car in gear, and drove back to the center of town.

Detective Ross looked disappointed when they told him Otto Schnell wasn't a spy.

"But you can't be sure, now can you, fellas? You'll monitor him, won't you?" He gave them a pointed stare, and Martin enjoyed Ross's displeasure.

Sam was diplomatic. "We're going to follow-up on a couple of items, but it seems there's nothing to worry about. False alarm." At Ross's skeptical look, Sam added, "They almost always are, Detective."

Ross scowled. "If you say so, you're the experts." He stood and shook their hands. "Just don't blame me if he gives secrets to the Nazis."

Martin wondered what secrets Ross supposed Schnell was finding in Gettysburg, but he let it go.

By the time they left the police station, it was after four-thirty. The regular work day was over. Martin glanced at his watch, realizing it would be after six o'clock before he got home, if they left now.

"I'll write up my report in the morning," Sam said, opening the car door. "I'll have you look at it before I give it to the chief, so you can add anything I forget." He glanced back at the police station. "Ross will settle down, and he'll tell Mrs. Richter and the others that it was all nothing. They can go back to their everyday lives, oblivious that Nazi and Commie agents roam the country, hidden among us."

"Do you mind if I make a phone call before we leave?" Martin asked, nodding toward a pay-phone a block down the street.

Sam looked at his watch. "If you're thinking of calling the office, nobody's there. It's after four-thirty."

"No, I need to call my wife to tell her I'll be late for dinner."

Sam chortled. "You young husbands, letting your wives rule the roost! If I decide to stay downtown for a couple of hours after work, or if I'm out here in the field following a lead, I don't call my wife to tell her I'll be late. She puts my plate in the oven and keeps it warm, and knows I'll be home when I get home."

Martin scowled. "I'm not asking her permission, it's just a courtesy call."

Sam held up his hands. "Alright, alright, don't get your dander up. I just notice that the younger generation lets their wives walk all over them sometimes, that's all. It was different when I was young. Men were *men*, you know?"

A sudden bolt of anger swept through Martin, and he started to ask what Sam meant by that. But the older man held up his hands again and hurried to add, "I didn't mean that for you, Martin. Just, you know, some of the younger men these days."

Martin nodded, barely mollified, and hurried toward the payphone. He inserted a nickel, asked the operator for long-distance to Washington, D.C., and gave the long-distance operator his telephone number. He inserted the amount she requested, and the line began to ring.

One advantage of sensitive government work was that they had a private telephone line—a rarity for anyone but the wealthy—in case the chief ever needed to call an agent at home to discuss something classified. They couldn't have someone listening in on a party line, hoping for gossip and getting much more.

"Schuller residence, Mrs. Schuller speaking," Becky's voice crackled over the line.

"Beck, it's Martin."

"Oh, hello, dear. Are you still at the office?"

Martin took a breath before continuing. "No, actually I'm in Pennsylvania. I came out here following a lead."

"I see." He could hear the ice in her tone, and pictured her frosty expression.

"It didn't pan out, so I'll be home tonight. I'll be late for dinner, though—keep a plate in the oven for me?"

The line was silent for a few seconds. "How late do you think you'll be? Will you be back in time to see the children before bed?" There was a distance in her voice that came through loud and clear, even over the crackle of the long-distance line.

"Oh, yes! I'll probably be home before you finish dinner. Probably around six thirty."

"Alright." She sounded unconvinced.

"I'll make it up to you," he said, not sure how he planned to do that. He could figure that out on the road.

Luckily, she supplied the answer. "Give the children their baths when you get home. Your dinner will keep."

As if on cue, he felt his stomach growl. "I'd be happy to. See you soon." He hung up before he had to insert any more change.

"Alright, let's go," he said to Sam when he reached the Dodge.

Sam shook his head and chuckled as he got behind the wheel. "Everything ok at home?"

"Of course."

Sam drove west out of town, toward Seminary Ridge.

"You ever been to the Gettysburg battlefield before?"

Martin nodded. "It was a required field trip when I was in high school."

"Did I ever tell you the Civil War was my special area of study when I was at college?" Sam asked.

"No, I don't believe you have."

"Yeah, that and the late antebellum, which got us into the Civil War. I've been to Gettysburg close to a dozen times. I know the fields and ridges backward and forward. Care for a tour?"

Martin thought of Becky's irritation, and shook his head. "It's been a long day, and I'd rather just get home."

Sam shrugged. "Suit yourself. I give a darn good battlefield tour."

"Thanks, some other time, maybe." *I just want to get home and see my kids*, he thought. *And my wife*, he belatedly added.

12

Monday, May 29, 1939

The breath caught in Martin's throat as he read the intercepted communiqué that arrived in the morning delivery from the diplomatic pouches.

An Information Officer at the American embassy in Berlin had come across a decoded message that the office of Admiral Canaris—the head of the *Abwehr*—had sent to the German High Command in Berlin more than a month before. The office of the U.S. Military Attaché in Berlin had intercepted the message and decoded it.

While the Military Intelligence Division and the Office of Naval Intelligence did not share with State the information gathered by their respective attachés at the embassies, it was not entirely unheard of that one of the assistant attachés, or support personnel, would accidentally leave something unattended on a desk for a period of time, and one of the embassy's Information Officers would just "happen" to stumble across it and copy it.

And it was by one such stroke of luck that the communiqué in Martin's hand had come into their possession.

In typical German military fashion, it was brief and to the point.

U-45 departed Bremerhaven 12 April 1939, 20:15.
Confirmed Schwarzkiefer aboard.
Will land beyond Montauk lighthouse and contact the skier.

There was a handwritten note to the side of the transcript, probably written by someone in the Military Attaché's office: "4 knots submerged = 43-44 days."

Martin quickly did the math, and found that forty-three to forty-four days would put them off the coast of Long Island on May 25th or 26th.

He bolted from his seat with the message and went to the chief's door. It was closed, but he knocked hard until he heard the chief shout, "Come in already."

"I've got a hot one, Chief," Martin said, laying the communiqué on the chief's desk. "German agent, landed off Montauk this past Thursday or Friday. Even if it took him two days to reach the city, he's probably in New York at this very moment."

The chief stood and began giving orders. "Have Hansen check the police blotters for the last four days from every police department between Montauk and New York City, see if anyone picked up our man—trespassing, peeping, loitering, you know the drill. If not, get ready to go to New York tonight. Trudy! I need requisition forms, on the double."

"I'm on it, Chief," Martin said, and hurried to Hansen's desk.

"This is Marty's last week of school, Martin," Becky said, sounding exasperated. "We said we were going to take the kids to the coast next week for the start of summer vacation."

"We'll go when I get back," he said.

Becky folded her arms and glared at him. "So what am I supposed to tell the kids about the trip? That it's postponed and I don't know when we're going to do it?"

Martin felt the irritation rising. Why couldn't she decide what to tell the kids, like always?

"Why not just tell them we'll go to the beach in a couple of weeks? They're kids, you don't have to be more specific than that."

Becky held her hands out in a helpless gesture, shaking her head. She walked over to the kitchen sink, stared at the wall a moment, and then spun around. Unexpectedly, she wore an almost triumphant expression.

"I think I'll ask my parents to come to the coast with me and the kids next week. It's not a far drive for them, I'm sure they'll be happy to." She added as a sort of afterthought, "You can join us whenever you get back from wherever you're going this time."

Something about the suggestion didn't sit well with Martin, but he couldn't put his finger on what exactly, or why. There was nothing wrong with Becky's parents joining them at the coast, and he could still meet up with them when he returned from New York. He had no argument against it.

"Alright, I'll send you a telegram when I get back to Washington, and I'll go out to the coast the next day."

She nodded without a word, and turned away to wash the breakfast dishes.

He hesitated a moment, not sure how to read her signals; then he walked up behind her, gave her a kiss on the cheek, and went out the door.

Tuesday, May 30

The shops in the Yorkville neighborhood on Manhattan's Upper East Side were all closed for the Memorial Day holiday as Martin walked past. He was dressed in the shoddy gray suit and fake mustache and glasses of his Augustus Graeter alias.

The rooming house on 88th Street where he had stayed in February was full, but late in the day on Monday he was able to find a room on 79th Street in the same neighborhood, close to a German butcher shop on 80th Street where he hoped to make some contacts.

No one here knew August Graeter, or seemed to recognize him—so for now, he hadn't had to recount the story of being arrested by the FBI and held against his will for three months.

The national headquarters of the German American Bund was located on 85th Street near Third Avenue, which was why his team chose that area last winter when scouting places for "Augustus Graeter" to stay. They had suspected a lot of Bund supporters lived nearby, and Martin had found those suspicions to be correct. He'd made the acquaintance of a few German nationalists in the area in February, and he intended to seek them out again.

There was a German restaurant with a biergarten on the next block. Martin hoped the biergarten would be open in spite of the holiday. He could get something to eat, and talk up the local Germans over a stein of beer. He often got good intelligence from casual conversations with people who had no idea they knew something significant.

As he reached the restaurant, he was happy to see that although it was closed, the gate leading toward the biergarten behind the restaurant stood open with a hand-written *"Wilkommen"* sign posted. He turned down the narrow walkway between the buildings and found the biergarten occupying a courtyard overlooked by several buildings.

It was not large as biergartens went, but he supposed in a densely populated and largely residential area, it was about as large as was practical.

Several people sat around tables, or on barstools at the big polished wood bar, which stood along the back wall of the restaurant. A radio behind the bar broadcast the Indianapolis 500, and most of the patrons appeared to be listening to the race—though Martin noticed they all seemed a bit subdued.

He walked to the bar and ordered a stein of Weiss beer. As the bartender poured it from the tap, Martin nodded toward the radio and asked in German, "What's happening with the auto race?"

"Floyd Roberts was killed a little while ago. Crashed through the barrier at more than a hundred miles an hour," the bartender replied, his German good, but carrying an unmistakable American accent. "Bob Swanson and Chet Miller are in the hospital. They said a couple of spectators were killed, too."

"My God," Martin said.

"You speak English?" the man on the barstool next to Martin asked him in German with a thick New York accent. He was a stocky man, probably mid-thirties, with light brown hair and pale blue eyes. His white dress shirt was open at the collar.

"Yes, I speak English," Martin answered in that language, in a perfect imitation of his parents' Pennsylvania Dutch accent.

"That's good, because my German's *nicht sehr gut.* My name's Fred Weideman."

"Augustus Graeter," Martin said, shaking his hand.

"Pleasure to meet you. I live in the neighborhood, just around the corner," Weideman said. "I haven't seen you around before—you new in the area?"

"New here, but not new to New York," Martin said, maintaining the Pennsylvania Dutch accent he'd heard daily as a child. "I used to have a room on 88th Street. Now I have a room on 79th Street, close to here. Moved in yesterday."

"You're from Germany?"

Martin made a sort of shrug. "I was born in Germany; but now it is in France, my hometown."

Fred Weideman made a little grunting sound. "I hear ya, bub," he said. "There were a bunch of people in the neighborhood who weren't too happy with what the Versailles Treaty did to Germany at the end of the World War, didn't think it was fair. Pretty hypocritical of Wilson, too—he talked so much about 'self-determination of nations,' but in the end he didn't extend that to Germans."

The sentiment piqued Martin's curiosity about Fred Weideman. What he'd expressed wasn't at all unusual among German-Americans twenty years earlier, and didn't *necessarily* indicate any sort of nationalist feeling now—but it could.

Martin decided to probe this a bit, but carefully.

"It was no good, but it was not the fault of the United States." He made a face before adding, "It was all the fault of France. They hate us. Now, in Alsace it is illegal to speak our own language in public; only French, or you pay a fine, maybe go to jail. It is no good in Alsace these days."

The look on Weideman's face—part curious, part sympathetic— told Martin this was likely new information to him.

"That's just not right," he said. "Here in America, we have freedoms. You can speak any language you want, and no one can tell you not to. Well—the *government* can't tell you not to, or the police. There are small-minded idiots out there that'll harass anyone they hear speaking a foreign language, but that's not how most Americans feel. Hell, we all came from somewhere, right?"

"That's good," Martin said, smiling. "Where are you from, Mr. Weideman?"

"I was born and raised here right here in Manhattan. My folks, too. My pop's folks came from Germany when they were children, but my mother's family has been in New York a long time. They're a little bit of everything, I suppose—English, Dutch, some other stuff too, I think. So I'm your typical American mutt."

He chuckled and took a long drink of his beer. "I like the food and the beer from my German side, but I don't speak very much German. *Ein Bisschen,*" he added with a grin, holding his fingers close together.

"Ah, not so bad, eh?" Martin said.

"Yeah, pretty bad, but I try. I come here a lot—like I said, I like the food and the beer. Gertrude in the kitchen makes a pretty mean Wienerschnitzel, and they get the sausages daily from the German butcher down the street. Oh, he's from Germany, by the way—the butcher, I mean. Been here a long time, I think, but he'd probably like to have someone from the old country to talk to, and it might make you feel at home here."

"Thank you, I will go there," Martin said.

The radio announcer's voice grew frantic. Louis Meyer's car had crashed in the backstretch at Indianapolis. Everyone in the biergarten fell silent, listening intently as the announcer described the events. The atmosphere was tense for several moments, until it became clear that Louis Meyer was unharmed. Then everyone seemed to exhale at once.

"Damn, I wanted him to win," Fred Weideman said.

"He's won three times already," the bartender said. "Who should win the Indianapolis 500 four times? Let somebody else have a chance to win it."

Weideman shook his head. "That's just jealousy. He's the best driver in the country. Why shouldn't he win again?" He looked at Martin. "Besides, he was born here in Manhattan, just like me."

"His parents were Alsatian," the bartender said, looking at Martin. Clearly, he'd been listening to their conversation.

Martin wasn't surprised. He'd found that bartenders could be a great source of information—they prided themselves on being good listeners as customers spilled their sorrows to them, and on keeping everyone's secrets—though they could usually be persuaded with cash. Martin didn't like resorting to bribery, but he wasn't above it if the need arose.

"You a married man, Mr. Graeter?" Weideman asked.

"No," Martin answered.

"Then I'll buy you another," he said with a grin, nodding toward Martin's empty stein, and raised his hand to order another round.

Martin chuckled. "Thank you. You are not married, either, then?"

"Not anymore," Weideman said. "Wife left me about a year ago, which was the nicest thing she ever did for me."

The bartender set the full steins in front of them, and Weideman raised his toward Martin. "Welcome to the neighborhood. *Prost!*" he said, and Martin clinked his glass on Weideman's.

The race was nearing its final laps, and the conversations around the biergarten ceased as everyone listened. Wilbur Shaw finished first, and conversations slowly resumed as the announcer described the festivities at the winner's circle. Weideman continued to listen, so Martin did as well.

When the radio announcer called out Shaw's average speed—115.035 miles per hour—Fred Weideman whistled and shook his head. "Can you imagine driving that fast? Trains don't even move that fast!"

He downed the last of his beer, laid a dollar on the bar, and put on his hat as he stood. "It was nice chatting with you, Mr. Graeter. I'll catch you around."

Wednesday, May 31

Martin found the butcher shop the next day, a few doors from the German restaurant.

Knowing that the butcher was an immigrant from Germany drew Martin's interest—the German immigrant community, far less numerous these days than just a few decades before, was where he was most likely to find Nazi sympathizers who might knowingly provide assistance to an *Abwehr* agent. At the least, they would likely provide assistance to a fellow German, even if they didn't know him to be an agent of the *Abwehr*.

And it was to German immigrants that a newly arrived *Abwehr* operative would instinctively go.

Martin arrived late morning, finding the butcher shop empty. Numerous cuts of meat—pork, veal, and beef—sat on display behind glass, while long chains of sausages hung from hooks on the ceiling over the counter.

A bell rang as he entered, and he heard a man's voice yell in a German accent from the back, "Boy! We have a customer." Then his tone grew less commanding. "We will be with you in a moment!"

"I've got it!" an adolescent male voice responded, and a thin boy came though the swinging door, wiping his hands on a bloody rag.

Martin addressed him in German. "I am new to the neighborhood, and I heard the butcher was from the Fatherland."

"Sorry, no sprechen deutsch," the boy said, mangling the pronunciation. "You speak English?" He had a strong working class New York accent, which sounded out of place in this middle class neighborhood, even in a butcher shop.

Martin switched to English, with the Pennsylvania Dutch accent. "Sorry, I heard the butcher was from Germany, so I assumed his children would speak German."

"He's not my pop," the boy said. "I just work here. Can I get you something?"

"Yes, I will take two of the knackwurst," Martin said, hiding his disappointment. He could be patient. It often took days to find out if a lead would pay off.

The boy took a large knife and climbed onto a stool. The butcher came through the swinging door as the boy was cutting off two sausages from the end of a long string.

The butcher was a portly man, about fifty years old, with thinning brown hair combed straight back from his red face. "Good morning, sir," he said in a thick German accent. "The boy is helping you, yeah?"

"*Guten Morgen, mein herr,*" Martin replied with a crisp nod, and continued in German. "Yes, he is."

"Ah! You speak German," the butcher said in that language. "You are from Switzerland, sir?"

"Alsace," Martin replied.

"*Ach,* I confuse the accents. I am from Essen, myself."

"You have been in America long?" Martin asked, eyeing the butcher's boy, who wrapped his sausages in brown paper. Martin saw no recognition in the boy's eyes, so he'd been telling the truth about not speaking German.

"Sixteen years," the butcher said. "It was very bad in Germany in those days. The inflation, a*ch*! I couldn't make a living. The money my customers would give me on Monday wouldn't buy me lunch on Tuesday! But in America, times were good. *Happy days are here again*, eh?"

He said the popular 1920s phrase in English. Martin faked a bemused look.

"I hear there is no shortage of work in the Fatherland these days," he said, and watched for the butcher's reaction.

The butcher gave him a shrug. "Yes, there is plenty of work in Germany now—but at what cost?"

He didn't elaborate, and Martin decided to probe a bit. "The cost does not seem too great for the people there. They are always smiling in the newsreels."

The butcher made a face. "For the cameras, of course they smile. They are afraid not to. My sister sends me letters, every month, and for the last five years her letters are always short. I can tell she is very careful what she says. I am not naïve; I can tell what is not there."

Martin nodded, sympathetic. He noticed the butcher's boy was standing there looking at him, the package of sausages in his hand, waiting as his employer and customer finished their conversation in the foreign language.

"Thank you," Martin said to him in English, careful to use the accent, and took the package. As he turned to leave, he looked back at the butcher and switched to German again. "Are there many people from the Fatherland in this neighborhood?"

"A few," the butcher said. "They mostly come to me for their meat, or to the Rathskeller restaurant down the block."

"Ah, yes—I visited the biergarten yesterday," Martin said. "Well, good bye, sir. And thank you."

"Have a nice day, sir," the butcher's boy said in English as Martin walked out.

Martin wasn't sure what he was going to do with a pair of uncooked sausages, when he didn't have a kitchen. He would figure that out later. For now, he tucked the package under his arm and walked west along 80th Street toward Lexington Avenue, and turned north. He walked a couple of blocks, and stopped at a deli for a sandwich.

After eating a corned beef on rye, he read the newspaper while he waited for the time to near one o'clock. At ten minutes before the hour, he folded the newspaper and tucked it under his arm with the package of sausages, and went north again.

At 86th Street and Second Avenue, in the heart of Yorkville, he found the Ketterman Print Shop. The sign on the door said they were closed for lunch, so he waited.

A few minutes later, he saw the figure of Stefan Ketterman walking forward through the shop. Ketterman saw him, and as he unlocked the door he took a quick glance up and down the sidewalk before motioning Martin in.

As soon as Martin was inside, Ketterman locked the door again. "Long lunch today," he muttered, and motioned for Martin to follow him toward the back office.

"I wasn't sure when I'd see you again, Mr. Graeter—or Mr. Smith, or whatever your real name is," Ketterman said.

"It's Mr. Graeter again today," Martin said, straight-faced, in his own voice. "I need to know if you've made any 'special' passports recently."

"Of course not," Ketterman said, with false sincerity. "Our agreement was that I wouldn't do that without contacting you, remember?"

"I'm sure you heard, I was swept up in an FBI raid at the Bund rally three months ago," Martin said. "You could have assumed from that news that our bargain was off."

"I might have heard something like that," Ketterman said. "I really can't remember."

Martin handed him a five dollar bill.

"Yeah, I heard about it. Some of the nationalists in the neighborhood knew something of it. They all speculated about what you'd been up to, to draw the attention of the FBI. I mean, they've been questioned before—you know, about their involvement with the Bund—but never arrested. So, rumor has it you're working with some secret organization, some German underground."

"How many knew?" Martin asked.

"Not many—ten, twelve, fifteen tops. But I can't say who all heard about it through the grapevine."

"I'll repeat my question," Martin said. "Have you recently done any passport work?"

Ketterman shrugged in exaggerated fashion, and Martin gave him another five dollar bill. "Yeah, sure. Couple of days ago, for this fella from Germany, needed some papers."

"What was his name?"

Ketterman scoffed. "His real name? Are you serious? They don't tell me that—they give me the name they want on the papers, and I pretend that's their name, even though I know as well as they do it's not."

"And what name was that?" Martin asked.

"Called himself Fritz Dendler."

"Did he speak English?"

"Some," Ketterman said. "But *nicht sehr gut*. He knows enough to get around. More than the last fella, anyhow—that 'Jan Hoffman,' the one who got arrested with you at the Bund rally—he could barely put together a sentence in English."

"Did you recognize his accent?" Martin asked. "Was it Bavarian, Swabian, Hessian?"

Ketterman shrugged. "I don't know accents in German, Mr. Graeter."

"You were born there."

Ketterman made a bigger shrug. "Yeah, sure—but I don't remember it. My parents' accent, *that* I know if I hear it. So I guess the most I can tell you is he ain't from Dusseldorf."

"Describe him."

"Young, like the last one, but not as skinny. Taller, too. This one was blond, hair wavy, blue eyes—you know, the Nazi ideal."

"Any idea where he was staying?" Martin asked, aware that his quarry may have moved on in the last couple of days.

"I told you last time—I don't get that involved. I don't know where their safe houses are, and I don't care to. I don't want to know who puts them up. All I want is to take their cash and give them the papers they ask me for. That's all I do, and that's really all, I swear."

Martin believed him. This wasn't going to be as easy as last time, when they knew in advance that the *Abwehr* agent, code-named *Immergrün*, was going to meet his contact at the Bund rally. He and Hansen had arrived in time to arrange with Ketterman to deliver the false passport themselves to *Immergrün* at the rally—and they would have nabbed him there, along with his contact, if it hadn't been for the interference from the blasted FBI.

This time, they knew little about the spy's agenda—only that he was supposed to locate *Der Skiläufer* and take his orders from him.

"Is there anything else you can tell me?" Martin asked, holding another five dollar bill just out of Ketterman's reach.

Ketterman eyed the money. "He asked how to get to Penn Station."

Penn Station, not Grand Central—so he was heading west. That could be anywhere—Philadelphia, Cincinnati, Cleveland, Chicago, Milwaukee, St. Louis, or even points beyond.

Damn it!

Martin moved the five dollar bill forward a few inches, and as Ketterman reached for it, he pulled it back.

"Did he say how long he's been in the States?"

"Not exactly," Ketterman said. "But he did mention that he was told before he left to seek me out right away—so maybe he'd been here a day or two? Who knows? Anyway, I told him I'd have the papers for him the next day, and to come back at three in the afternoon. He was here at three o'clock on the dot, he handed me the cash, I handed over the passport, and he left."

Martin handed over the five dollar bill. "You think he went directly to Penn Station?"

"Maybe," Ketterman said with a slight shrug. "He didn't have any baggage, but he might've been dressed for travel. He was wearing a nicer suit the second time than he was the first day."

"Thank you, Mr. Ketterman," Martin said, touching the front rim of his hat. "I'll be in touch. If you think of anything more, you'll tell me when I come back—got it?"

"Got it."

"And no more passport work for you," Martin said over his shoulder as he walked back through the store. "I hear one word about you doing that again, I'll have you arrested faster than you can say jiminy crickets."

He didn't look back at Ketterman as he unlocked the door and let himself out.

He took the subway to Grand Central station, noting as he got on the train that he'd left the package of sausages at Ketterman's shop.

114

At Grand Central he made for the Grand Hall, finding the nearest bank of pay telephones, and waited with the mass of humanity that also wanted to make a call. It took five minutes to shoulder his way into a phone booth. He put a nickel into the slot and asked the operator for long distance to Washington, D.C. When the long distance operator came on the line, he gave her a phone number and asked to reverse the charges.

"What name, sir?"

"Mr. Schuller."

He waited as the line rang; Trudy answered, "State Department."

"Long distance from New York, will you accept the charges from Mr. Schuller?"

"Yes, operator, I'll accept the charges."

"Go ahead please."

"Hello, Mr. Schuller. How's the trip?"

"Decent," Martin said. "Is Mr. Hansen in the office?"

"Yes, I'll put you through. One moment."

"How is it going up there, Martin?" Hansen asked a moment later.

"I've hit a dead end, Joe," Martin said. "He went to Ketterman two days ago, got a passport, and asked how to get to Penn Station."

"Yikes. He could be almost anywhere now. Not California, anyway—in two days, he could have made it as far west as Denver, but no farther than that."

"More likely somewhere in Pennsylvania or the Midwest," Martin said.

"Sure, but that doesn't exactly narrow it down much."

"Go over with me again what we know about *Der Skiläufer.*"

"Not that much, you know—but it'll still take a few minutes. The chief isn't going to like the bill for this call."

"I'll take the rap for it," Martin said. He listened as Hansen recounted the little tidbits they'd gleaned about the purported cell leader. It took a little more than three minutes, and he felt no better when Hansen had finished.

He'd hoped he had forgotten something, some little thing, but he hadn't. He sighed and rubbed his forehead.

"Alright, thanks, Joe. I've got to go before this call gives the chief a heart attack. I'll telegram when I need you to come out, the usual."

He hung up the receiver, opened the door, and almost got run over on his way out of the booth by the next man shouldering his way inside.

The only thing left to do was to go back to Yorkville and see if he could coax some nugget of information out of the German immigrants who frequented his local butcher, or the biergarten.

To start from scratch.

13

Martin returned to his old neighborhood. He walked to the tailor shop on 88th Street that occupied the ground floor of the building next to the boarding house where he had stayed in February.

"*Rolf Pfluger, Skilled Tailor*" was etched in the glass on the doorway.

The shop appeared empty, but at the sound of the bell ringing from the doorway, a middle-aged man's voice shouted from the back in a thick German accent. "I'll be right with you!"

A moment later, a man in his mid-forties came through the curtain that hung in the doorway to the back workroom. He had dark hair, graying at the temples, and wore a white dress shirt and a navy blue vest buttoned up. His navy blue slacks were crisply pressed, and matched the vest and the neck tie—it was a three-piece suit without the jacket. Martin saw the jacket hanging on a peg beside the curtained doorway.

The tailor recognized Martin—Augustus Graeter—right away, and Martin saw the apprehension in his gray eyes.

"Good afternoon," he said, hesitant, and in English.

"Good afternoon, Mr. Pfluger," Martin replied in German, with a crisp nod.

Pfluger's smile seemed forced, nervous even. He switched to German.

"Greetings—Mr. Graeter, wasn't it? We have not seen you in the neighborhood in a long time. It has been months, hasn't it?"

He stepped forward and continued in a lower voice, though the shop appeared empty. "We heard you were arrested at the rally," he said, his gaze intense. "We heard you were taken away by the FBI. When you did not return, we assumed you were in prison."

Martin made his best modest shrug. "For a little while, yes. They could not keep me long, for lack of evidence."

Pfluger glanced back at the curtain for a second, then motioned Martin toward the front of the shop. He locked the door and pulled the shades.

"My wife is working in the back," he whispered. "There is no one else here. Tell me—were you the courier?"

Martin didn't let his surprise at the question show. He stared back at Pfluger and said nothing.

As he suspected, Pfluger took this as tacit acknowledgment, and felt free to open up a little more.

"We knew there was a courier, but we did not know who it was," he said. "You went to the rally because you were taking the—the 'package'—to the Skier, weren't you?"

Again, Martin said nothing, but made the tiniest of shrugs.

"Is that why you are back now?" Pfluger asked, almost breathless. "Is there another 'package' to deliver to the Skier? I mean, we have heard rumors, but..." he trailed off.

"The rumors are true," Martin said, and didn't elaborate.

Pfluger nodded, a firm gesture, and took a step back. "It is dangerous for you to be here," he said, only slightly louder than his previous whisper. "I cannot help you right now. After the rally in February, I was questioned several times. I was not arrested, but I knew they were on to us. They may even now be watching us. You must leave and not come back. I'm sorry."

He started to raise the blinds.

"Do the patriots still gather at the Burnett Fountain?" Martin asked.

The apprehension returned to Pfluger's eyes. "Yes," he said, and hesitated.

"Go on," Martin prodded.

"The gatherings are irregular now, in case they are watching. And we—all of us—only go to every other one, to keep them guessing. Now leave, please. I'm sorry." He unlocked the door.

"Thank you," Martin said, and slipped out.

The Burnett Fountain stood at the south end of the Conservatory Garden in Central Park, off Fifth Avenue and 104th Street. Martin went there that afternoon on the off chance that a few of the local German Nationalists would gather there after work, before the dinner hour.

On this warm afternoon, children ran around the conservatory garden, squealing and laughing, relishing the beginning of their summer vacation, while their mothers—already weary looking—walked behind them in twos and threes, commiserating.

Martin sat on an empty park bench, watching the children and thinking of his own. They would probably be on the beach now, splashing in the surf, or building sand castles while Becky read a book under an umbrella. He felt a touch of sadness about missing these moments with them, but shoved that aside. He allowed himself only a few moments of reverie, and then his mind began mulling the questions before him.

Who was this courier who had taken *Immergrün* from his unknown safe house to the Bund rally at Madison Square Garden? Clearly, Pfluger and the others around him did not know the true identity of the courier, or else he would not have so readily believed it was "Augustus Graeter."

So was there much that he could learn here from them, should any of them arrive this afternoon?

If they were not in the know, there were obviously others who were. But where would he find them? He began to suspect he'd be better off returning to his new neighborhood on the southern end of Yorkville, visiting the German butcher shop on 80th Street, and the Rathskeller biergarten.

He exited the Conservatory garden and walked south down the park side of Fifth Avenue for more than twenty blocks. Just past the Metropolitan Museum of Art, he crossed over when he reached 80th Street and headed east.

This was the wealthy part of the Upper East Side, lined with large brownstone mansions where the upper class had fled in the previous decades, as midtown high-rises had displaced them and their earlier Victorian mansions farther south along Fifth Avenue. He passed Madison and Park avenues, and crossed Lexington Avenue into Yorkville.

Yorkville was a middle class area, and more than half of the area's residents were German-American—though most were second, third, or fourth generation Americans these days, and it was not exclusively German, like the old *Kleindeutschland*.

For most of the nineteenth Century, the *Kleindeutschland* had been several miles south, surrounding Tompkins Park. During the height of German immigration, the area between Avenue A and Avenue D had been almost exclusively German, and middle class. But by the late 1890s, the influx of poorer eastern European immigrants spreading north from the Lower East Side tenements had begun to push the German-American community out. Many of them migrated up the east side to the newer Yorkville neighborhood, and for the last forty years this had been the center of German-American culture in New York City.

It was late in the afternoon when he neared the German butcher shop. He was surprised to see a line out the door—and even more surprised that the line was mostly middle-aged men, rather than housewives.

Jackpot, he thought as he got into line. But he changed his mind after greeting the three men in front of him, and realizing they were all American. Judging by their accents when they returned his *"Guten tag"* greeting, they were not fluent speakers of German.

He decided to give up, and instead went around the corner to his boarding house. He would clean up, and then go to the biergarten.

An hour later, he rounded the corner from Second Avenue onto 80th Street. The sun sat lower in the western sky, resting just above the roofs of the buildings on the opposite side of Central Park, and the heat of the day was moderating.

As he reached the alleyway leading back to the biergarten, he saw the butcher's boy come out of the shop—dressed in a stylish black suit, matching fedora, and shiny new black shoes. The seeming incongruence of his appearance made Martin stop in his tracks for a second.

"Did you forget something?" a familiar voice behind him said in English, sounding amused.

"Oh, sorry," Martin said to Fred Weideman, with a sheepish look. Then he nodded down the street. "I was just surprised to see the butcher's boy dressed in such a fine suit. I could never afford such a suit, so how can he on a shop boy's wages?"

A strange look of disapproval came to Weideman's face. "It's not his wages that buy Mr. Spooner the nice clothes," he said, his words cold-edged. "It comes from what he charges for his, um, *services*." He shook his head. "Looks like he must be off for a date, or whatever you call it."

Martin wondered what illegal activity the boy might engage in. He gave Weideman a bemused look in hopes he would elaborate.

Weideman leaned close, and muttered just louder than a whisper. "They say for five dollars, he'll, um, 'oil your sausage' for you; or for twenty he'll put your sausage inside his bun."

121

He pursed his lips and shook his head. Then he gave Martin a wary look. "I didn't think that was your sort of thing, though, Mr. Graeter."

Martin felt his cheeks flushing hot. He stammered "No, *mein Gott*," then looked away, embarrassed.

Weideman chuckled. "I didn't take you for a faerie," he said. "It's also said that Mr. Spooner sells dope, if you're into smoking funny cigarettes."

Martin smiled a sheepish smile. In truth, he hadn't smoked marijuana in almost ten years.

Weideman leaned in again, and whispered. "Yeah, alright, so maybe I've bought marijuana cigarettes off him a few times. It took the edge off after my wife left me. It's not like I'm a dope fiend or anything."

He started down the alley toward the biergarten, and Martin followed.

There was a decent crowd in the biergarten for a Wednesday evening, Martin thought, pleased. Most of the tables were occupied, and while most of the conversations were in English, he heard a couple of conversations being conducted in German, with native accents.

Just what he'd hoped to find.

Friday, June 2

Martin went to the biergarten on 80th Street late in the afternoon. Earlier in the day, he had visited the German butcher shop, and this time he made the acquaintance of a few men and women from Germany.

The butcher's boy—"Young Mr. Spooner" the patrons called him— had begun to remember him, and greeted him as "Mr. Graeter" when he came in that day.

Martin had learned that many of the German-born patrons of the butcher came to the biergarten on Friday and Saturday evenings, so he made a point to arrive early and get a good seat in the middle of the courtyard, where he would be able to hear any conversation.

He saw Fred Weideman arrive shortly after five o'clock, and he smiled when he saw Martin siting at a table in the middle of the garten. "Hello, Mr. Graeter," he said, standing at the bar but facing sideways.

"Hello, Mr. Weideman. It is a pleasure to see you again."

"Getting comfortable in the neighborhood?" Weideman asked, then turned to the bartender and ordered a stein of beer.

"Yes, thank you for asking."

"Did that shipment arrive today?" Weideman asked the bartender.

"Yes, sir. It arrived before lunchtime, like you promised. Mr. Kraus said your first beer tonight is on the house."

"Thank you, Paul," Weideman said, raising his stein in the bartender's direction. Then he walked over to Martin's table, nodded at the empty chair across from him, and asked, "Would you mind if I joined you?"

"Not at all, thank you," Martin said.

"You're getting to be a regular here," Weideman said as he sat, and took a swig of his beer.

"Yes, it is a nice place. You do business with the restaurant?"

Weideman nodded as he took a long drink of his lager. "Yes, glasses and china. I'm a regional salesman for Showalter Glassworks. I have a lot of regular customers in Yorkville, including this charming little venue. The good beer and the wienerschnitzel aren't the only reasons I come here so often."

A small part of Martin hated that he couldn't tell Weideman that he'd met Maximilian Showalter a couple of months before, but he knew he wouldn't be able to think of a plausible story for a common laborer such as Augustus Graeter to have met the wealthy industrialist.

"What sort of work do you do, Mr. Graeter?"

"I am currently looking for work," Martin said. "I make a little money doing odd jobs, but I have not had steady work in almost two years."

"A very common predicament," Weideman said. "What did you do before?"

"I was a bookkeeper," Martin said. It was the most common skill that he knew how to do, in case Weideman recommended a position with one of his clients.

A curious look came to Weideman's face. "There should be plenty of work of that type available these days," he said. "Businesses are expanding again, and just about everyone needs a bookkeeper."

"They hire Americans first," Martin said with a shrug, trying to sound nonchalant about it. "They won't hire an immigrant like me when there are three or four Americans who also apply."

This seemed to satisfy Weideman, who nodded with a sad sort of resignation on his face. "I'm sure that's common. Perhaps I can recommend you to one of my midtown clients. Do you have a nicer suit you can wear to an interview in an office?"

Martin shook his head. "This is my only suit."

"That's too bad," Weideman said. "But I can give your name to any of the shopkeepers around here when I hear they need some day labor, in any case."

"Thank you," Martin said, and raised his stein. "That is very kind of you."

"Don't mention it."

The biergarten was beginning to fill up as evening fell. Several of the German immigrants he had met at the butcher shop recognized him and nodded in his direction as they took seats. He nodded back, and greeted them in German.

"I see you're settling in," Weideman said. He finished the last of his beer, and stood. "If you'll excuse me, I'm going inside for dinner. Good evening."

"Good evening, Mr. Weideman," Martin said with a nod.

He spent the next hour engaging in conversation with some of the Germans he had met, little more than idle chit chat, but getting them comfortable.

The odds were, at least one German-born resident of the area was helping the *Abwehr* agents after they landed, giving them safe haven until they could move on.

Was one of them nearby right now? Only time would tell. He would have to be patient.

Wednesday, June 7

Martin was walking down the sidewalk from his boarding house toward the biergarten late in the afternoon when he saw a familiar, though unwelcome, figure leaning against a wall, staring at him with a sardonic smile.

Martin slowed down, and Special Agent Reginald Sloan walked to him.

"Shake my hand, and then start walking with me," Sloan said, extending his hand.

Martin did as instructed. It was a safe enough bet that no one around here knew who Sloan was. They walked south down Lexington Avenue.

"I've wondered when I'd see you back here," Sloan said, his voice low enough that only Martin could hear.

"What do you want?" Martin asked, not hiding the irritation in his voice.

"We want to know who you're tracking in New York," Sloan said.

"Why should I tell you that?"

"Because this is our territory," Sloan said. "And we're responsible for Federal law enforcement here in New York. So if you're tracking the sort of man we think you're tracking, we want to know about it."

"What will you do if I don't tell you?"

Sloan chuckled. "Let's not find out, shall we?" He pointed toward the subway station across the street, and they waited for a break in the traffic to cross 77th Street and go down the stairs.

"I can't tell you, it's classified," Martin said from the corner of his mouth as they descended the stairs.

"We'll see about that," Sloan said, following Martin through the turnstile and pointing him toward the platform for downtown-bound trains.

"Where are we going?" Martin asked.

"The Waldorf Astoria," Sloan said.

Martin wondered what FBI big-wig had arranged a room at the Waldorf, just to have a chat with him. He was hardly a big fish. Something was up.

They got off at 51st Street, ascended to street level, and walked a block west to Park Avenue, then south to the Waldorf Astoria. It was a fairly new hotel, having replaced the old one on 34th Street less than a decade before, when it was torn down to make way for the Empire State Building. Martin felt eyes on him as they crossed the lavish lobby, and he felt shabby and underdressed for the venue.

The elevator operator gave his clothes a side-glance as he followed Sloan into the car. "Sixteenth floor," Sloan said.

After stepping off the elevator, Sloan guided Martin down the long hallway to the end. He rapped on the door in a sequence, and it was opened by a short man with slicked-back brown hair, wire-rimmed glasses, and a thick brown mustache. He gave Martin a smug look, and stepped aside as Sloan put his hand on Martin's shoulder to guide him inside.

Another man, black-haired and with a darker complexion, sat at a desk in front of a Poulsen Wire Recorder, wearing a pair of ear phones and making small adjustments to dials on the recording machine. He stood up when he saw Sloan.

"Mr. Schuller, allow me to introduce Agent Anderson"—he indicated the man who had opened the door—"and Agent Pagliaro"—the man at the recording machine. "They'll be assisting me."

"I'm to be interrogated?" Martin asked, a little surprised. The fancy recording device concerned him. And so did the location—why wouldn't they want to talk at their headquarters downtown? What was the reason for the remote location?

"If you'd prefer it that way," Sloan said. "I'd rather it be a conversation."

"Like I said before—I won't be able to tell you very much. I'm sure most of what you'll want to know is classified, and I'm not at liberty to discuss it."

"I have security clearance," Sloan said.

"Then you can file a request with my superior at State."

"Has another Nazi agent landed? Is that who you're tracking? Hoping he'll lead you to The Skier?"

Martin's jaw set. "I can't discuss it."

"Cut the crap!" Sloan said, scowling. "What makes you boys at State think you can do better at this counter-espionage stuff than we can? We've been doing infiltration and reconnaissance far longer than you. We perfected it busting up the Mob. You might have read about some of our successes in the newspapers. You wanna ask Al Capone if we're any good at this? How about Doc Barker and Alvin Karpis? Should I go on?"

"I'm not exactly an amateur detective, Special Agent Sloan," Martin said, his eyes narrowing.

Sloan and Anderson both smirked.

"He don't know what a real pro is," Anderson said to Sloan.

Sloan didn't respond, and kept his eyes on Martin. "Have a seat, Mr. Schuller. Make yourself comfortable." He pointed at the chain next to Pagliaro and the Poulsen.

Martin had had enough. "I think I'll be leaving," he said.

As he started toward the door, Anderson appeared in front of him, and drew up close to his face.

"Sit down, wise guy."

Martin stared down into Anderson's eyes, refusing to blink. When he spoke, his tone was confident and steady. "Do you fellows suspect me of some crime? Do you have probable cause? If not, you can't keep me here."

"Shut up," Anderson said, his voice angry but also a touch whiny.

Martin chuckled. He'd pricked the little bully. His voice shifted from confident to commanding. "You might be able to get away with unlawful detention of anarchists, or communists—but you know as well as I do you won't be able to get away with it with me, a U.S. government employee. You know this, Sloan. Harassing a government officer performing his official duties—that could cost you your job, couldn't it?"

"Shut up and sit down!" Anderson said, giving Martin a shove.

Martin's hand came up in one swift move, the heel slamming into Anderson's chin and sending him reeling back. Anderson stumbled and fell, blood pouring from his mouth.

"You fuckin' bastard!" Anderson shouted, wiping his mouth and starting to scramble up.

"Anderson, stop!" Sloan shouted from behind Martin. "Go clean yourself up and cool down," he ordered, pointing at the bathroom.

Anderson glowered at Martin as he stormed past, slamming the bathroom door.

Sloan pointed his finger at Martin's face. "Have it your way, Schuller. Yeah, you're free to go—but see how you do. You just made an enemy of the FBI."

Pagliaro looked aghast. "But Boss! He just assaulted a Federal officer! We can't let him go—we can hold him now."

"I *am* a Federal officer," Martin said, forcing down the butterflies that filled his stomach. They were right—they could arrest him for striking Anderson. It wouldn't matter that Anderson had assaulted him first. What had he done?

Martin picked up his hat from where it had fallen on the floor when Anderson shoved him. He put it on his head, nodded at Sloan, and let himself out.

He spotted them as soon as he reached the top of the stairs from the subway station at 77th and Lexington. Two men in dark suits and hats, lounging against the stone wall of a building, stared at him as he emerged into the daylight. The moment he began walking up Lexington Avenue, they followed him, keeping about ten steps behind.

He took a round-about way home, and they stayed with him. At one intersection while he waited for the light to change, he turned around and stared at them. They stared back.

"Can I help you, gentlemen?" he asked, using the Pennsylvania Dutch accent he'd adopted for Augustus Graeter.

"No, we're just out for a walk," one of the men said, with exaggerated innocence.

They followed him all the way to the boarding house, and as he stepped into the vestibule he spun around, prepared to fight if they followed him inside. He was not by default a violent man, it ran counter to his upbringing—but he could do what he must.

He saw the men continue down the sidewalk, passing his building as if they were just minding their own business.

Martin waited a half hour before venturing out again. He spotted a different pair of men across the street, watching the front of his building. He began walking toward the butcher shop, and they followed him, about twenty feet behind this time.

They waited on the sidewalk until he came out, and Martin felt a deep unease settle into his belly at the thought of everyone in the neighborhood observing that he was being watched. If he was too hot, no one would talk to him.

The same two were waiting for him when he came out of his boarding house a while later. They followed him to the biergarten, lounging at the entrance of the alley until he emerged an hour later, and followed him back home.

As Martin closed the door of his room and pulled the shade, he seethed in silence. The room was stuffy, with no breeze coming through the open window, and he undid his tie and unbuttoned his shirt. He stood for a moment and stared at the floor, brooding. Then he bunched up his shirt in his fist, and tossed it across the room.

"Damn it!"

14

Friday, June 9, 1939

Everywhere he went the next day, a pair of men followed him. He counted at least four different pairs on a seemingly random rotation, but they were always there.

On Friday morning, he went to Grand Central Station, waited for a phone booth, and placed a call to Washington. The two men following him that morning leaned against the granite wall opposite him, arms crossed, watching.

"Trudy, I need to speak to the chief," he said when he'd been connected.

"He's got someone in his office right now, but I'll see if he'll take the call."

"It's urgent, Trudy."

"Alright, I'll see what I can do."

Thirty seconds later, she transferred him through.

"What's the urgency, Schuller?" the chief asked.

"The FBI's interfering again," Martin said, not hiding his irritation. "They won't let me alone this time." He recounted their surveillance of him for the last day and a half, and finished by saying, "I can't do a damn thing like this."

"Get out of there," the chief said. "Go straight to Penn Station and get on the next train back. I'm aborting the mission for now."

"We can't let them get away with it, boss."

"You let me take care of that," the chief said. "Just get back to Washington on the double."

"Yes, sir," Martin said, and hung up.

He eyed the two agents as he squeezed out of the telephone booth and through the crowd. He headed through the corridors toward the cross-town subway line that ran between Grand Central and Penn Station.

The two men followed him, standing about ten feet from him on the platform as he waited for the next train. When it arrived, they got on right behind him and hung on the rail a few feet from him, staring him down the entire ride.

At Penn Station they followed him all the way to the ticket counter, waiting near the clock as he purchased a ticket for the Washington Express.

They followed him from the ticket counter toward the terminal, but as he went down the stairs they hesitated, talked it over, and then only one of them followed him down to the platform.

Martin assumed the other had gone to make a phone call. He could imagine the conversation with Sloan, informing the special agent that the interloper from State was heading back home with his tail between his legs. "We drove him off, Boss," he imagined the man saying with a big gloating grin.

The remaining agent stood about a dozen feet from him, watching while he waited, and as the train arrived in a cloud of hissing steam and passengers disembarked—until the conductor announced over the loudspeaker that boarding had begun for Washington, D.C.

As Martin walked down the aisle of the train car, he looked out the window at the platform and saw the agent walking along beside the train, keeping watch.

Martin took a seat, and the agent stopped, leaned against a steel beam, and watched.

When the train finally began to move, the agent took a few more steps, keeping watch until he was out of sight.

Martin felt the tension of being followed slip away, but in its place rose anger at being driven out of New York. He ripped off his fake mustache and banged a fist on the arm-rest.

"Sons of bitches," he muttered.

Martin went directly to the Old Executive Office Building from the train station when he arrived midday. He got strange looks from the office girls as he walked through the typing pool, and even from the old black janitor who was dumping waste paper baskets into a bin as he passed, and Martin realized he hadn't changed clothes.

"Aren't you a sight," Trudy said as he entered the office.

Hansen looked up from his desk and laughed. "Why, as I live and breathe, if it isn't the elusive Augustus Graeter!" he hammed.

Martin shot him a look. He wasn't in the mood.

Hansen's grin faded. "You missed all the excitement around here yesterday," he said.

"Oh?"

"The king and queen of England were in town," Hansen said. "The chief let us all go outside and watch as the royal motorcade arrived at the White House."

In his irritation over his unceremonious departure from New York, Martin had completely forgotten about the much-ballyhooed royal visit to the U.S. No British monarch had ever visited the country before—not even during colonial times.

"I'm glad you got to enjoy yourselves," Martin muttered.

"They're going to be in New York tomorrow, at the World's Fair," Hansen continued.

"I'd rather not talk about New York right now, if you don't mind."

Hansen caught his tone, and returned to his work.

"Yes, sir," Trudy said, and hung up the phone on her desk. She spun her chair around and faced Martin. "The chief wants to see you, Mr. Schuller."

Martin could see from the look on Trudy's face that this wasn't going to be a fun conversation. He took a deep breath, pushed himself up from his seat, and marched to the chief's office door.

"Close the door, Schuller," the chief barked.

Martin complied, noticing that the chief had not offered him a seat. He swallowed hard, and kept his face placid with effort.

"Did you strike an FBI agent?"

Straight to the point. Martin nodded. "In my defense, sir, he got physical with me, and I—"

"Shut your mouth," the chief said, a deep scowl wrinkling his forehead. "I don't want your excuses. The Under Secretary got a call this morning from J. Edgar Hoover himself, demanding your head on a God damned silver platter. All I want to hear from you right now is why we shouldn't fire you this moment."

Martin swallowed hard again. He could feel the sweat on his upper lip, and his stomach seemed to have tied itself into knots.

"Well, sir, I learned some good information." He recounted all he had learned about *Schwartzkiefer*'s movements, the courier, and the FBI's apparent ignorance of it.

The chief stared at him as he spoke, unblinking, eyes narrow, unmoving. When Martin finished, the chief released a long, frustrated sigh.

"This is the second time the blasted FBI has spoiled one of our investigations, but that is not an excuse for what you did, understand? Alright, fine—you can get back to work. But you're on probation because of this, Schuller. You make us look bad again, and you're done."

Martin swallowed his pride, and bowed his head in acquiescence. "I understand, sir."

The chief looked down at the papers strewn across his desk, made a dismissive wave with his hand, and Martin slunk out.

Martin got home from work that afternoon wound as tight as a piano string. The boss was still furious, and kept shouting at everyone in the office about the slightest error. Martin left at precisely four-thirty, and so did everyone else.

He knew the apartment would be empty, which at least meant peace and quiet this evening. He figured he'd take a bath, have a beer, and pack his suitcase for the coast. That was one good thing about coming back early, he reasoned—he could get to the beach with the kids only a few days after they got there, and he wouldn't miss much of their vacation.

The thought of their happy faces when he showed up made him smile as he unlocked the apartment door and stepped inside.

He saw the envelope on the mantle as soon as he hung his hat on the coat rack. It bore only his first name, in Becky's elegant flowing handwriting.

He tore it open, a sense of dread sinking into the pit of his stomach. He unfolded the single sheet of stationary with her monogram at the top, and read the short note.

> *Martin,*
> *Please do not come to Delaware. I don't want to see you. I*
> *am leaving you. The children and I will stay with my parents*
> *for the foreseeable future. I can't continue to live this way. I'm*
> *sorry,*
>
> *Becky*

He crumpled the paper and tossed it onto the living room floor. He marched down the hall to their bedroom and flung open the door. Her clothes were missing from the closet, and from all of her dresser drawers.

He rushed to the kids' room, but all he found were their beds, carefully made. Their clothes, toys, puzzles and books were gone. Everything was gone, including their teddy bears.

He began to shake. Whether it was rage or sorrow he wasn't sure. He didn't care.

There was still plenty of daylight, and he walked south along 17th Street NW toward downtown, taking quick, agitated steps in spite of the heat. He normally paid attention to everything and everyone he passed, but he was too distracted this evening, his thoughts whirling in his head.

When he reached Pennsylvania Avenue, he looked across at the Old Executive Office Building. He didn't want to think about work in his sour mood, so he turned east and didn't look at the giant old building again. After a short block, the buildings fell away, and the North Lawn of the White House spread out to his right on the opposite side of the avenue, while the semi-wooded expanse of Lafayette Park stretched northward on his left.

He turned into the park.

He walked the perimeter, still agitated and barely noticing his surroundings. The shade offered relief from the early evening sun, and he took off his hat, wiping the sweat from his brow. He continued with his hat in his hand.

He stopped, hot and sweaty, when he reached the statue of General Lafayette at the southeast corner of the park. The trees provided shade, but seemed to hold in the muggy air. He found a nearby park bench under the arms of a giant oak tree and sat down, fanning himself with his hat. He loosened his necktie and unbuttoned the collar of his shirt.

Now he tried to relax and distract himself by looking around the park. It was a warm evening, and the park was full of young people, probably the residents of all the rooming houses and apartment buildings that lined the park and the nearby side streets, fleeing the stuffy heat of the indoors for the relative fresh air of the park.

The government bureaucracy had doubled in size over the last six years, since President Roosevelt began his New Deal programs. The rooming houses and apartment buildings in this part of Washington were crammed beyond capacity with young government clerks and secretaries, sometimes three or four to a room.

The people Martin saw walking around Lafayette Park this evening all looked happy. He'd often overheard groups of young staffers inside the Old Executive Office Building talking about how bad things were in their home towns, or how boring and backward their little rural towns were compared to Washington. He supposed that even being crammed into little apartments with multiple roommates had to be better than what most of them had left behind.

He was envious of their happiness.

There were far more men about than women this evening, Martin realized as the sun sank behind the buildings and a soft shadow fell over Lafayette Park. Several of them smiled at him as they walked by. Probably Southerners or Midwesterners, he supposed—smiling at a stranger was not something one did in Pennsylvania.

A lone young man sat down on the opposite end of the park bench, smiling at Martin.

"Hot one tonight, isn't it?" he said with a sort of flat nasal accent from somewhere such as Wisconsin or Minnesota. His collar was open, and the next button also, and his sleeves had been rolled up past his elbows.

Martin nodded.

"You meeting some friends?" the young man asked.

"No," Martin said, and continued to watch people walk by.

"Me neither," the young man said. After a moment, he added, "But I'm probably going to a party over at the YMCA in a couple of hours."

Martin grunted and nodded as his only acknowledgment. He wished the young man would just mind his own business and let him sit alone and think.

"I haven't seen you around here before."

Martin shook his head. "I don't usually stay downtown after work."

"You work for the government?"

Martin really wished the guy would stop talking. "State."

"Oh, just around the corner over there," the young man said with a grin, pointing toward the towering façade of the Old Executive Office Building a block away. "I'm the opposite direction, at Treasury. I'm a bookkeeper."

Martin nodded. He wanted solitude, but supposed he'd have to get up and go somewhere else to find it. He stood and put his hat on.

"There's privacy back there in the woods," the young man said, nodding his head back. "I mean, if you're new to this."

For half a second, Martin wondered what he meant; then he noticed the young man's hand slowly rubbing his crotch, and realized he had an erection tenting the front of his pants.

Something inside him snapped. Normally, this would have been a minor aggravation, something he would have ignored and walked away from—but after everything that had happened that day, first in New York, then the office, and then at home, his anger exploded.

He backhanded the young man across the mouth, sending him sprawling across the bench.

"Hey! Cool it, fella—I didn't mean anything!" the boy said as Martin grabbed a fistful of his shirt and tugged him up to his feet.

He pulled his arm back and slammed his fist into the young man's stomach.

The boy doubled over and began to sob.

Martin let go and stepped back, going suddenly cold as he had a flashback picturing a group of Nazi Stormtroopers beating up a pair of "degenerate perverts" on a street corner in Berlin in 1933. Fingers of ice crept up his spine as he realized how easily he had fallen into that role, and his breath caught in his throat.

But the young man's crying filled Martin with contempt, and he turned and stormed off.

"You could have just said no, you big jerk!" he heard the boy yell after him.

The groups of young men and women walking along the path parted before he reached them, and they all watched him march past, wide-eyed.

Damn them all, he thought as he turned toward home.

Martin knew he'd overreacted. *I shouldn't have hit the kid.* The thought kept repeating itself. The young man's actions hadn't been sufficient provocation to attack him.

Still, he had a difficult time feeling truly remorseful. He had done nothing to encourage what happened, after all.

He'd been caught fighting in the school yard a few times when he was a boy in Reading, and he remembered his father's stern disapproval. Violence and fighting were frowned upon in the Pennsylvania Dutch culture in which he'd grown up—not just among the pacifist sects, but among the Reformed and Lutheran as well.

The image of his father's deep scowl and the memory of his Bible-laced rebukes firmed Martin's resolve. He might have overreacted, but he wouldn't admit he'd been in the wrong.

But that night, he lay awake for a long time, picturing the young man's crying face, unable to forget the hurt he saw in it.

Later he dreamed he stood and watched as Nazi Stormtroopers beat the young man unconscious. When they turned around, he saw his own face on each of them.

Hutson

15

Monday, June 12, 1939

As if he'd conjured it up, on Monday when Martin got home from work there was a letter from his mother in the mail box. It was addressed to *Mr. and Mrs. Martin Schuller*, as usual, and Becky typically read them first.

Martin cringed to think of what his parents would say when they found out Becky had left him. He put that out of his mind for now, and opened the envelope.

The letter was long, more than three pages, in his mother's flowing script. Becky had had a hard time learning to read it when they were first married, and Martin had to help her decipher words—until she'd learned to read the characters of the elaborate German script on all of the storefronts in Austria, and from then on she'd been able to read his mother's letters without assistance.

There was the usual news about families in Reading, his siblings, things that had transpired since his mother's previous letter the month before, and finally a reminder that they had not seen them since Christmas.

He and Becky usually took the kids to visit their grandparents in Reading around county fair time in the late summer. That was an event Martin always associated with good memories from his childhood, and he loved sharing that experience with his own kids. The thought of going to the Berks County Fair this summer without Becky made his stomach hurt.

Maybe I can convince her to come back before then, he thought, but knew it wasn't true even as he forced himself to think it. She was never coming back to him. This had been building for too long, and he had done nothing to stop it.

Would he be able to take the kids with him to the fair? He was sure Becky wouldn't object, but he would have to ask. There were so many things that needed to be discussed with regards to the kids—but he knew that if he called her right now, he would get angry, and they would begin yelling at each other over the long distance line. That would only waste time and money.

Still, they had to talk sooner or later. He could write her a letter, but waiting for a response could take days, even weeks if she stalled.

He decided a week was a good enough amount of time to calm his emotions so that they could have a rational conversation. He made a note on the calendar hanging from the wall in the kitchen, and then tried to put it out of his mind.

Wednesday, June 14

The phone on his desk rang shortly after eleven o'clock that morning, and Martin stared at it for a second before answering, his stomach seeming to fill with butterflies. He rarely got personal calls at work, but he wondered if it was Becky calling from the hotel in Rehoboth Beach.

He answered after the second ring. "Schuller."

"I have a call for you from an FBI Special Agent, Reginald Sloan," Trudy said.

That caught Martin by surprise. "Long distance, from New York?"

"No, it's a local line, Mr. Schuller."

What the hell does he want? And why is he in Washington?

"Go ahead and put him through, Trudy." When the line clicked, he said, "This is Martin Schuller."

"Mr. Schuller, I'm glad I found you in your office. This is Special Agent Sloan, from the New York office of the Federal Bureau of Investigation. I'm sure you remember me."

Martin scowled at the smug tone. "I'm surprised to hear from you. What can I do for you, Mr. Sloan?"

"I'm in Washington for the day, and I'd like to take you to lunch—just you and me, no tricks."

Martin took a couple seconds to recover from his shock. "Alright, where?"

"You tell me, you're the expert around here. I hardly know Washington."

"You must be calling from over at the Justice Department." That was three quarters of a mile away, down Pennsylvania Avenue.

"That's right."

"Are you buying?" Martin asked.

"Of course."

"Good. Then let's meet at the restaurant in the Willard Hotel at noon. It's on 14th Street NW, a block north of Pennsylvania Avenue, big hotel, you can't miss it."

In addition to being about halfway between their locations, the Willard was a Washington landmark, the first choice among visiting dignitaries, and a prime dining location for the powerful—too expensive for Martin's budget, but if the FBI was paying the bill he'd take advantage.

"OK, I'll see you there. And remember, Schuller—just us."

"Just the two of you?" the chief scowled. "Hmm, I'm not sure I like the sound of that."

"What do you think they're up to, Chief?" Martin asked.

"I haven't the foggiest idea, but we need to find out. Have Hansen go somewhere nearby, someplace he can watch the front of the hotel while you're there, so he can see if there's any funny business. Take separate routes so it doesn't look like you went together, in case they've got someone watching, too."

"I wouldn't be surprised," Martin said.

"Me neither."

Sloan was waiting for him at the entrance to the restaurant when Martin arrived. He looked irritated.

"Pretty ritzy place," he said with a scowl as Martin approached. "You fellas at State must be used to a lot higher living than a humble policeman like me."

"I've never eaten here before," Martin said with a chuckle. "It's popular with the higher ups, though—cabinet members, members of Congress, foreign ambassadors—folks like that."

Sloan's scowl deepened. "I see. You think you can give me the squeeze because you know I want something."

"I chose the Willard because it's about midway between State and Justice—but if you'd like to suggest another location, I'd be happy to consider it," Martin said with false congeniality.

"I told you, I don't know Washington." Sloan shook his head. "Let's get a table."

After they sat, a young black man in a spotless white uniform filled their water glasses. Martin thanked him, and noticed the briefest of scowls cross Sloan's face.

Martin cut right to the chase. "Why are you in Washington, Special Agent Sloan?"

"It's Special Agent *in Charge* Sloan now," Sloan said, lighting a cigarette. "I got promoted recently, and put in charge of the bureau's efforts to crack the cell that reports to this *Skiläufer* fellow. We have reason to suspect they're mostly legal U.S. residents, or even citizens— which is why you boys at State are in over your heads with this one, since you're limited to tracking foreign agents using false passports."

Martin hid his irritation. "You and I both know the *Abwehr* has sent agents over here to contact *Der Skiläufer*'s cell. You arrested *Immergrün* in February, as you recall; and recently, we were both tracking *Schwartzkiefer* in New York."

"That's true," Sloan said, nodding. "We believe German Intelligence made contact more than a year ago with someone already here, someone with established ties to Germany, so they could communicate without suspicion; and they've sent agents here to assist him with whatever his cell is up to. We have reason to believe that all of the cell members belong to the German American Bund—thus our interest in the rally at Madison Square Garden.

"When we arrested you and that Evergreen fellow, we assumed you were part of the cell. We knew from our sources that Augustus Graeter was supposed to be a legal U.S. resident, and we thought you'd be able to lead us to this *Skiläufer* fellow. So now you see why you disrupted our investigation with your little undercover operation. We'd been tracking these people for almost a year at that point, and the Director expected results that we weren't able to deliver because of you."

He frowned, and leaned forward. "I'm sure you're aware that Director Hoover is not someone you'd care to disappoint, Mr. Schuller."

Martin nodded. "I understand your predicament," he said, and left it at that.

The waiter began to stop at their table, and Sloan waved him away.

"I know without a doubt that we have more information than you fellas at State—but I also believe you know some things that we don't."

"I'm sure that's true," Martin said, noncommittal.

Sloan watched him for a moment, as if waiting for him to say more. Martin stayed quiet, and stared back.

Finally, Sloan broke eye contact. "Listen," he began, sounding slightly exasperated. "I don't care if you boys at State are the ones to catch this *Schwartzkiefer* fellow, as long as I can bust *Der Skiläufer* and his ring. Remember—most of them aren't using those fake passports you boys are so concerned about, and some of them might even be Americans—so you can back off and let us do our job."

Martin shrugged. Sloan was right about that—if the ring members were Americans or legal residents, that was outside of State's purview.

"So you think an exchange of information will be mutually beneficial," Martin said.

"Yep—you scratch my back, and I'll scratch yours, Mr. Schuller."

"Why should I trust you, after the way your men treated me in New York last week?"

Sloan's eyes narrowed. "Because your country's security depends on it."

Martin couldn't argue with that. He would likely never get an apology for his treatment at their hands, so he tried to put it out of his mind and move on.

"Even so," he said. "What I told you in New York still stands—most of the information you would want from me is classified, and I haven't been given authorization to share it with anyone outside of our department."

"Get authorization."

"That's not so easy," Martin said.

"Why not?" Sloan asked with a deep scowl. "I'm authorized to tell you information about this German agent you want, this *Schwarzkiefer*. I didn't have to jump through too many hoops to get that."

He leaned back and folded his arms, a smug sort of half-smile spreading across his lips. "But maybe I'm higher up than you are, and I can get that sort of authorization easier than you can. Maybe I overestimated you."

Martin felt his gut clench, as if it had been punched. "I'll see what I can do for you, Special Agent Sloan."

"I appreciate that, Mr. Schuller," Sloan said with a grin that seemed false. "In the meantime, why don't you give me at least a little something I can take back to my superiors this afternoon, some nugget of information to show we're making progress with our cooperation."

A thought occurred to Martin.

"You're meeting with Hoover himself this afternoon, aren't you?"

Sloan's expression was unreadable. "The Director is very interested in busting this ring."

He hadn't confirmed, but Martin could read between the lines. "Then I'll tell you this much—I suspect that the latest *Abwehr* agent—*Schwarzkiefer*—is an Austrian."

Sloan seemed to consider this a moment. "Interesting. What makes you say that?"

"His code name means Black Pine—"

"Yes, I've had the translation for some time."

Martin ignored the interruption. "Which is a species found only in the Alpine regions of Austria."

A tiny appreciative smile spread across Sloan's lips, and he nodded. "No one in the bureau's been able to come up with that," he said. "We noticed the pattern of code names—*Immergrün* meaning 'Evergreen' and *Schwarzkiefer* meaning 'Black Pine'—but we didn't consider that would give us clues to their origins. Of course, that Evergreen fellow wasn't from Austria."

"No, he was Bavarian," Martin said.

"Yes, he was. How did you know that?"

"His accent," Martin said. "I've been to Bavaria, many times. It's the German state that borders Austria. I couldn't say if that's significant to this cell run by *Der Skiläufer*, but it could be."

Sloan rubbed his chin. "*Der Skiläufer*—'the skier.' Don't think we haven't had agents all over Golden, Colorado, looking for someone like him—but we haven't found a thing. The German American Bund doesn't have a base of support out there, for one thing. Not many recent immigrants in that area. The Coors brothers founded their brewery out there in the 1870s, and brought over a whole bunch of workers from

Germany—but that was decades ago. The German-American community in Colorado seems completely loyal to the United States."

Martin hadn't thought of Golden, Colorado, and that irritated him. It was a little enclave of German settlement in the far west, easy to forget—but it was near ski resorts.

"I take it you've also checked out all of the ski resorts in Vermont, New Hampshire, the Adirondacks?"

Sloan nodded. "No trace of the man we're looking for."

"What about Michigan? Wisconsin?" Martin asked. "There are large German-American communities out there, and I think they've got some ski resorts."

"No luck," Sloan said.

Martin shrugged. "Sorry, I'm out of ideas."

Sloan waved over the waiter. "Let's get some lunch. Maybe the food will help our thought processes."

The waiter came over and took their orders. It never escaped Martin's notice that waiters in Washington restaurants were always white, but the men who filled water glasses were inevitably black—serving the white guests but having little interaction with them, while the waiter who spoke to the diners (and received the tip) was white.

Ever since Germany enacted the Nuremburg Laws four years earlier, restricting the roles that Jews could hold, Martin had been keen to notice these things that he'd never paid attention to before, right here in America.

It disturbed him, though he never said anything—except to Hansen, who agreed with him that there were things you could change, and things you could not.

What he *could* do was stop Nazi agents trying to infiltrate American society and spread their hateful ideology.

**

Midway through their lunch, Martin saw Congressman Barbour enter the restaurant with a pair of younger men, both mid to late thirties and well-dressed in expensive silk suits.

"Who's the big shot you're staring at?" Sloan asked, following Martin's gaze.

"That's Congressman Barbour. I met him a few months ago at a charity event in Philadelphia that my mother-in-law was part of." Martin chuckled. "He offered me a job, actually. I turned him down."

"Looks like a pompous jerk," Sloan said.

"How do you know I'm not offended by your assessment of my friend the Congressman?"

"Ha!" Sloan smirked. "I didn't become a Special Agent in Charge without being able to read people pretty good, Mr. Schuller. That man *is* a pompous jerk, and you think so too."

Martin didn't argue.

"Did he know the kind of work you do for State?"

"Some of it," Martin said. "Not the undercover work."

"If you don't mind me asking—how does a man of your position get to rub elbows with a congressman at a charity event?"

Martin watched Sloan for a couple of seconds; he seemed genuine, which surprised him. "You mean you FBI fellas haven't dug into my past already?"

Sloan made a slight shrug. "Some."

"I told you—my mother-in-law was involved with the group putting on the event." He left it at that.

"And what group would that be, if you don't mind?"

"The Daughters of the American Revolution."

"Ah, the DAR," Sloan said with a knowing tone. "I've got an aunt who's part of the DAR back in my hometown. I always thought they were a bunch of stuffy old dames, thinking they're better than everyone else. All concerned with their bloodlines and making a big show of how patriotic and charitable they are. No offense to your mother-in-law, Schuller."

Martin couldn't help but smile. "None taken. I kind of agree with you."

"I thought you would."

Sloan finished off the food on his plate, wiped at his mouth with the linen napkin, and pushed it all away.

"Listen—see if you can talk your bosses into sharing some of your intel on this *Skiläufer* character. Tell them what I told you, that he's in the country legally, and so it's not under your jurisdiction. Let them know that if we locate him, we can help lead you to that foreign agent you're looking for, that *Schwarzkiefer*. Then we both get feathers in our caps. Think you can do that for me?"

"I'll see what I can do," Martin said.

"I guess that's as good as I'm going to get today, huh?" he said as the waiter came and took their empty plates.

"I guess so," Martin agreed.

"Well it ain't much for the expensive meal I bought you," Sloan said, his humor laced with a touch of bitterness.

Martin shrugged and stood up. "I'd best be getting back to my office. I can reach you in New York after today?"

"Yeah, I'm going back tonight." Sloan's expression was unreadable.

"Then I'll be in touch," Martin said, turning to leave. "Thanks for lunch."

He didn't look back as he walked out of the restaurant.

"Interesting offer," the chief said a half-hour later, after Martin finished recounting the conversation. "Do you trust him?"

"Not entirely," Martin said.

"Good, me neither. Still, we don't have any leads on *Schwarzkiefer* right now. The trail's gone cold, correct?"

Martin hated having to admit that. "That's correct, Chief."

The chief leaned back in his chair and stared up at the ceiling in thought. "Tough call—let me think about this a while, and ponder all the possibilities."

"Should I call Sloan tomorrow and tell him we'll get back with him later?"

The chief shook his head. "He'll figure it out when he doesn't hear from you."

"You got it," Martin said, and smiled as he left the chief's office.

Hutson

16

Monday, June 26, 1939

Martin couldn't believe his ears. As the news sank in, he shook his head in disbelief and disgust.

"So what's to become of us?" Frank Hooper, one of his fellow Intelligence Analysts, asked the chief.

"You keep doing your jobs," the chief said. "No one's out of work here. We still own all the intelligence that the overseas missions send us, and we still have to sort it out. That remains our number one job. The only difference is that when we detect a foreign agent, either in or coming to the United States, we've been ordered to hand that intelligence over to the FBI. They'll handle the investigation and arrests."

"So no more undercover work," Hansen said. He sounded bitter.

"No more undercover work," the boss agreed. "We leave all of that to the Bureau from now on. And remember, it's not just us—MID and ONI also have to share their domestic counter-espionage intel with the FBI."

"Military Intelligence, the original oxymoron," Sam Watts said in an attempt at levity.

Martin stared at the side of the chief's desk, saying nothing. He kept replaying in his mind the smug way that Special Agent Sloan had interrogated him after his arrest at the Bund Rally in Madison Square Garden in February, and again in the Waldorf Astoria a few weeks ago. And now these FBI agents—who had no foreign sources of intelligence—were solely responsible for keeping the United States safe from foreign spies.

They had won, and it made his blood boil.

"You don't have to like it," the chief was saying, and Martin looked up to see the chief looking at him. "But this is by order of the President, so no argument. And as Assistant Secretary Messersmith has pointed out, this change frees up State to focus on building better foreign intelligence networks, centered around our overseas missions. Now get back to work, everyone; we've still got a lot to do."

Martin sat back at his desk, but couldn't concentrate on the paperwork in front of him. He kept stewing.

Those smug FBI agents had won.

Becky had won.

And he had lost.

"Damn it!" he muttered, loudly enough that the guys around him heard, and gave him side glances.

Hansen got up and patted him on the shoulder. "Come on, let's go out and grab a beer."

Martin wasn't normally one to leave the office early, or to shirk his duties at work, but he nodded and got up, grabbing his hat and following Hansen out the office door without a word to Trudy or anyone else. He walked beside Hansen in silence as they crossed the typing pool, loud with the metallic clacking of keys.

Fifteen minutes later, they sat at a bar up the street, a bottle of Löwenbräu in front of each of them.

"Slimy FBI bastards," Hansen said, taking a swig from his bottle. "It's not right. It's just not right."

"J. Edgar Hoover," Martin replied, pronouncing each piece of the name slowly, deliberately. "He's gonna run everything before you know it."

"They say he's got cabinet after cabinet full of blackmail material on every major government official," Hansen said. "What do you suppose he's got on the Secretary?"

Martin stayed silent. It wasn't Secretary Hull who had to fear being blackmailed. He'd heard whispers about Under Secretary Sumner Welles, however, and his supposed preference for black men. Perhaps Director Hoover had evidence to blackmail Welles. Martin wouldn't be shocked.

"So tomorrow I've got to hand over all of our material about *Der Skiläufer*," Martin grumbled. "After we've resisted sharing it with those FBI fellas for two weeks, now the bastards have won."

He swallowed the last of the beer in his bottle, and raised his hand to order another.

"Will Becky get sore if you come home drunk?" Hansen asked, raising his own hand to order another beer.

Martin smirked. "She'll never know it—she doesn't live here anymore."

He hated admitting that. He wasn't exactly sure why he had, either. He hadn't said a word to anyone before now.

"Oh brother, she left you?" Hansen asked, an incredulous look on his face. "Jesus, Martin—I'm really sorry to hear that, buddy." He put his hand on Martin's shoulder.

"Don't be, it's for the best." As much as it hurt to admit that, Martin knew it was true.

"This round is on me," Hansen said.

"No, don't do that, I'm fine," Martin said, scowling. The last thing he had ever wanted was anyone's pity.

"I insist," Hansen said, firm. "It's the least I can do."

Martin shrugged, indifferent. "Thanks."

"You're hardly alone, you know," Hansen said after their beers arrived. "They say one in four marriages end in divorce these days."

And preachers have been predicting the fall of American society for the last twenty years because of it, Martin thought. "So I'm a damn statistic."

"That's not what I meant."

"I know what you meant," Martin said. "It was a good try, anyway. I appreciate it."

Hansen looked around, though there was no one sitting near them at this hour. Even so, his voice was quieter when he continued, leaning in.

"What do you think of what the chief said, about expanding the foreign intelligence networks around our overseas missions?"

Martin shrugged. He didn't want to think about work right now, but at least they'd moved on from the subject of his marriage. Besides, he didn't have any better topic of conversation.

"It means we'll be busy—we'll get more information to sort through, maybe better information. Who knows? But we won't be able to do anything about it, unless we share it with another agency, so what's the point?"

"You don't think the country will be better off if we all cooperate?"

Martin didn't want to think about that, even if it was probably true. He didn't respond.

"I think that's why the President wants to consolidate domestic counter-espionage under one agency," Hansen continued.

"But not us," Martin said, and took a long pull on his new beer bottle.

Hansen nodded. "Yeah, I know how you feel, buddy. I feel the same way. I'm just trying to look on the bright side."

"Well do it with someone else," Martin replied. His tone was harsher than he'd intended, but he didn't apologize.

"Sorry," Hansen muttered, and turned away.

They both faced forward, drinking their beer in silence for a while.

The bar began to fill up after four-thirty, when the government offices all closed for the day. Martin wasn't in the mood for a crowd, so he laid a dollar on the bar to pay for his first beer, told Hansen he'd see him at the office tomorrow, and left.

A man in a dark blue suit stood waiting at the entrance to Martin's apartment building, and when he saw Martin coming up the walk, he approached him.

"Martin Schuller?"

"Yes?"

The man handed him a thick envelope. "You've been served." He walked away without another word.

The return address was the Philadelphia County Clerk of Courts, and Martin felt his heart sink into the pit of his stomach. Then he got angry, and he marched up the stairs, threw open his apartment door, and tore open the envelope.

As he suspected, it was a petition for dissolution of marriage— Rebecca Ann Schuller, petitioner. William G. Walsh, Esquire had filed as attorney for the petitioner.

Of course. Martin felt a deep cold inside. His father-in-law might be a jerk, but he was a damn successful attorney. Martin knew he could never hire an attorney half as good as William Walsh, and that this whole affair was going to go Becky's way.

"Damn it!" he shouted, crumpling the envelope and tossing it on the ground. He let the pages of the petition fall to the floor, and he sank onto the couch and rested his forehead on his hand.

Friday, June 30

For most of the week, Martin and his coworkers went through their active files, flagging any item pertaining to foreign agents in the United States, so that Trudy could type up copies for the FBI.

The whole exercise irritated Martin, a constant reminder that his favorite part of his job had been taken away. He was sullen and quiet all week.

The work was also dull, since this was old intelligence. It failed to keep his mind off Becky, the kids, and his impending divorce.

Late that morning, as he worked his way toward the end of his *Skiläufer* file, he perused the documents about Dr. Atherton and his eugenics misdeeds. He'd decided not to flag any of these for copying, when something caught his attention.

He stopped and stared at a name on the page.

Bernard Gold, the attorney in Philadelphia who had won a settlement against the hospital where Atherton had worked.

The attorney who had gotten the best of William Walsh.

Would he be willing to take a divorce case if it meant going up against William Walsh again? Martin supposed Gold might jump at the chance.

He told himself he couldn't afford it. Bernard Gold was obviously an accomplished trial lawyer. That didn't come cheap. These days, you couldn't get a good attorney for less than two dollars an hour. One as prestigious as William Walsh might charge more than triple that.

But what would it hurt to just ask?

Martin stared at the name on the page for several minutes, his pulse accelerating. He could sit and brood over his anger for weeks, or even months—or he could do something.

His entire life, Martin had always opted to take action. That had gotten him into trouble sometimes, he had to acknowledge—and he'd faced consequences—but he couldn't stand to let things happen to him.

This made him think of Susan. He'd grown sullen after she left, powerless to stop it. He hated that powerless feeling more than anything. He reminded himself that he'd been seventeen, and others held all the cards.

He wasn't powerless now.

He bolted from his seat and put on his hat. "I'm going to lunch a little early today, Trudy," he said as he walked out the door.

He found a payphone on the street corner outside the Old Executive Office Building, and waited a moment while a young woman in a dark dress finished a call. Then he hurried into the booth, deposited a dime, and asked the operator for long distance to Philadelphia.

The long distance operator came on the line, and he asked for the business listing for Bernard Gold, attorney at law.

"I have that listing, sir," the operator said a moment later. "Please deposit ninety cents for the first three minutes."

Martin fished the coins out of his pocket and inserted them in the slot. After he'd finished, the operator said, "I'll connect you. One moment."

After Gold's secretary put him through to the attorney, Martin got right to the point. Long distance was expensive, after all.

"Mr. Gold, my name's Martin Schuller, and I'm calling long distance from Washington. You don't know me, but my father-in-law is William Walsh."

"Yes, I'm familiar with Mr. Walsh," Gold said, gruff. "What can I do for you, Mr. Schuller? Are you one of his associates?"

"No sir, I'm getting divorced from his daughter."

There was a momentary pause on the line. "I'm very sorry to hear that, Mr. Schuller." Gold didn't sound sorry at all. Martin could almost picture the man smiling. "Do you have representation, may I ask?"

"That's what I'm calling about, actually."

"I thought that might be the case. I can tell you, I'd be more than happy to go up against that son-of-a-gun again, if you'll pardon the expression. Do you and Mrs. Schuller have any children, by any chance?"

"Yes, three."

"Even better. And are she and Mr. Walsh trying to keep you from seeing the children?"

Martin felt his gut tighten. "I haven't seen them in a month."

"We'll fix that," Gold said, his voice oozing confidence. "Mr. Schuller, I'll take your case for half my usual rate. I normally charge two-ten an hour, but I'd take your case for a dollar-five."

Martin's heart soared, and he couldn't help the big grin that spread across his mouth. He could afford that. He fought back the excitement, trying not to sound overly eager.

He pretended to consider for a couple of seconds, and accepted.

"Excellent!" Gold said, sounding excited. "I'll need a retainer of twenty dollars to cover some of my anticipated costs. Then once the dissolution of your marriage is final, we'll settle up for the rest of my time and bill you. How soon can you come into the office to go over your case?"

"Well, I live in Washington," Martin said, and paused to think. There were regular trains that left for Philadelphia, and he could easily catch one shortly after work most days, and get to Philadelphia around six o'clock. "Would you be available this evening?"

"No, I don't work late on Fridays," Gold said, and Martin felt suddenly foolish—of course Gold didn't work on the Jewish Sabbath. "Can you meet on Sunday?"

"Yes, I can come up on Sunday. What time?"

"The earlier the better—unless you're a religious man?"

Martin chuckled. "Not particularly."

"Then let's say eleven o'clock, and bring anything with you that you think might help your case. Good day, Mr. Schuller."

Martin smiled to himself as he walked back to the building. He'd have to start skimping on lunch, getting the cheap sandwiches, but things were going to work out. He could just imagine William Walsh's face when he realized they wouldn't get to take advantage of Martin, not this time.

Now if he could only figure out what to do about the blasted FBI.

17

Friday, July 28, 1939

Martin let off the gas pedal as his car came up behind a black horse-drawn buggy east of Lancaster, and he eased the maroon 1938 Desoto onto the other side of the road to pass.

When he'd first learned to drive as a teenager, he and his friends used to get a kick out of speeding past the Amish buggies and frightening the horses. They would howl with laughter. Now, he was more respectful—and more than a little ashamed of the reckless younger version of himself.

"Whoa! Dad, did you see that?" Marty said from the passenger seat after they'd passed. "They were driving an old-fashioned buggy, like they used to in the olden days! And they were dressed like it, too."

"You've seen the Amish before," he reminded his elder son. Then he realized Marty might have been too young to pay any attention before. "They're a church—Pennsylvania Dutch, like me—but they believe in keeping separate from outsiders, and keeping the old ways. No cars, no electricity."

"Why?" Marty asked, frowning.

Martin shrugged. "I think they believe modern conveniences make life too easy, and hard work brings them closer to God. I heard once that they think the devil likes laziness."

"So no radio?" Marty's eyes were wide.

"Is that so hard to imagine?" Martin asked with a grin, reaching over to rumple his son's hair. "We didn't have radio when I was your age."

"How old were you when you got radio, Dad?"

"Oh, about fourteen, I think."

"Wow!" Marty sounded amazed, and Martin had to laugh.

"I see cows!" Stevie's excited voice called from the backseat.

"Brown cows," Jackie said.

Martin chuckled. "You'll see a lot of those at the fair tomorrow."

It was about a four-hour drive north from Washington to Reading, and as they passed through eastern Lancaster County they had about twenty miles to go. Becky had sent the kids by train from Philadelphia to Washington right after Marty's eighth birthday, and it irritated Martin that she hadn't come with them. Couldn't she stand to see him at all?

It was the first time he'd seen the kids in eight weeks, and they ran up to him when they got off the train and saw him waiting on the platform, excited shouts of "Daddy! Daddy!" making his heart melt and hurt at the same time.

They'd stayed at home one night, and this morning they hit the road in a rented Desoto sedan.

"Daddy, I'm hungry," Jackie complained from the back seat.

"We'll be at Grandma's house in less than half an hour," Martin said. "We'll have lunch when we get there."

"More cows!" Stevie shouted. "Moo! Moo!"

They passed through downtown Reading a little after noon. The center of town hadn't changed much since Martin was a child, tidy store fronts in brick buildings along the street. The only difference was that all window signs were in English only—a change he could vividly remember when he was nine years old, hardly older than Marty was now, when the country had entered the Great War against Germany.

His father had been slow to take down the bilingual signage in the front windows of his grocery, until one night someone put a brick through the window and spray-painted "HUNS" across the front door. It had been shortly after dinnertime, and they'd heard the breaking glass from upstairs. Martin remembered sweeping up broken glass with his brothers and sisters while his father and an uncle nailed plywood over the window.

They had never experienced prejudice like that before—not in Berks County, where forty percent of the population was German-American—and it stuck with Martin.

That week, their bilingual window signs had been replaced with English-only signs.

"There's Grandma and Grandpa's store," he said, pointing at the storefront as they drove past. He turned at the next light, and turned immediately into the alley that ran behind the building. He parked the car by the back door.

His mother came out the door as he climbed out of the car, wiping her hands on her apron. A broad grin cracked her wrinkled face as she saw the kids scrambling out of the back seat, and she held her arms open wide.

"Oh, my little dumplings! Come give your Grandma a big hug and kisses." Anna Schuller was a fifth-generation American, but her Pennsylvania Dutch accent sounded as if she'd come from Germany as an adult twenty or thirty years ago. Here in Reading, that wasn't unusual.

"Grandma!" the kids ran into her arms, and she smothered them with kisses.

"Can we have a cookie?" Stevie asked.

"Of course you may," Anna said with a firm nod.

"After lunch," Martin said.

"After lunch, he says," Anna said, winking at her grandchildren. "I'll give you a cookie when he's not lookink, yeah?"

She put her arm around Marty as they walked in the back door. "Marty Schuller, you get taller every time I see you."

The narrow stair case beside the back door led to the living quarters above the store. She sent the kids scrambling upstairs, and turned to her son.

"You have a kiss for your mother, Martin?"

He gave her a kiss on the cheek. "Hello, Mutti," he said. "Thank you for letting us visit."

Her expression grew stern. "I haven't told your papa the news," she said, pointing a finger at him. "He wouldn't let you stay here if I had, so I didn't."

"Thank you, Mutti."

"Your *Oma* is staying at your uncle Henry's house, so you can have her room. You know she's been staying here since your *Opa* died two years ago."

"I remember," Martin said. "Is Papa in the store?"

"Of course," Anna said. "He'll close for lunch soon. I made fried chicken, since the grandchildren don't eat sauerbraten."

He detected a note of reproach, but ignored it.

The kids were already in the living room when he reached the top of the stairs, playing with his parents' cocker spaniel, and laughing as she licked their faces. Martin watched them for a second, then walked toward the mantle, which was lined with framed photographs.

The largest was a sepia-toned picture of the Schullers' six children, from the spring of 1925. Martin had to chuckle as he looked at it. The seventeen-year-old version of himself stood straight and tall, staring into the camera with a super serious look. His blond hair was parted down the middle and plastered back in the fashion of the day, and his starched shirt collar stood up to his chin.

His two younger brothers stood on either side of him, wearing the identical brown suit to his; while their three sisters sat in chairs in front of them, their knees carefully covered by the hems of their dresses, hands folded across their knees. He remembered their mother would never let them wear skirts higher than their knees, no matter how much they complained.

Martin remembered that day well. This was the last portrait of all six of them together; his eldest sister, Helen, then nineteen, got married two months later. Mutti had been very particular about that portrait.

He heard her setting the table in the neighboring dining room, so he joined her there. She set the table, and then counted the dishes. "Too many sweet," she pronounced, walked back into the kitchen, and fetched a bowl of vinegar coleslaw from the ice box.

She took a platter of fried chicken from the oven last, and set it in the middle of the table. "I heard your father closing up the store," she said, though Martin wondered how she'd heard anything over the noise the kids were making in the other room.

"Kids, come in for lunch," he called.

His mother swatted at his shoulder. "They are not goats, they are *children*." She gave him one of her stern looks, and he looked away.

"Oh boy, fried biscuits!" Marty said as he took a seat, reaching for one of the fried balls of dough.

Anna swatted at his hand before he could take one. "Wait for your grandpa, or he will be grumpy."

David Schuller came through the door a moment later.

"Hello, Papa," Martin said, standing.

"Ah, Martin—you decided to visit us finally." Then he looked at the kids, and his stern expression changed to a grin. "Hello, my little ones."

"Can I have a fried biscuit now, Grandpa?" Marty asked.

"Of course—after we say grace."

Marty withdrew his hand again, disappointed.

"Bow your heads, children," Anna reminded them. "Close your eyes."

Martin bowed his head out of respect for his parents, but he didn't close his eyes.

David Schuller said grace in German. "Merciful Lord, for the bounty of your gifts, make us eternally grateful to you, and to your Son. Amen."

"Amen," Anna echoed.

Marty reached for a fried biscuit the second they had finished with grace, and took a spoonful of apple butter for it.

"What did you say, Grandpa?" Jackie asked.

David Schuller gave his son a side glance, the kind that said in an instant *'You still haven't taught your children any German.'* Then he translated the prayer for his granddaughter.

"Why is Rebecca not with you and the children?" he asked Martin. "Will she join us later today? Or tomorrow?"

"It's just me and the kids this visit," Martin said. "Becky's in Philadelphia with her parents."

He got glances from Marty and Jackie, and he gave them a half-smile. Stevie was too busy gnawing on a chicken leg to pay any attention to the adult conversation.

"Your children are not goats, Martin Schuller," his father said with a scowl.

Martin was about to retort that he was an adult who didn't need his grammar corrected, but he held his tongue. At least his father hadn't dug deeper into Becky's absence—yet.

"Jacob is coming to dinner tonight with his family," his mother said. Then she looked at Marty and Jackie with a smile and said, "You can play with your cousins tonight."

"That'll be nice," Martin said.

He got along reasonably well with his middle brother, most of the time. Depending upon his mood, Jacob could either be a buffer between Martin and their parents, or he could join on their side in a game of "gang up on Martin." He wondered which Jacob would show up tonight.

"Everyone will go with us to the fair tomorrow," his mother continued. "All the children and grandchildren."

"That'll be quite a crowd," Martin said.

He was the second of six children, and the eldest son. All of his siblings had three of four children apiece—except for his youngest sister, Louisa, who was pregnant with her first. At last count, his parents had sixteen grandchildren, all younger than twelve.

"How's business, Papa?" Martin asked, taking the subject away from family and all of its potential pitfalls.

"Better these days," David Schuller said. "It had gotten really bad again last year, I think your mother told you. But this year, the factories are hiring again, and the people are spending a little more on their groceries."

"I'm glad to hear it," Martin said, trying to sound enthusiastic.

"You'll see after lunch. You're working in the store with me this afternoon."

Martin suppressed a groan. He should have expected that.

He took a slice of rye bread and spread a dollop of the dark mustard on it. He smiled as the horseradish rushed into his sinuses and tingled. He looked at his eldest boy.

"Hey Marty, try some of that bread with the mustard. It's good."

"Like this, Marty," David said, taking a slice of rye and spreading a dollop of mustard on it, then popping it in his mouth.

Grinning at being asked to copy his father and grandfather, Marty took a piece of the bread, carefully put some of the mustard on it, and took a bite.

Martin and his father both laughed at the face Marty made, and the tears that spilled over from his eyes. David Schuller slapped his grandson on the back, roaring with laughter.

"How you like that? Pretty good, yeah?"

Marty smiled through his coughs and sniffs, and nodded his head. "It's good," he said, his voice a hoarse whisper.

"You want some more?" Martin asked, but Marty shook his head. "No, thank you."

"That's alright, it's an acquired taste." He winked at him.

**

Martin stocked shelves that afternoon while his father walked the aisles, greeting customers—usually in English, but sometimes in German—and running the register. The ones David greeted in German usually took the time to converse for a few moments.

"Good afternoon, Mrs. Dierdorf."

"Hello, Mrs. Kandt."

"Very nice to see you today, Mrs. Schroeder."

Martin noticed after a while that the customers his father greeted in German were all older than forty, and most of them he remembered from when he was growing up. Most of their families had lived in Reading for as long as the Schullers—which was about two hundred years.

"Good afternoon, Mrs. Schmidterman," his father said in German to an older woman in a navy blue dress who came in around three o'clock, white haired and pleasantly plump.

"Good afternoon, Mr. Schuller. I see Martin is working in the store today. Hello, Martin."

Martin looked up from his work and recognized his brother Jacob's mother-in-law. It had been nearly ten years since he'd last seen her, and her hair had been salt and pepper then.

"Hello, Mrs. Schmidterman," he said in German.

"Have you come back to Reading to work for your father, then?"

Martin had to smile as he shook his head. "No, ma'am. I still live in Washington. My children and I are visiting for the weekend."

"They came for the fair," David Schuller said.

"Ah, good," Mrs. Schmidterman said, beaming. "You should be sure to come by the bake tent—I have entered a cake in the contest. You should have a piece, and then vote for me."

"We'll do that," Martin said.

"I won the red ribbon last year for my blueberry cake. This year I will settle for nothing less than the blue ribbon."

"Best of luck," Martin said. "Excuse me, please. I have to get back to my work."

Martin was tired when they sat down to dinner that night, and his back was stiff. He wasn't used to manual labor anymore. He looked at his father, in his mid-fifties now, and wondered how he could still do it six days a week.

They were eleven around the table, and the room rang with laughter and conversations that switched from English to German and back again.

Martin was used to that, though he knew it baffled his kids, who looked around the room with bemused smiles.

When he was growing up, the conversations around the dinner table had been fully bilingual, and for Martin and his siblings they sometimes even switched from German to English—or vice versa—in the middle of a sentence. He noticed that Jacob and his wife Mary still did that, though not necessarily mid-sentence anymore; but their three kids used mostly English, only using German to answer the adults if addressed in that language.

His mother had made a big pork roast with enough potatoes to feed a small army, and Martin ate more than his fill. It had been a while since he'd eaten really good cooking.

"Mutti said you spent the afternoon working in Papa's store," Jacob said, nodding at Martin's back one of the times that he put his hand on it and stretched. "Bring back memories?"

"That it did," Martin replied. "Every afternoon after school for years."

"Well, not *every* afternoon—at least not for you," Jacob said. "Not once you started playing football."

"That was just a different kind of work," Martin said, stiffening.

His sophomore year of high school, fifteen-year-old Martin had been tapped to play tight end on their varsity football team. They practiced every weekday afternoon from August through November—which took him away from his chores at the grocery. That, plus the fact that his father disapproved of his new friends from the team—incidentally, most of whom were from English-speaking families—caused a bit of friction at home for the next three years.

"Always seemed to me you had a lot of fun playing football," Jacob said.

So this is how it's going to be tonight. "It was fun," Martin said. "It's too bad you never experienced that, Jake."

Jacob's smile seemed forced. "I guess we all got to live vicariously through you on Friday nights."

Martin shrugged. "Playing varsity football is what earned me a scholarship to U Penn." He enjoyed the look of jealousy that briefly passed across Jacob's face.

"What are you boys talking about?" their father asked from the end of the table, one eyebrow raised in a dubious look.

"That Martin's not used to hard work like he had to do today," Jacob said.

"I wouldn't put it that way," Martin replied, keeping his cool with effort as his cheeks flushed.

"*Ach*, what kind of hard work do you do, sitting behind a desk in Washington, D.C.?" his father asked.

"It's good work, Papa."

David Schuller waved his hand dismissively. He switched to German. "Always thought you were better than the rest of us, going to college and getting the fancy government job, never having to do manual labor. Is that why you almost never come home to see us?" He shook his head. "When you come home tired at the end of a long day of hard work, you know that you accomplished something good, with your own hands, something you can see. *That* is work you can be proud of."

Martin answered him in English. "I can see the good work that I do every day, Papa—just not with my eyes. I guess you would have to be able to look beyond the obvious to see it, though."

One of the frustrations about not being able to fully discuss his work with family was the lack of understanding of its importance he got in return. He accepted that frustration begrudgingly.

His father stared at him for several seconds. "There is the attitude I told you about—better than everyone else."

"David, that's enough," Anna said in German. Then she looked at Martin and continued. "Of course you do good work, Martin. You are very smart, and always have been very smart. You are like me, yeah? Always thinking. We are proud to tell people that you work for the government in Washington, D.C., doing important things."

"You give him airs, the way you carry on about him," David Schuller said, continuing the conversation in German. "No wonder he married the rich English girl—who is too good to come with him to visit us, I might point out."

Martin and his mother exchanged a quick glance. Neither said a word.

Martin looked over at his kids, who were too engrossed in play with their cousins to notice the tension around the adult end of the table. He was glad for that.

He looked at Jacob and faked a smile. "I saw your mother-in-law in the store today."

Jacob also forced a smile to hide the tension. "Oh? I guess that doesn't surprise me, since she's always shopped at Papa's store."

"It's funny to see people after all these years, looking the same, mostly, but older than I remember them."

"I guess we don't notice, since we see them every week."

"Martin, if you stay through Sunday, you can come to church and see everyone again," his mother said, in English like them. "I know everyone at the church will be happy to see you."

171

Her hopeful expression almost broke his heart; but half a second later he remembered how vicious and judgmental everyone at the church had been fourteen years ago.

"I don't think so, Mutti."

"The children should have the opportunity to grow up in the church, Martin," Anna Schuller said with a slight note of reproach.

"We go to church with our other grandparents," Marty said. "They're Episcopalians, and I get to have a drink of the wine every week."

Martin cringed at the reference to "every week." He hoped no one read into that.

"There won't be any wine at the Reformed Church," David Schuller said to his grandson. "It is not a communion week, and we would have grape juice in any case." Then he looked at Martin and addressed him in German. "And how often do they get to visit with their other grandparents?"

"That's not my doing," Martin said, terse. "You'll have to ask Becky the next time you see her."

"Ah, I see," David Schuller said, and ate his meal in sullen silence.

"Talk about the church makes Papa grumpy," Jacob said in English, trying to sound light about it. "I think he's still sore about the switch from German to English, even though it's been thirteen years."

"I had stopped going by then," Martin said.

"And then the merger bothered him for a long time."

"What merger?" Martin asked.

"The Reformed Church merged with the Evangelical Synod five years ago," Jacob explained. "It made sense—both denominations have German heritage, and the Evangelical Synod is half-Reformed anyway."

"But the Lutheran half is obvious in their liturgy," David Schuller mumbled in German. "Very high church."

"We got a new minister a couple of years ago," Jacob explained, staying in English. "A young one, who came out of the Evangelical Synod—so Papa thinks we've gotten a little too high church lately."

"Reverend Koenig is a good preacher," their mother said. "He gives wonderful sermons. Even your father usually likes them." She gave her husband a stern look, but he ignored her.

"Come to church if you want, or stay home if you want," he muttered in German. "You always do what you want anyway."

"But the children can come with us," Anna said, looking at Martin.

If I can still stand to be here on Sunday, Martin thought. Right now, he doubted it.

Hutson

18

Saturday, July 29

"Lots of cows!" Stevie shouted as they entered the cattle barn at the fairgrounds.

"Do you want to try milking one?" Martin asked his children.

"Can we?" Marty asked.

"Of course. Let's see…" Martin looked around for a cow with a swollen udder. "There, that one needs it. Let's go ask the farmer." He guided them toward that stall, where a blond teenager scooped up manure with a shovel.

"Would it be OK if my children tried milking your cow?" Martin asked.

"OK by me," the boy said, and pulled over a stool.

"Show me how?" Marty asked the boy, who grinned and squatted on the stool.

"Here, like this."

After each of the kids had a turn—Stevie couldn't grip the teat hard enough, and ended up squirting a bit in his eye, which made his brother and sister laugh—they moved on toward the exit. Martin had left his parents' home right after breakfast to get some alone time with his children, but it would be time to meet the rest of the family soon.

"Hey Dad, those people over there are dressed like the ones in the buggy yesterday," Marty said as they neared the exit. "But they have a radio in the stall. You said they don't listen to the radio."

"The Amish don't," Martin said. "Those are Mennonites. They're almost the same, but they use cars and electricity."

As they walked by their booth, Martin heard the teenagers chattering among themselves in German. Unlike most of the other Pennsylvania Dutch, the Mennonites and Amish weren't Anglicizing. He was surprised by the twinge of sadness that brought him, a sudden sense of loss.

The crowd increased as the morning advanced, and Martin told his kids to hold hands so they wouldn't get separated. He held onto Marty's shoulder, and guided them toward the band stand in the center of the fair grounds.

"Dad, can I have a funnel cake?" Marty asked, pointing to one of the concession stands.

"I want one, too, Daddy," Jackie said.

"Me too!" Stevie echoed.

"After lunch, kiddos. You can split one."

His family stood in a cluster near the band stand—all except his older sister, Helen, and her family. Martin shook hands and kissed cheeks all around, and after a moment of shyness the kids gravitated to the cousins they'd seen at dinner the night before.

His sister Helen came hurrying up a few minutes later, looking tired—no, downright harried—three rambunctious kids in tow, plus one sullen twelve-year-old boy beside her with his hands in his pockets, and a husband who looked as if he wanted to be anywhere else.

Martin kissed his sister and shook hands with his brother-in-law, Al Schneider, who gave him a half-hearted smile and half-hearted greeting.

"Oh, hey there, Martin. How're you doing?" Like Martin, he was wearing brown slacks and a white button-down shirt, collar open. Only Martin's father was wearing a tie, though he'd taken off his jacket in the growing midday heat, and carried it draped over his arm.

"Are we ready for some lunch?" David Schuller asked his wife, and when she agreed he leaned down and addressed his grandchildren. "Do you children want some hot dogs? Or maybe some pretzels? Maybe both, huh?"

This was greeted with enthusiastic cheers from the kids. They followed their grandfather like the pied piper toward the concession stands, shouting their orders as they went.

Helen held back, and Martin stayed with her. She gave him a tired smile as she tucked a stray strand of sandy blond hair behind an ear.

"I say we let Papa deal with them for a while," she said.

"Rough morning?" Martin asked.

"They're all rough mornings these days," she said, genuine sadness coming to her tired gray eyes. "Robbie complained about absolutely *everything* this morning. I swear, there is no pleasing that boy these days. It doesn't matter what his father and I say or do, we're wrong."

"I bet Papa tells you to take a belt to him."

Helen grimaced, and then shook her head. "Not recently, thank goodness. He's gotten too big for that. Besides, Papa isn't always right. You should be the first person to agree to that."

"I'll say," Martin muttered, nodding.

"Speaking of not being able to please someone," Helen said, with a touch of bitterness.

"I know exactly how you feel," Martin said.

She gave him a challenging look that surprised him. "No, you don't, Martin. You moved away—you haven't really had to deal with Papa's expectations in years. Not that I blame you. But I still live here, so I have to hear it all the time. To hear Papa tell it, I'm raising a bunch of spoiled brats because I'm not strict enough or firm enough, and give them *anything* they want." She scowled. "I don't give them anywhere near everything they want, which is why Robbie fights with me all the time."

"That's rather ironic criticism, coming from the man who snuck my kids candy before dinner last night," Martin said, trying to add a little levity.

Instead, her expression grew dark. "You told him he was a big hypocrite once. You remember? It was a Sunday afternoon, and Albert and I had come over for dinner. We'd been married about a year, and you had just graduated from high school. You and Papa got into another one of your arguments over—" she stopped, embarrassed.

"Yes, one of those arguments."

She smiled, a sheepish sort of half-smile. "Yes. And you actually started *shouting* at him across the table. I think I dropped my fork. Food might have fallen out of Jacob's mouth, it hung open so wide. You called Papa a hypocrite and a tyrant—and I'll never forget it, you were jabbing your finger at his face, and he stood up and raised his hand to smack you, and you knocked it away. I think he was as stunned as the rest of us. You stomped out, and I don't think anyone said another word. Papa went into the other room, and Mutti started clearing dishes. We all just sort of stood there for a moment, and then we started clearing too. But nobody said anything. It was the strangest sensation—like the moon had fallen out of the sky or something, and no one wanted to believe it was true."

"I called him hypocrite and a *judgmental* tyrant," Martin corrected her, staring off at his father, who beamed as he handed hotdogs and pretzels and cotton candy to his grandchildren.

She laughed a little. "That's right. I can't believe you remember it that well, after all these years."

"Apparently, so do you."

She looked at him, and stared into his eyes. "It was never the same after that. Something went out of Papa, and he was never the same. He tried acting the same, but it seemed somehow forced. You got to him, you know."

Martin shrugged, saying nothing. If what Helen said were true, he didn't feel like gloating over it.

She sighed. "It's going to be like that between Albert and Robbie someday, I can feel it. We're already building toward it."

"But Al's not like Papa," Martin said. "They couldn't be more different personalities."

She shrugged. "Yes and no. But that's not the point—my husband and my son are at each other's throats all the time, and Robbie's only twelve. You think *you* were strong-headed? Try arguing with your nephew."

Martin didn't tell her he wasn't half as strong-headed as the supremely stubborn David Schuller. Or that she was thinking of the eighteen-year-old version of himself that she remembered, and not the thirty-one-year-old man who stood next to her now, practically a stranger.

"So before everyone comes back, are you going to tell me what's going on with you and Becky?"

He looked at her, surprised, and she laughed.

"You're a lot more transparent than you think, Martin. I'm not stupid, you know. In spite of that impenetrable façade you put up sometimes, those of us who know you know how to read what's going on."

"Maybe you don't know me as well as you think."

She shrugged again. "Fine, don't tell me. We'll all just speculate after you leave."

That got him. "She left, two months ago. Took the kids and went home to Philadelphia." He paused, staring at his kids, stuffing their faces and looking as happy and normal as any other kids. "She filed for divorce a few weeks ago, so it's over."

He felt Helen's hand on his arm.

"I'm really sorry, Martin. That must feel terrible."

He wanted to tell her she didn't know the half of it, but he kept it to himself.

"May I ask what happened?"

He hesitated, but then decided to give her the basics. "I was away a lot for work. She didn't like it much—at all, really—and she started trying to get me to leave government work, and go work for her father or one of his cronies in Philadelphia. I wouldn't do it, and the last time I was away, I came home to find them gone."

"I'm sure that was hard for Becky, to be alone a lot," Helen said, quiet.

That stung, and Martin turned away, scowling. How dare she take Becky's side, instead of her own brother's?

Their family was making their way back to where Helen and Martin stood, so Martin put on a happy face.

"Don't you two want anything to eat?" his mother asked them.

"I'll get a brat in a little bit," Martin said.

"It's a *Bratwurst*," his father said. "It's only two syllables, why so lazy you only say one?"

Martin ignored him, and glanced at his sister instead. She took a deep breath and gave him an encouraging smile. Then they both started to laugh.

"What on earth is so funny?" David Schuller asked, but they shook their heads and looked away. He looked at his wife and said to her in German, "This generation, they'll be the ruin of us."

Anna Schuller shook her head at him, then slipped her arm through his as they followed behind their extensive brood.

"I want to ride the Ferris wheel!" Marty shouted. "Can we, Dad?"

Martin grinned. "Sure, why not? We can all ride together." He took his two youngest kids by the hand, and they followed behind Marty toward the delighted squeals and shouts of the midway.

19

Sunday, July 30 - Lower Manhattan

Police Detective Thomas Crenshaw had seen this countless times before, and it hadn't made him sad in years. The victim was young—probably seventeen, maybe sixteen, definitely not older than eighteen—with the swooped hair and crazy silver suit of a hep cat. His young skin was perfect—except for the ugly purple and black bruises across his throat in the shape of two large hands.

The forensic photographer circled the body, which was sprawled between thick stands of bushes behind a grove of trees in the southwest corner of Washington Square Park, in the heart of gritty Greenwich Village. The early morning light was still soft, and his flash bulb created a startling blast of white light.

Crenshaw turned to the patrol officer who had been first to arrive after an old lady walking her dog had found the body and called the police from a payphone across the street.

"You didn't touch anything, right?" Crenshaw asked.

"I felt for a pulse," the cop replied, swallowing hard.

"Neck or wrist," Crenshaw asked, stifling a sigh.

"Neck," the cop said. "Was that wrong?"

"It'll be fine," Crenshaw said. "Your prints are on file with the force, so we'll know it wasn't you if we find someone else's prints as well."

The cop blanched, and Crenshaw chuckled. "I'm just messing with you. Now tell me about our victim."

"He was cold when I touched him," the cop said.

"Did you talk to the lady who found him?"

The cop nodded. "She didn't recognize him. But some of the others who passed through the park a few minutes ago did—said he was a local dope pusher and, um..." The cop glanced away, embarrassed.

"And what?"

"And a known prostitute," the cop said, whispering. "I guess that's Greenwich Village for you, Detective—a boy prostitute and dope pusher." He shook his head in obvious disdain.

Crenshaw didn't tell him how many times he'd arrested queer prostitutes in this part of the city.

This one was fully dressed, however, and the knees of his pants were clean—in fact, his clothes were spotless—so he probably wasn't killed after performing any deviant sex acts for money. Possibly a drug deal gone bad, but just as likely something else.

"Did you get a name yet?"

"No sir, Detective. The witnesses I talked to wouldn't admit to actually knowing the kid. They just said he worked the neighborhood, and they thought he lived around here somewhere."

"Did you check his pockets for identification? Money?"

"Yes sir, Detective, sir. His pockets were empty."

The photographer nodded at Crenshaw that he was finished, and walked away. Crenshaw put on a pair of black leather gloves and began moving the kid's head to either side, getting a good look at the hand prints around his throat. Whoever had strangled the boy knew exactly what they were doing—they'd squeezed hard enough and in just the right place to crush his wind pipe.

"Are you the detective in charge?" a deep voice said behind Crenshaw.

He turned to see a man in a dark blue suit and matching fedora, standing over him and looking down.

Crenshaw stood and took a step back.

"That's right. You are?"

"Special Agent in Charge Reginald Sloan, FBI. This is a Federal investigation now, we'll take over from here."

Crenshaw, like most city cops, didn't like the Feds and the bossy way they took over crime scenes. "You think this was mob related or something?" he asked, pointed.

"Or something," Sloan said. "Don't worry about it. I'm federalizing this investigation, and it's no longer your concern, detective. We'll take it from here."

"I'll need to call my captain first," Crenshaw said, but Sloan chuckled.

"Our office is on the phone with your captain as we speak, detective. Why don't you go get a cup of coffee? There's a shop over the other side of the park, across from the arch."

"Right," Crenshaw said, eyeing the half dozen FBI agents that spread out around them. He touched the rim of his hat, nodded at Sloan, and took his leave.

"Damn Feds," he muttered under his breath as he stomped away.

Sloan looked down at the youthful face of the murdered boy. That was him. He couldn't say he was too surprised, though he'd hoped to talk with him.

"Get the film from that NYPD photographer," he ordered one of the agents standing beside him, and the man hurried off. "Canvass the area," he said to the others.

They crept across the ground nearby, looking for any trace left behind by the killer.

"There are footprints over here," one of the agents called, and Sloan hurried over. They were faint, but definitely the outline of a man's dress shoe in the dusty ground behind the bushes. He could trace their path over to the sidewalk that ran down the center of the park. Judging from their angle, the killer was moving north toward the arch and Fifth Avenue.

"Get a camera over here," Sloan ordered. "Snap close ups of each print, and a few wide-views of the whole set."

He went back to the body.

He put on gloves and slipped his hands under the head. He felt the back of it, fingers running slowly along every inch of the skull. No fractures that he could tell, and no blood. So, strangulation it was. He'd assumed as much, from the nature of the bruising; it didn't seem post-mortem, but he'd had to check.

They had a medical examiner they could use who would be able to do a thorough search for any other injuries, but before they transported the body, Sloan wanted to look around a bit more.

He checked the pockets, pants and jacket, but found them all empty. No wallet, no spare change, no pocket watch—the killer had wanted it to look like a robbery.

"Hey, Agent Sloan, sir!" one of his men called from the other side of the park, near the arch. "Pagliaro found the kid's wallet."

"Where?" Sloan asked, jogging over toward the arch.

"Where'd you find it, Pagliaro?" the first agent shouted, and Sloan turned on him with a scowl.

"Keep your damn voice down, O'Neal!"

"Sorry, sir."

Sloan saw Pagliaro coming down the west side of Fifth Avenue toward the park, and Sloan met him on the corner across from the arch.

"Found it in the garbage, a couple of blocks up Fifth," Pagliaro said. "Almost to Ninth Street."

"You're sure it's the kid's?" Sloan asked.

Pagliaro nodded, and opened the well-worn leather bi-fold to reveal the kid's identity papers. "Gregory Spooner. And there's about thirty bucks in cash."

"So definitely not a robbery," Sloan said, with a sense of satisfaction. That was a lot of money, especially in this neighborhood. "Bag it, and we'll dust it for prints."

But Sloan was beginning to suspect they wouldn't find any fingerprints that didn't belong to the victim. He'd seen set ups like this before. Their killer would have been careful.

"Have Anderson call our doc, and let's get the body down to the morgue," Sloan said. He saw a group of New York cops standing a half-block down Waverly Street, staring at them. He ignored them and turned away.

"Territorial sons of bitches," he muttered as he marched back toward the body.

Hutson

20

Martin stood next to his car and watched his kids wave from the back seats of his parents' Studebaker. He'd declined his mother's invitations to join them at church without elaboration.

After they'd driven out of sight, he got into the rented Desoto and drove the opposite direction.

It was less than a mile up 9th Street to the familiar house on Douglass Street, and he slowed as he drove past it. The familiar porch swing still hung to the side of the front windows. He remembered summer evenings on that swing, holding hands with Susan while her parents kept surreptitious watch from the living room window.

He hadn't come by here in more than nine years—not since before he and Becky got married. The last time he'd walked by had been in December 1929. He stood on the corner in the cold for a long time on Christmas Eve, watching for any sign of Susan.

There had been none, of course; there had been no sign of Susan in Reading for four years by then. He'd watched for her all around town, to no avail. He knew, of course, that in a city of a little more than 100,000 people, he wouldn't necessarily bump into her if she returned; that's why he'd always made a point to ride past her parents' house on every college break, multiple times, to see if she were around.

A few times, her father saw him walking or riding his bike down their street, and he stood on their porch, arms folded, and glared at Martin until he was out of sight.

187

But Martin refused to be intimidated. He knew better than to knock on the front door—not after that first time, in late November 1925, when Mr. Powell threatened him with a shotgun if he ever came looking for Susan again. He told Martin then that she'd been sent away, and he was not to go looking for her, ever.

It was the coldest sort of cruelty, Martin felt with bitterness, that he was never given even the tiniest indication of what had happened to Susan after that, or to the baby they had created. He had no idea if it was a boy or a girl, if it lived with Susan or with adoptive parents, if it lived at all, or where in the world either of them might be.

The reaction from his own parents had been only marginally better. He'd sat on the couch in their living room, hands trembling—alone, since Mr. Powell had already forbidden him from ever again seeing Susan—a scared seventeen year old telling his parents that he had gotten his high school girlfriend pregnant.

His mother cried and prayed. His father scolded him with a vehemence he had never before seen, for his 'carelessness and immorality.' He quoted Bible verses endlessly, long after Martin stopped listening.

The church community scorned Martin, which infuriated him. For all their talk of forgiveness of sins, they had shown him no forgiveness. After his eighteenth birthday three months later, he started skipping Sunday mornings at home whenever he could get away with it, so that he wouldn't have to go to the Reformed Church with his parents and feel the icy stares and harsh judgment all around him.

He stopped attending church all together after he graduated from high school, which was what prompted that horrible fight with his father a few weeks later.

As he crept past the house, he wondered if Susan's family still lived there. On the far side of the block, looking back in his rearview mirror, he saw Mrs. Powell cutting roses from the bushes along the side of the house. She looked old and gray, and stooped from age and worry.

188

He hit the accelerator and hurried away.

He drove around town for a while, indulging in a rare sense of nostalgia as he looked at soda shops and movie theaters where he used to hang out with friends when he was a teenager. He drove past his old high school, then got out to walk around the football field where he had played three years.

He stood under a goal post for a while, remembering all the passes he caught, including quite a few touchdowns. The forward pass had become ubiquitous by the time he started playing football in the fall of 1923, and his big hands had made him a natural receiver.

He knew it was football, as much as his grades, that had gotten him out of this town. His grades were good enough for state college, but probably not for the Ivy League University of Pennsylvania, if he were being honest. Either way, his parents wouldn't have been able to pay tuition, so the football scholarship to Penn had saved him.

He got back in the car and drove to his parents' place. They were back from church, and as he reached the living room at the top of the stairs, his father looked up from the newspaper he was reading in his arm chair.

"Where have you been?" he asked.

Martin couldn't tell from his tone if he was cross, or just curious.

"Just around, seeing places I used to go."

"Hmm," David Schuller grunted, and looked back at the newspaper.

Martin noticed the paper was the Reading Times; when he was younger, his father had always read the local German language newspaper. Martin thought he remembered hearing it had gone out of business ten or twelve years ago.

"It's time for me and the kids to leave."

His father looked up from the newspaper again, lowering his reading glasses to stare at his son. "I thought you were leaving tomorrow."

189

"Change of plans."

David Schuller scowled. "You shouldn't travel on the Sabbath."

"You know I don't care about that," Martin said.

"Do you care that your mother is making dinner for six? What should she do with the extra food, huh? What about the extra work she did making dinner for you and your children?"

"I'll talk to her," Martin said, and walked into the kitchen.

"Hello, Mutti," he said, kissing her cheek. "Where are the kids?"

"The children are in your guest room," she said, not pausing in her meal preparation. "I put Steven down for a nap; Jacqueline and Marty are reading to themselves."

"I think we need to leave today, Mutti—this afternoon. We're leaving within the hour."

She stopped chopping vegetables and stood still for a few seconds. "I see," she said, not turning around. "You can't wait another hour more? I'm making Sunday dinner. You like pot roast."

"I don't think that's a good idea," Martin said. He wasn't going to sit through another meal listening to his father's criticism. He'd had enough.

She stood there for a few more seconds, and then slowly turned around to face him. "You break your father's heart, you know."

"You reap what you sow. Isn't that what Papa says?"

She scowled. "Don't be impudent. He's still your father, and you should respect him."

Martin shook his head. "He's the one who makes that hard. Papa never changes."

She cocked her head to the side. "Do you really expect him to?"

"Yes." Martin spun on his heels and marched toward the spare bedroom.

Stevie was asleep under the covers of the large four poster bed, while Jackie and Marty sat above the covers, leaning back against the pile of down pillows, books open on their laps. They looked up as he came in.

"Hi Daddy!"

"Hi Dad."

"Pack your things, kiddos. We've got to leave."

"I thought we were staying with Grandma and Grandpa one more night," Marty said.

"Change of plans, kiddo," Martin said. "What do you say we go to New York? How about Coney Island? You enjoyed the midway rides at the fair yesterday—Coney Island's are bigger and faster."

Marty grinned. "OK!"

"I can't ride the fast ones," Jackie said with a small pout. "They said I was too little."

"I'll buy you all the cotton candy and cracker jacks you can eat," Martin told her with a smile, giving her a kiss on the forehead. "Be quiet while you pack your suitcase, and don't wake up Stevie yet."

Thirty minutes later, he woke Stevie and told him they were going to leave and go to an amusement park. The four-year-old rubbed his eyes and nodded, and Martin lifted him out of the bed and set him on the floor. Stevie shuffled down the hall following his brother and sister, and Martin carried the two suitcases.

Martin stood at the top of the stairs as the kids hugged and kissed his parents. Then he kissed his mother's cheek, thanked her for the hospitality, and turned back toward the stairs.

He nodded at his father as he turned. "Good bye, Papa." He walked down the stairs without shaking his father's hand.

Sadness, regret—even anger—had been buried away long ago, but seemed to resurface every time he came here.

He buried them deeper, and locked them under a concrete vault.

"OK, climb in kids," he said after he closed the suitcases in the trunk. "Coney Island, here we come!"

He hit the gas and sped away, not looking back in the rearview mirror.

The road northeast from Reading took them into the Lehigh Valley. This was hilly country, with green wooded slopes rising up around deep valleys full of towns and farms. Like Reading and Lancaster, this area had been Pennsylvania Dutch country for a long time, though in the middle of the last century the burgeoning iron and steel industries and textile mills here had attracted tens of thousands of immigrants from every part of Europe.

The highway wound alongside the Lehigh River, and many of the small towns in the western part of the valley still had the same Pennsylvania Dutch feel as neighboring Berks County; but later, as they drove into Allentown with its countless smokestacks belching black soot into the sky, there was little sign of that remaining.

Martin knew there were still families like his in Allentown—he'd known a couple of their sons at the University of Pennsylvania— but they were surrounded by the industrial American melting pot. He knew for a fact that many members of the German American Bund resided in the Allentown and Bethlehem area, though he assumed most of them were the product of recent immigration, rather than Pennsylvania Dutch.

In fact, the Bund owned a large club and camp ground at Sellersville, about twenty miles south of here, and about twenty-five miles east of Reading.

He began to wonder if *Schwarzkiefer* had been headed to Sellersville when he asked Ketterman for directions to Penn Station six weeks before.

Why hadn't he thought of that? Why had he been so stupid? He cursed himself for overlooking something that obvious.

He considered turning off the highway and heading down to Sellersville; but he looked over at Marty on the seat beside him, and in the rearview mirror at Jackie and Stevie in the backseat, and knew he couldn't disappoint them after promising them Coney Island.

Besides, he reminded himself—that was no longer his job.

He made a mental note to call FBI Special Agent in Charge Sloan— after he got back to the office in a couple of weeks.

After Allentown, Bethlehem, and Middletown, the highway passed through Easton. As they started to cross the bridge over the Delaware River toward New Jersey, he glanced down at a barge on the river, loaded with iron ore, and he pointed it out to the kids.

"See that? It's taking that iron down the river to Philadelphia," he said.

He noticed a factory on the river's edge where the barge was passing—the Showalter Glassworks, with white smoke rising from its twin smokestacks.

Our paths cross once again, he mused to himself. Strange how things sometimes randomly popped up over and over again.

He focused his attention on the road ahead. "Look, kids," he said pointing toward the "Welcome to New Jersey" sign as they passed it on the opposite side.

Hutson

21

Monday, July 31, 1939

Sloan lit a cigarette as he waited in the back seat of the Studebaker. Agent Anderson stood guard outside, his pistol in his hand, giving a menacing glare to anyone passing by the entrance to the alley. Agent O'Neal did the same at the other end.

The car was parked in a narrow alley in Harlem, between 133rd Street and 134th Street off 6th Avenue. Rusty iron fire escapes rose up the grimy walls of the brick buildings on either side of them, and garbage littered the ground just feet from trash cans. A street lamp on 133rd Street illuminated the entrance to the alley—where Anderson stood—and another on 134th street illuminated the exit behind them; in between, it was mostly dark, except for the little light from windows in the tenements above.

The car's back door opened, and Agent Pagliaro shoved a young black man into the back seat; Pagliaro slid in beside him, his gun in his left hand resting on his lap.

"You're Alan Carmody?" Sloan asked the young man.

"Yes, sir." There was a slight tremble in his voice, and he looked tense in spite of his obvious efforts not to. He wore an orange shirt and a silver-blue necktie under a coffee brown suit. His hair was short, and the curls were smoothed by the oil he used when combing it straight back from his face.

"How do you know Gregory Spooner?" Sloan asked, getting right to the point.

"Sir?"

Sloan pointed a finger at Carmody's face. "Don't play dumb with me, boy. We found your name on a slip of paper in Mr. Spooner's apartment downtown, along with the names of a couple of negro jazz clubs in Harlem—Minton's Playhouse and The Hamilton Lodge. How'd he get those? Were you providing him a reference?"

A nervous grin broke across Carmody's lips. "Oh yeah, Greg. Young white boy, right? Tall and kind of skinny?"

Sloan slapped Carmody across the chin, not hard, but enough to let him know he wasn't playing around. "Cut the act—we know you know who we're talking about, so stop yanking our chains, got it? Now tell me how you know Mr. Spooner, and what you and he had to do with those clubs."

Carmody looked frightened, and said nothing.

Sloan tried a different tack. "Listen, Mr. Spooner was found murdered yesterday morning—so if you don't want us to treat you like a suspect in his death, you'd better start spilling about how you knew him, and what the nature of your relationship with him was."

"You're cops?" Carmody asked.

"FBI. Now start talking."

"I met Greg about a year ago, over at the 125th Street Station—"

"Was he selling dope?" Sloan asked. Then his eyes narrowed. "Or selling sex?"

Carmody's mouth hung open for a second after the second question. "I don't know nothing about none of that," he said. "He was just this stray kid, new in the city, and I helped him out."

New in the city, my ass, Sloan thought. Gregory Spooner was from the Bronx.

"How'd you help him out? Give him a place to stay? Food? Maybe a warm bed to share with you?" Sloan's tone was sharp.

Carmody glanced nervously between Sloan and Pagliaro. Then he began talking, his nerves making him chattier.

"Yeah, alright so we bunked up a few times. We weren't hurting nobody. I took him around a few clubs, met some cats, we cut the rug together, stuff like that. I helped him look for a job, got him steady."

"You get him into the business?" Sloan asked, eyes narrowed.

"No sir, I ain't got nothing to do with none of that," Carmody said. "But word gets around, see, and offers start coming down, so then Greg puts it together a bun boy can make some serious moola in the Big Apple, and he took off."

"You see him much after that?"

Carmody shrugged. "Couple times, yeah. Couldn't help it. I had it bad, I guess. He worked for a butcher down the east side, but I found out he was selling Cadillacs on the side, plus taking dough for the gobble and bend, so I didn't want nothing more to do with him after a while."

Selling Cadillacs—street lingo for ounces of cocaine. Heavier stuff than the marijuana they'd been told about. It made Sloan raise an eyebrow. And as for 'gobble and bend,' he got the imagery, and his lips pursed.

"What about recently?"

Carmody looked nervous, sitting silent and playing with his fingernails.

"If you don't tell us what you know, boy, Pagliaro here'll take you up to the Bronx, dump you in an Italian neighborhood, right on the corner where the Guido boys hang out, and see how long a sissy nigger queer like you lasts, OK?"

Carmody swallowed hard. "Yes, sir. I saw Greg a few weeks ago; a month maybe. I was at this swing joint down on 112th Street and Seventh, and he came in. I was with some fellas, and he come up to me and wants to talk. Said he took this job a while back, and now he was in trouble."

"What did you talk about?"

"Nothing much. I told him it served him right, the way he'd been acting. You act like a hoodlum, you gonna have bad shit come down the line, sooner or later."

"Did he say what the job was?"

"Not too much," Carmody said with a shrug. "He said it started out real simple—take this package here, and tomorrow there's cash in your mail box. Next thing he knew, he was being told go somewhere, and some foreign man will meet him, and he was to take the man somewhere, wherever he said. He was supposed to dress nice, and they were supposed to act like they were businessmen."

Carmody swallowed hard, and hesitated before continuing. "He said he did this twice, but he put it together they were up to some nasty business, so he told the man he wasn't going to do it no more. But the man threatened to break his arms or something if he backed out—said there was more to be done, and they couldn't have no turncoats running their mouths off."

"Did he say what kind of 'nasty business' it was?" Sloan asked.

Carmody shook his head. "No, sir. He just said it was real bad. He seemed terrible scared. Asked if he could stay with me for a while and lay low."

Carmody's eyes began to well up a little, and he fell silent.

"You turned him down?" Sloan asked.

"Yes, sir," Carmody said, his voice breaking a little. "Maybe I should've took him in, huh? Maybe he wouldn't have got hisself killed."

Sloan scowled at the last minute show of conscience. It would have been one thing if he'd bought Carmody's act of innocence and righteous indignation at Spooner's nefarious activities—but he knew better.

"You're the Alan Carmody who got arrested May 1937 with three other colored men, convicted of making pornographic movies for sale on the black market? Stag movies with only stags, wasn't it? No dames, according to the record."

Sloan enjoyed the panicked look in Carmody's eyes. "Seems you served a year at Sing Sing for that, released July 1938—just in time to meet sixteen-year-old Gregory Spooner, young man new in the city and all alone at 125th Street station. How fortuitous for you."

"I put those days behind me, sir," Carmody said. "I ain't done nothing like that since I got out of the big house. I was trying to go clean, and that's why I couldn't have Greg doing wrong like he was."

Pagliaro grabbed him by the collar, a sour look on his face. "You weren't trying to go *too* clean, if you was bangin' a sixteen-year-old white boy."

Carmody swallowed hard. "That was nothing but private business, like I told you before. It was strictly between me and Greg. We weren't hurting nobody, and we kept it to ourselves, see? There weren't no money, or nothing like that."

Sloan motioned for Pagliaro to let go, then he stared at Carmody hard, menacing even. "So if the NYPD searched your room right now, they wouldn't find any pervert queer pornography stashed in a drawer somewhere?"

Carmody swallowed hard again, but said nothing.

"Would it spark your memory about what Greg told you a few weeks ago if we were to go up and have a look around?" Sloan asked, watching him closely.

Carmody's eyes grew slightly wider. "No, sir. I told you all I know, and that's the God's honest truth. Greg didn't tell me no more than that, I swear, sir."

Sloan looked at Pagliaro and motioned toward the door with his head. "Get him out of here."

Pagliaro opened the car door and stepped out. Carmody started to follow, but Pagliaro grabbed him by the lapels and hauled him out, dumping him unceremoniously on the ground.

"Nigger faggot," he said, and spat on the ground near Carmody's feet. He turned up the alley and whistled before climbing back into the Studebaker.

Agent Anderson moved from his sentry post at the head of the alley, and got into the driver's seat, O'Neal beside him. A few seconds later, the Studebaker drove away in a burst, its back tires tossing up dust and grime into Alan Carmody's face.

22

Thursday, August 3, 1939

It was a four-hour drive from Coney Island in Brooklyn, down the length of Long Island to Montauk—a distance of one hundred and twenty miles—and Martin spent most of it in silence while the kids slept in the back seat.

Marty stayed awake the longest, reading a book in the front seat beside Martin, but somewhere past Islip he fell asleep, too, his head resting on Martin's arm.

It was peaceful having silence in the car while he drove. There was no Becky around to intrude on his solitude. He mused about how nice it was to be able to make the spur-of-the-moment decision to leave Coney Island and head to Montauk instead, without having to ask anyone what they thought about that. No Becky to tell him it was a bad idea, or not what she had in mind.

Martin hated having to stop for gasoline, but the tank was nearing empty as they reached Westhampton. There was still forty-five miles to go, and he knew the car wouldn't make it the full distance without a fill-up.

A man in a white uniform came out of the filling station as Martin pulled alongside the pump. "Fill her up, and check the oil," Martin told him.

A passenger train sped past on the track that followed alongside the highway, pulled by one of the sleek new diesel engines, all silver steel and rounded edges. Martin watched it, amazed at how much faster and quieter it was than a steam locomotive.

Ten minutes later, they were on the highway again heading east, through farmland and tidy Yankee villages. Sand dunes covered in scrub grass blocked the view of the ocean.

At Southampton they began to pass large beachfront houses with long, gated driveways. Most were cedar shingled, with immaculate landscaping.

The new summer retreat for the wealthy of New York, Martin thought. He wondered if Newport, Rhode Island was still where the old-money families summered. Perhaps these were the *nouveau riches* from the post-war boom years of the 1920s.

These giant beach houses stretched from Southampton through Bridgehampton and East Hampton, taking up a large proportion of the oceanfront acreage.

After East Hampton, the houses thinned, and so did the traffic. The land became emptier, with grassy sand dunes on the right, and a mix of forest and farms on the left. He slowed through the little fishing village of Amagansett, and found open highway on the other side. He floored the gas pedal as he passed a sign saying "Montauk, 9 mi."

Here, the dunes were unbroken by development, with dense forest on the left.

This was the perfect landing spot for *Abwehr* spies, he realized. He'd known they usually landed somewhere between Montauk and Amagansett, but he had never seen the area. Now, it made perfect sense.

As he zoomed past a sign saying "Montauk, 4 mi," he hit the brakes, pulling off onto the sandy shoulder. Marty stirred as the car came to a stop, and he sat up, looking at Martin with sleepy eyes.

"Daddy?"

"Just stopping for a minute, buddy," Martin said, putting his hand on the back of his son's head. "I'm going to climb that dune and look at the ocean, if you want to come with me."

Marty nodded without a word, and slid to the passenger side door.

Martin killed the engine, and walked around to meet his eldest son. "Come on," Martin said.

There was a narrow trail through the tall grass, probably made by animals who lived in the scrub, and they followed it up the slope. It was a relatively high dune, probably twenty feet above the highway behind them, but the slope was gradual.

The sound of crashing waves grew louder as they crested the dune. The slope dropped off more steeply in front of them, down to a wide sandy beach. Martin stood still at the top, looking out over the vast expanse of ocean. Marty came up beside him, and Martin put his hand on his son's shoulder.

They stood together in silence for a few moments, watching the waves.

In his mind's eye, Martin imagined this spot on a moon-lit night; in the distance, a gray submarine surfaced a half-mile off shore. Its hatch opened, and three men climbed out. One of them inflated a yellow raft, and he climbed aboard with an oar and a small suitcase while the other two held it in place next to the submarine. They pushed him off, and he paddled for the beach. The submarine waited in place until the raft hit the beach, and then the men on top climbed down the hatch, and the sub disappeared beneath the waves.

"Dad?"

Marty's voice broke his reverie, and he looked down at his son. "It's nice here, isn't it?" Martin asked.

Marty nodded. "Can we go down to the beach?"

Martin shook his head. "Not here. We'll go to the beach later, after we check into a motel. Let's go."

They trudged back down the landward side of the dune toward the car. Jackie and Stevie were still asleep in the back seat when they got in. A moment after pulling away, Martin told Marty to wake them up.

"We're almost there," he told his two youngest as they sat up in the back seat, rubbing their eyes.

Motels lined the beach side of the road as they entered the little town of Montauk, many still with damaged roofs and boarded-up windows from last year's hurricane. He found a two-story motor lodge with a vacancy sign, painted a worn shade of blue, and pulled up to the office. The kids came inside with him.

"How far is it to the lighthouse?" Martin asked as he signed the guest card for their room.

"About four miles," the lady behind the counter said in a nasal Yankee accent. She was a few years older than he was, with frizzy red hair pulled back from her face. She pointed out the window. "You go a few blocks to the center of town, take a left, go a couple more blocks, and take a right at the big hotel. You'll see signs for the lighthouse. You take that road out of town."

He thanked her, and she handed over a room key.

Their room was on the second floor, plain, with two double beds, and a pair of nautical paintings on the walls—one with a sailboat on a gray wind-swept sea, and the other of a tall white lighthouse on a bluff.

"Let's go get some lunch, eh?" Martin said after they'd unpacked their suitcases into the drawers of the room's dresser. "After lunch, you kids want to go check out the lighthouse?"

"OK," Marty said.

They walked to a little restaurant a few blocks away, between the town center and the oceanfront motels. The kids ate hot dogs, while Martin indulged in local clam steamers. After lunch, they walked back to the motor lodge and got in the car.

The road east from Montauk wound up into the hills away from the ocean, through scrub woods and limestone outcroppings. After what seemed too long, and a few minutes after Martin had begun to wonder if they were on the wrong road, the woods fell away and an open lawn spread out between the road and a big bluff over the ocean. Right in front of them stood a four-story white lighthouse.

Martin parked the car in a gravel lot on the opposite side of the road. "Come on, let's go have a look."

They crossed the grassy lawn, which inclined uphill toward the lighthouse. Beyond the lighthouse, the ground fell away in steep bluffs, and large waves crashed against giant boulders at the base.

A gray-haired man in a dirty white shirt and dark trousers, his face weathered and stubbled, emerged from the lighthouse and shouted, "You're on government property."

Martin showed his badge. "Federal agent. I want to a look around."

The man eyed the kids, but turned away without a word.

Martin stood facing east and pointed across the endless expanse of dark water. "The ocean goes on unbroken for three thousand miles that way," he said. "Nothing but water between here and Portugal."

"Wow!" Marty and Jackie said, almost in unison. Stevie was throwing rocks over the bluff.

"Wanna swim to Lisbon?" Martin asked with a crooked grin.

"How long would it take to swim across the ocean, Dad?" Marty asked.

"I don't know—no one's ever done it."

"How long do you think?"

Martin shrugged. "It takes a big steam ship ten days to cross it, and they go pretty fast," he said. "If you tried to swim it, I bet it would take you more than three months to get across—if a shark didn't eat you first."

He added this last with another sly grin at his kids, and he leaned down and tickled the two younger ones from behind, sending them into startled squeals.

"Are there lots of sharks?" Marty asked.

"In the whole ocean? Oh yes, thousands."

"And they eat people?"

Martin saw the concerned look on his son's face, and chuckled. "Sometimes—but not very often. You don't have to worry about a shark eating you, son."

Marty didn't look convinced.

Martin chuckled, and squeezed his son's shoulder. "Come on, kiddos—let's go inside."

Martin carried Stevie on his back, and followed his other two children up the narrow circular stairway inside the lighthouse. As he should have guessed, Jackie tired out early and didn't make it farther than halfway; he had her take a seat next to the window on the small landing that marked the half way point, set Stevie down beside her, and told them to wait there while he and Marty went the rest of the way.

At the top, Martin climbed onto the platform, then held out his hand to help his son up. They stood in the stuffy glass enclosure, and looked out at the three-hundred-and-sixty-degree view.

"See that land way off there?" Martin asked, pointing north to a hazy green shoreline far in the distance. "That's Connecticut and Rhode Island. And back that way you can see Montauk, where we're staying."

He swept his hands to the south and east. "Nothing but ocean for thousands of miles in either of those directions. That's what's kept this country safe all these years."

From obvious enemies, at least.

He had always been proud of his role in keeping the country safe from the sneakier ones; but now he felt his role had been diminished, and there wasn't a thing he could do about it.

206

"Come on, let's go back down and get your brother and sister," Martin said, patting Marty's shoulder. He stepped down off the platform, and reached up to help his eight-year-old down.

"What do you say we go to the beach for the rest of the afternoon?"

"I don't want to go in the water," Marty said.

"Why not? You went in the water at Coney Island—that's the same ocean as here."

"I'm scared of sharks," Marty said.

Martin chuckled, and squeezed his son's shoulder. "Don't worry, buddy—I won't let anything bad happen to you. I'll keep you safe, I promise."

Hutson

23

Monday, August 7, 1939

"Of course we're aware of it," Sloan's voice said over the telephone. "You didn't think we weren't, did you?"

"No, of course not," Martin said. "I'm only suggesting that you might need to give it another look, to see if *Schwarzkiefer* was headed for Sellersville."

"We've had the grounds under surveillance for months," Sloan said.

"And?" Martin asked, impatient.

"That *Schwarzkiefer* agent hasn't gone there."

"You know this for certain?"

"As I said, we've had it under surveillance for months. We know all the regulars. Any newcomers are investigated and identified. No one new has shown up there and been unidentifiable since before this *Schwarzkiefer* arrived. Everyone who's been there this year is in the country legally."

Martin tried to hide his disappointment. "Have you infiltrated them? Made sure everyone's papers are legitimate?"

Sloan's tone became exasperated. "Listen, Schuller—you let us handle this. We know what we're doing. And like I told you a couple of months ago, we're way more experienced at this kind of thing than you boys at the State Department."

"Just trying to be of help," Martin said, his voice clipped with irritation.

Sloan sighed. "I appreciate that. You get any other bright ideas you think we haven't thought of yet, give me a ring."

The line clicked off.

"Jerk," Martin muttered, and returned to the paperwork on his desk.

"You did what you could," Hansen assured him as they walked out of the office at four-thirty that afternoon. "It seemed like a good suggestion, and from the sounds of what that Agent Sloan told you, they've got it pretty well covered."

"Yeah, sounds like it," Martin said, not one hundred percent convinced.

"*Schwarzkiefer* is probably embedded somewhere in the Midwest," Hansen continued. "But it's not our problem anymore, so let Sloan and his men worry about it."

Easier said than done, Martin thought. They'd spent more than a year trying to crack the identity of *Der Skiläufer*, and he still hadn't completely accepted that the FBI was in charge of that from now on.

They rode down the elevator in silence, packed among a dozen other civil servants going home for the day. After they exited the Old Executive Office Building into the hot afternoon, Hansen asked Martin if he'd paid much attention to the news while he was on vacation.

"I checked out the newspapers every day. Why do you ask?"

"It seems as though Hitler's rhetoric has amped up again," Hansen said. "Kind of reminds me of the way he carried on before the Munich conference—only it's Poland this time."

Martin nodded. He'd noticed that, too. "He's been ranting about Danzig and the Polish corridor since the beginning of the year, though," he pointed out. "And then he went and sent tanks and troops into Czechoslovakia instead. This could be another diversion."

Hansen shrugged. "I suppose so. Doesn't feel like that, though."

"I agree," Martin said. "But I'm always suspicious of Hitler's motives. I wouldn't rule out anything."

"Have you seen any intel that would suggest a different target?" Hansen asked, lowering his voice. "I haven't."

"No, I haven't either," Martin said. "But Germany lost territory to a number of countries after the World War—Denmark, Belgium, France of course—and his ultimate goal has always been to regain all the lost territories."

Hansen looked doubtful. "He hasn't made any ranting hysterical speeches about any of those other countries of late."

"No, he hasn't," Martin agreed.

"I'm thinking, if Hitler's getting ready to invade Poland, he'll probably send an agent over here—like he did with *Immergrün* in February, which turned out to be right before the invasion of Czechoslovakia. And there were others before the Sudetenland, and before Austria."

"It's a definite pattern," Martin said. "Maybe he wants to take our political pulse before each action, as much as stir up support for their 'noble cause.'"

They walked in silence for another block, until they reached Rhode Island Avenue NW, where Hansen always turned off to head home. He paused at the corner.

"You have plans this evening, Martin?"

Martin shook his head. "Just to make something for dinner, do some reading, maybe listen to the radio for a bit. Why?"

"There's a new pizza joint near my place off Logan Circle—want to go split a pizza with me?"

Martin shrugged. After a week alone with his kids, he could use some adult company. "Sure, why not? What time?"

"How about six o'clock?"

"OK, what's the address?"

Hansen gave him the address, Martin repeated it once to commit it to memory, and they shook hands and parted.

Martin found the pizza place, Luigi's, a few minutes before six. Hansen was already sitting at a table when he walked in. He stood and waved as Martin came through the door.

"Thanks for the invitation," Martin said as he sat down.

"Any time. We bachelors need to stick together." Hansen motioned for the waiter, who brought over a carafe of red wine. "I figured after all this time, you're probably getting tired of the solitude every night."

"It's not so bad."

In truth, he had gotten a little tired of it. He was used to a fair amount of solitude whenever he was on an undercover mission—but those had usually been two weeks or less, and allowed him to get absorbed in the task at hand. It had now been eight weeks since he came home to find Becky and the kids gone, and he was beginning to get a little stir crazy at home alone.

"If you want to know my opinion, there's more good things about being a bachelor than there are bad," Hansen said with a grin, and began ticking them off on his fingers. "Freedom to do what you want, go where you want, stay out as late as you want, without having to answer to anyone. You can leave your clothes on the floor without hearing about it from anyone, you can eat what you want, and it's cheaper—all good things, my friend."

Martin shrugged. "I suppose so."

"And if you get tired of being by yourself, there's a whole city full of people out there."

Martin thought that sounded overly optimistic, but he just shrugged again. He looked down at the menu. "What kind of pizza do you want to get?"

"They make really good pizza here," Hansen said. "I like just about anything on the list—except anchovies, no taste for that stuff. Tell me what you like, and that's what we'll get."

They ordered a pizza, and Hansen poured wine into their glasses.

"Have you seen that new British spy comedy, 'Clouds Over Europe?'" he asked.

Martin shook his head. "I took the kids to see the new Donald Duck movie, about a picnic on the beach with Pluto. It was a hoot, and the next day at the beach on Coney Island the kids kept reenacting some of the scenes. We also saw the latest Shirley Temple flick, 'Susannah of the Mounties.' Typical silly Shirley Temple story, but the kids liked it a lot."

Hansen shook his head. "Buddy, you need to get out and see some grown-up pictures."

Martin ignored his comment. "You're a fan of spy stories?"

"Sure," Hansen said with a half-shrug and a smile. "Why not? They're fun, if you don't take them too seriously. This picture was a comedy, so no danger of that. Laurence Olivier, Valerie Hobson. I'm a big fan of Laurence Olivier, so it was a shoo-in I'd go see it. And it was a funny picture. A bit of British farce, plus danger from enemy moles in an airplane factory, so what's not to like?"

Martin chuckled. "I think my problem is, I can't ignore all of the inaccuracies. I don't know how to not take them too seriously, as you say. They get pretty sensational, don't you think?"

"Oh, that's part of what makes them so fun," Hansen said. "I take it you don't read much Graham Greene, then?"

Martin shook his head. "I prefer Hemingway or Fitzgerald, and lately Steinbeck. If I'm going to read a novel, I want to believe it."

"Fair enough," Hansen said. "I like Fitzgerald, but Hemingway can be a little heavy, don't you think? I like books to be fun to read, otherwise what's the point? If I can go out to a bar and have more fun, I'll do that."

"Hemingway's a big fan of bars," Martin said, joining in the fun. "You might run into him at one sometime, and have to defend your assessment of his writing."

"Ha! He might charge me like a bull, so no thanks."

Martin laughed. It occurred to him later that he hadn't laughed much in months. Maybe that was why he'd enjoyed the Donald Duck cartoon so much with the kids the week before. Either way, this night out with Joe Hansen was exactly what he'd needed without knowing it.

After they'd eaten their pizza and drunk their wine, they walked out of the restaurant into a steamy August twilight.

"Thanks again for getting me out of the apartment tonight," Martin said, and turned to leave. "See you at work tomorrow."

"I'm going to go grab a nightcap—care to join me? It's only eight o'clock."

"Thanks, but I'll pass tonight. Good night, Joe."

"Suit yourself. Good night, Martin."

24

Friday, August 11, 1939

It was almost four o'clock before Martin came across the
bombshell—one decoded message buried in a stack from this morning's
deliveries from the diplomatic pouches, which made his breath catch.

The cover letter itself was intriguing. One of the second secretaries
at the U.S. Embassy in Berlin noted that the decoded message had been
given to him the night before by a diplomat at the British embassy with
whom this second secretary was friendly after hours.

Martin remembered from his days at the embassy in Vienna how
this worked, and how much diplomacy and exchange of information
occurred at cocktail parties rather than during normal hours of
operation. Still, this struck him. The British secret services among were
the most secretive of them all, right up there with the Soviets. They
never gave away information for free, not even to their closest allies
during times of war.

When he and two others had been trained as undercover
counterintelligence agents in Virginia in 1935, one of the old adages
that was drilled into their heads was that while there were friendly
nations, there were no friendly intelligence services. Still, the British
were extreme even by secretive intelligence service standards.

So that struck him first. Then he read the message, and his heart
skipped a beat.

1 June, 1939

Made contact with The Skier 30 May, Deutschhorst Country Club. At his command, infiltrating Conservative Coalition. Will meet a Congressman tomorrow. The Fatherland's cause will be heard in American halls of power. Next broadcast three days.

Black Pine.

The notes the British service had made indicated it was a radio broadcast originating from somewhere near the mid-Atlantic coast of the United States.

Martin checked his report from his last abortive undercover mission in New York; as he thought, he met with Ketterman on May 31st, and had been told that *Schwarzkiefer* had been there a couple of days before.

Schwarzkiefer must have gone straight to Penn Station the day he picked up his false papers; that was how he was able to contact *Der Skiläufer* the next day, May 30th.

While Martin was working laboriously in the biergarten and butcher shop in Yorkville, his quarry was making contact with an American Congressman.

What was the false name he'd used for his papers? There it was— Fritz Dendler. His pulse quickened.

Martin wondered how long it would take to track down a Fritz Dendler on the appointment logs of up to four hundred and thirty-five Congressmen.

Or if there would even be such a record.

Still, there was one clue to narrow it down—the Conservative Coalition was the name given to a semi-formal association of Congressmen and Senators, first organized two years ago, to oppose all expansion of FDR's New Deal programs. Martin supposed it wouldn't be too difficult to find a list of names—Hansen probably knew them by heart. They would be mostly Republicans, but if they were southerners they'd be Democrats.

He got up and stepped over to Hansen's desk.

"Hey Joe, how easy would it be to get a list of Congressmen in the Conservative Coalition?"

Hansen shrugged. "Just Congressmen, and no Senators? I could probably come up with that in twenty minutes. I could probably name a bunch of them for you right now, off the top of my head—but if you want the full list, we've got a directory of members of Congress I can reference to make sure I don't miss anyone."

"Just twenty minutes, huh?" Martin said.

"Sure," Hansen said with a grin. "I'll know them all by name when I see them listed in the directory. It won't take long, probably less than twenty minutes."

"Care to wager a beer on that?"

Hansen's grin widened. "You're on."

"Start now," Martin said, and glanced at his watch as he turned back toward his own desk.

Seventeen minutes later, Hansen tossed a sheet of paper onto Martin's desk. "You owe me a beer, buddy."

"Thanks!" Martin said, and began perusing the list. He recognized some of the names—but the one that jumped out at him was Congressman Barbour, from Pennsylvania.

"Get your wallet ready, because it's almost quitting time," Hansen said, but Martin was distracted. "Did you hear me?"

"Sorry, what?" Martin looked up at him, unaware that he was still standing there.

"I said to get your wallet ready, it's almost quitting time."

Martin held up a finger as he stood, a collection of papers in his hand. "I've got to talk with the chief first. Hang out a little while."

**

The chief's forehead knit into a tight knot as he read the papers while Martin summarized what he'd learned.

"You've got to get this to the FBI right away," the chief said. "This shouldn't wait until Monday. Call up that Agent Sloan as soon as you get back to your desk." He handed the papers back to Martin.

Disappointment morphed into anger in the pit of Martin's stomach as he left the chief's office. He walked back to his desk in an anger-induced fog.

"You ready?" Hansen asked, his hat already on his head.

Martin hesitated a second. "Yes, I am."

He threw the papers into a desk drawer, locked it, retrieved his hat and followed Hansen out the door.

He and Hansen were sitting at a bar on 15th Street NW, having a round of beers that Martin had bought, when Hansen asked him about the list of Conservative Coalition members.

"What did you need that for?"

"A hunch," Martin said, and didn't elaborate.

"Oh?"

Martin looked around. The bar was packed with government employees enjoying a Friday evening happy hour after work. "I'll fill you in later," he said, keeping his voice as quiet as he could and still be heard over the boisterous crowd.

"Alright," Hansen said. "But tell me this—did your hunch pan out?"

"I'll let you know soon."

Hansen shook his head. "Congress is out of session right now, so you'll probably have to wait a while."

Martin stared at him. "What did you say?"

Hansen looked confused. "I said that Congress isn't in session right now, so it'll probably be a while before you find out if your hunch panned out."

But Martin was already looking away, his mind turning over the possibilities.

"What's the matter?"

Martin smiled at his friend, trying to seem unconcerned. "Nothing, don't worry about it. I was thinking about something from this afternoon."

"Stop thinking about work," Hansen said. "It's Friday afternoon. Say, why don't we make a night of it? What do you say?"

But Martin was downing the last of his bottle of beer. He laid a couple of dollars on the bar. "Maybe next Friday," he said. Putting his hat on, he hurried out the door.

Hutson

25

Saturday, August 12, 1939

Martin leaned against the corner of the building early in the morning as Stefan Ketterman came down the sidewalk from Second Avenue toward his shop on 86th Street.

Martin wasn't wearing the fake mustache, glasses, or shabby old suit of his Augustus Graeter cover, so he had his hat pulled low over his eyes. There were few people out at seven-thirty on a Saturday morning, but he was still cautious, lest someone in the neighborhood recognize him.

Ketterman was almost upon him before he realized who Martin was. There was a hesitation in his step when it dawned on him, but he glanced around and continued to the front door of his print shop, unlocked it, and held it open just long enough for Martin to follow him inside.

"I haven't made any fake passports since you were here last, I promise," Ketterman said as he locked the door behind him.

"That's not why I'm here," Martin said. "I've got a job for you."

Ketterman gave him a wary look. "You want me to make fake papers for someone you're trying to catch?"

"No—for me," Martin said. "I want you to make me a membership card for the Bund, and don't pretend you don't know what it looks like."

Martin stood outside of the two-story brown brick building in downtown Eastbury, Pennsylvania. This was a small town of about two thousand people, and little was happening in the center of town at four-thirty on a Saturday afternoon.

This particular building was located a couple of blocks from the two-block business district, where a few women with baskets over their forearms went from little store to little store; and the block in between was occupied by the Presbyterian Church, a red-brick building with a tall white steeple.

The sign in front of the building announced that it was the district office of Congressman Barbour. The building was locked, and the interior dark. Martin realized he shouldn't have expected anything else on a Saturday afternoon in a small town—though on the phone he'd been told to go there.

A dark green Packard Touring Car pulled up a few minutes later, and a uniformed chauffer got out of the driver's seat, walked around to the passenger-side rear door, and opened it. He stood aside, but no one exited.

Martin stepped closer, and saw the Congressman seated inside, looking up at him.

"Go on, get in. We're not staying here."

Martin climbed in the back of the car, and the chauffer closed the door.

"I thought we'd go out to the house, have a cigar and some brandy," the congressman said. "I confess, I was surprised to hear from you again, after all this time. But then, perhaps I shouldn't have been so surprised, given the changes in your work a few weeks ago."

Martin knew he shouldn't be surprised that Congressman Barbour knew about that. He wondered just how much the congressman did know.

"I am hopeful I haven't burned my bridge," Martin said, trying to sound hopeful.

"No, not at all," the congressman said, waving a hand in the air. "Tell me, how is your father-in-law these days? I haven't had the pleasure of encountering him or Mrs. Walsh recently."

Martin's stomach clenched. He forced a smile with some effort. "I'm not quite sure myself, sir. It's been a busy summer, and I haven't been out to Philadelphia since that time when I met you at the gala in March."

The congressman gave him an appraising look. "So you came all the way out here, from Washington, all on your own?"

Martin forced the smile again. "That's right. My father-in-law doesn't actually know I'm here." He hesitated before adding, "And neither does my wife."

The congressman's eyebrows shot up in surprise. "Oh? Really? That is bold of you, Mr. Schuller."

He pulled a cigar from his pocket, offered it to Martin, who shook his head. He lit the cigar, took a puff, and blew it toward the front of the car.

"I like your style, Mr. Schuller. I need bold men such as you, who will take action when it's called for. We are living in dynamic times, and men of action will be called upon to act in the best interests of their country."

Martin had little doubt that the congressman's definition of the "best interests of their country" was different from his own.

"That's what I have made my life's work, sir—until recently, anyway." Martin's regret was unforced, even if the words he said were. "So you can see why I'm more interested in your previous offer than I was before."

"Absolutely!" the congressman agreed. "I can't blame you one bit, son. I'm glad you called again. Ah, here we are."

The car pulled into a circular gravel driveway in front of a large, old two-story house built of giant field stones, with black shutters on the many windows. It was probably four thousand square feet, Martin estimated—a small mansion.

As the car door opened and Martin stepped out, he was mesmerized by the view—the house sat on top of a hill overlooking the Delaware River a mile or so to the east. The valley floor below was green and wooded, broken by the occasional farm field and house along the river road.

"Come along inside, and we'll discuss particulars," the congressman said behind him.

They entered a narrow hall that bisected the house, with an open staircase in the center that led up to a partial balcony. A silver chandelier hung above the entry, and on either side of Martin were a formal parlor and dining room.

The butler took their hats, and Barbour led Martin into a large study and library with book shelves on two walls rising all the way to the ten-foot ceiling, as well as part of a third on either side of a large fireplace. Photographs lined the dark wood mantle. A giant window with a view of the valley occupied the other wall, and a large mahogany desk sat in front of it, facing into the room. An expensive-looking Persian rug covered most of the floor.

"Have a seat," the congressman said, motioning toward one of two leather chairs that faced the desk. He took a decanter of brandy off the top of a nearby credenza, poured a small measure into two glasses, and handed one to Martin.

"This is my second time in Congress, you know," Barbour said after he'd sat in the chair behind the desk. "It was my honor to serve this district for fourteen years—until I was narrowly defeated in '32. The people were right to be angry then, misdirected though their anger was.

"I spent six years in the private sector, and listened to our state's business leaders. I was able to return to my previous seat in Congress last year, when the majority of our district came to their senses and realized that Franklin Delano Roosevelt's socialist policies weren't fixing the Depression."

Martin noticed the congressman didn't mention his not-so-narrow defeats in 1934 and '36, before he was finally successful at regaining his seat in '38—a year in which the Republicans made big gains in both houses of Congress, due to the sharp recession that had undone nearly half of the economic growth since the New Deal began in 1933.

The congressman continued, turning his chair toward the fire place and pointing with his brandy glass toward the mantle. "I heard from our business leaders that we need government policies that will help businesses by removing obstacles to their growth, not putting burdens on them so that we can finance handouts."

"May I, sir?" Martin asked, putting his hands on the arms of the chair as if to stand, while nodding toward the mantle.

"Absolutely," Barbour said, and took a puff on his cigar.

Martin walked toward the mantle and looked at the pictures. The largest one in the center appeared about ten years old, based upon the style of their suits, and he recognized the congressman standing beside William Vare, a Philadelphia businessman who had been the most powerful Republican political boss in Pennsylvania at the time.

In other pictures, Martin recognized the congressman with Rodman Wanamaker, the Philadelphia department store magnate; Eugene Grace, president of Bethlehem Steel; Charles Schwab, former head of Bethlehem Steel; John D. Rockefeller, Jr., the Manhattan real-estate tycoon, and son of the late Standard Oil founder; J.P. Morgan, Jr., the New York banker who was one of FDR's sharpest critics; and on the end was the congressman with an obvious father-son pair, the younger of whom was Maximilian Showalter.

"That's quite a notable group," Martin said as he walked back to his chair.

A proud smile stretched across Barbour's face. "Indeed. It was men such as they who made this country great. Our leaders in Washington would do well to remember that."

Since neither Morgan nor Rockefeller had significant ties to this part of Pennsylvania, that was interesting.

The J.P. Morgan, Jr. connection in particular piqued Martin's interest—the banker was known to have made millions of dollars in loans to Germany and Italy. In regards to Italy in particular, it was widely believed in the State Department that those loans were responsible for financially propping up the Mussolini regime.

"When we met before, you said that you were looking for someone who could help businesses in the district gain access to German markets," Martin said.

"Yes," the congressman said, nodding and leaning forward, elbows on the desk. "Germany has one of the strongest economies in the world—and certainly the fastest growing one—so naturally American industries would do well to have access to those markets. I could use someone like you on my team, someone who knows international diplomacy, speaks German, and can navigate Washington red tape. You were in the diplomatic corps at one time, I understand?"

Martin wondered if Becky's family had provided that information back in March, or if the congressman had looked into his background.

"Yes, I was a Foreign Service officer in Vienna for two years."

"Excellent! So you know how to talk to diplomats. Businesses look to their government for assistance in international trade; my office receives inquiries all the time, and I could use someone on my staff who can work with German diplomats here to grease the wheels in Berlin."

"So I could stay based in Washington?" Martin asked. "I wouldn't be expected to return to Pennsylvania and live in-district?" He knew that was Becky's main wish when the offer was first floated.

The congressman chortled. "Absolutely you can stay in Washington! That's the best place for you, if you're going to make the connections and do the work I want you to. You can even make use of the contacts you already have over at State—and in return for their cooperation with our office, I can be persuaded to help them out when the next round of appropriations comes up on the House floor."

Martin always hated that side of diplomacy—the tit-for-tat mentality of governments, even internal. He understood that was how the game was played, that was how deals were made and action taken, but it didn't make him comfortable with the process.

"When we spoke in March, you made a generous offer of compensation." He watched the congressman's face.

"Yes, I believe I offered you one hundred and fifty dollars a week," the congressman said, stubbing out the end of his cigar.

"One hundred and seventy, actually, sir."

Barbour chuckled. "You have an excellent memory, Mr. Schuller—but you came to me this time. I'll offer you one hundred and fifty."

"No," Martin said, and started to stand.

"Now, don't be hasty, Mr. Schuller," the congressman hurried to say, motioning for Martin to sit back down. "I can be reasonable. Let's say, one hundred and fifty-five."

"One seventy."

Barbour's eyes narrowed. "I'm being reasonable in this negotiation, Mr. Schuller—why can't you be equally reasonable?"

"I would hardly call it reasonable to start negotiations at twenty dollars below your initial offer." Martin's voice was flat, his gaze unwavering from the congressman's eyes.

Barbour shook his head. "That offer was almost six months ago. A reasonable man would say it expired long ago. We are beginning this negotiation from scratch."

It occurred to Martin that it might not be so critical for Congressman Barbour to lure him away from State, now that State was no longer working directly to apprehend *Abwehr* agents in the United States.

"I'm sure you understand, Congressman Barbour, that the type of work you are suggesting I do would benefit greatly from entertaining German diplomats socially—and that this would require a townhouse in a reputable part of town; in Georgetown, perhaps. Those don't come cheap, sir."

"No, they don't," Barbour agreed, eyeing Martin closely. "But even on one hundred and seventy a week, a townhouse in Georgetown would be out of reach."

Martin wasn't entirely sure how much a townhouse in Georgetown cost, but he was certain the congressman knew. He would never know if Barbour was bluffing about that—and the congressman probably knew that.

He decided not to address it. "But it would be enough to rent a suite at the Willard Hotel, which would afford the same opportunities for entertaining dignitaries—and in a more convenient location."

Barbour seemed to consider this in silence for a moment. He swirled the brandy in his glass and watched Martin.

Martin sat perfectly still, staring back, and waited.

Finally, the congressman leaned forward, set his glass on the desk, and nodded. "Alright, Mr. Schuller, I'll offer you one seventy—but that is my final offer." He held his hand out.

It made Martin's stomach turn to do it, but he took the congressman's hand and shook it. "It's a deal, sir."

26

It was late on Saturday night when Martin arrived back at Union Station in Washington. He was tired from the long day, but also keyed up from the day's events. He didn't want to go back to his empty apartment and go to sleep yet, so he found a payphone and called Joe Hansen.

The line rang ten times without an answer, and Martin hung up, retrieving his nickel from the coin return.

Hansen sometimes spoke of going to bars downtown on Saturday nights, on Ninth Street NW, with a salacious grin that earned backslaps from the other men in the office. There was a notorious strip of burlesque clubs there, and for a swinging bachelor like Hansen it was a fun place to spend a late Saturday night.

Martin debated whether to go there and look for his friend. Hadn't Hansen told him recently he should start enjoying his new bachelor life? And wasn't he right about that, after all?

Why the hell not? He hailed a taxi in front of the station.

There was a certain seedy quality to the neighborhood along Ninth Street NW, a few blocks north of Pennsylvania Avenue from E Street to H Street. The taxi driver suggested the Gayety Theater as the best place to start.

"It don't look like it from the street, but it's a big theater," he said between puffs on a cigarette. "Big auditorium, lots of seating, big stage—and the gals don't shy away from kicking their legs up in the air while they do their numbers."

The driver let him off at Ninth and H streets, and Martin saw the theater marquee a couple doors south. It looked no bigger than a regular store front, just like the driver had described, and if it weren't for the long line of men of every conceivable age and class queued up down the block, Martin wouldn't have thought much of it.

He decided it wasn't worth it to wait in the line, so he strolled the sidewalk, fascinated by the crowds. Mostly men, but a few gaudily dressed women as well—"brassy broads" was what the type was often called these days. As he observed the men, most of whom wore fairly shabby suits, it occurred to him that a man such as Augustus Graeter would be right at home here.

There were also a large number of U.S. Navy sailors and marines, in uniform, traveling in packs, and all of them clearly drunk. Loud and bawdy, occasionally cat-calling the women who passed by, they were clearly enjoying their shore leave in the nation's capital.

Bouncers guarded the entrances to the clubs, and kept a close eye on every man entering. Martin supposed the level of drunkenness on display could lead to brawls and property damage, not to mention injury to club employees.

This wasn't the sort of crowd that he was comfortable being in close quarters with, so after wandering a few blocks he decided to head home after all. It would be almost a two-mile walk from here, so he began looking for a taxi.

Then from the corner of his eye he caught sight of Hansen coming out of one of the burlesque clubs, one arm around a red-haired young woman that Martin recognized from the halls of the Old Executive Office Building, and the other arm around a short but muscular marine in the tan uniform normally worn on shore leave.

They were a half-block down and moving away from where Martin stood, heading south down Ninth Street. Martin realized Hansen would never hear him call his name, so he began hurrying after them, hoping to catch up within the next block.

He had almost caught up with them when they disappeared inside a dark club, one that lacked the gaudy neon lights that most clubs used to display themselves. When Martin reached the door a few minutes later, he noticed the windows were all blacked out—not unusual—but there were no posters on display of scantily-clad burlesque girls like nearly every other club on this strip. There was no burly bouncer keeping watch at the door, and the only ornamentation at all was the name "Carroll's" in gold etching on the door.

Martin went inside. It was dimly lit, so he paused for a second to let his eyes adjust.

There were tables in the front and back, and a small open space in the middle where crowds of patrons—mostly, but not exclusively, men—gathered with beer bottles and cavorted. An elderly woman stood behind the bar, and two younger women worked as waitresses for the tables.

There were several groups of sailors and marines here, Martin noticed, but also along the edges of the room were small groups of much more effeminate-looking young men—the kind he saw so often in the halls of the Old Executive Office Building, the office boys, the "faeries."

Odd mix, Martin thought of the patrons.

As he walked toward an open spot at the bar, he saw Hansen at the far end, talking in an animated fashion with the shorter marine, who stood quite close to him. The red-haired woman they'd come in with stood several feet away, talking with two other women, one of whom was wearing a man's suit.

It was then that Martin figured out what sort of establishment this was.

"Get you something to drink, honey?" the elderly lady behind the bar asked.

231

Martin glanced at her, but then looked back toward Hansen and his marine companion. Hansen was putting his hands on the marine's arms as he spoke, and then touching him on the shoulder, and grinning so wide you could almost see his full set of teeth.

"First time here, honey?" the elderly bartender asked him, touching his arm. "Don't be nervous, sweetie. Have a drink, and you'll relax."

Martin looked back at her. "No, thank you," he said. "I think I'll just leave."

She shrugged. "Suit yourself, fella. We're open seven nights a week, if you change your mind."

He turned toward the door, and as he turned he caught sight of Hansen and the marine, mouths pressed together and arms around each other. Hansen's right hand slipped down to cup the marine's backside.

He felt his stomach turn sour. He marched for the exit, putting on his hat and keeping his eyes down.

The sound of chairs falling backward, followed by shouting, caught his attention before he reached the door, and he looked over to see a tall red-haired sailor and a blond marine grabbing each other by the collars, and pulling their fists back. A skinny young faerie boy beat a hasty retreat from the chair between them and took cover in a group of other faeries.

One of the waitresses appeared between the sailor and the marine before either had a chance to throw a punch, her hands on their chests, shoving them apart. It was an almost comical scene—the small, thin young woman with wavy brown hair and bright red lipstick, shoving around two servicemen who each probably weighed almost twice what she did.

"Knock it off, fellas!" she said, stern as a school marm. The bar went silent. "You start a ruckus in here, and somebody out there's gonna call the cops. And none of us want that, do we?"

232

The sailor and the marine released each other's collars, and glowered at each other as they straightened their uniforms.

Not wanting to stick around a second longer, Martin lowered his face and hurried out the door.

Monday, August 14

"Hey Martin, come look at this."

Martin had avoided talking to Hansen all morning, so he sighed as he got up from his desk and went back to stand beside his coworker's.

"This came from the British Embassy this morning," Hansen said, handing over a couple of papers. "What do you think of that?"

Martin read both messages, which were radio broadcasts the British had intercepted at listening posts in Canada, and deciphered.

18 June, 1939

Black Pine integration successful. Better prepared than earlier arrivals. Earlier failures due to lack of training before deployment. Advise Abwehr send more men as prepared as Black Pine, and increase diligence of training regimen.

-The Skier.

The second was a reply to the first:

22 June, 1939

To the Skier: message received and acknowledged. Will take recommendations to leadership. Continue work as previously instructed.

A thrill ran through Martin. This was gold.

"Very interesting," he said, handing the pages back to Hansen. "What do you think?"

"I think *Der Skiläufer* is expecting reinforcements soon," Hansen said. "I'm going to show this to the chief, and recommend telling our information officers at our missions in Germany to be extra watchful for signs the *Abwehr* is getting ready to send someone."

Martin was troubled by something else.

"The British have been acting a lot more cooperative lately, don't you think? First that radio communiqué on Friday, and now these two. What do you make of that?"

Hansen watched his face for a second. "You think the British know something that's about to happen."

"I do."

"So they're trying to bring us over to their side, by giving us these little tips about *Abwehr* agents in the States—is that what you're thinking?"

"More or less," Martin said. "I'll go in with you to see the chief."

"Sure, let's go now."

Martin followed behind Hansen as he entered the chief's office. It was his find, Martin would let him present it.

"Got something, Chief!" Hansen said with a grin as he handed over the two pages. "These came from the British embassy, radio transmissions they picked up at stations in Nova Scotia."

They waited in silence for a couple of minutes while the chief read.

"Interesting. What's your assessment?"

Hansen went first. "I think we should instruct all Information Officers at our missions in Germany—and potentially other countries in Europe, too—to be on increased alert for any chatter concerning *Abwehr* agents bound for the States. I think more of them are coming, based upon *Der Skiläufer*'s request."

"Or already arrived since this was sent," the chief said.

Hansen shook his head. "Not likely, not this soon. *Der Skiläufer* specifically requested that they be better trained than earlier agents, and that takes time. I'd say this month is the earliest a well-trained one could be sent, or even next month."

The chief shook his head. "The *Abwehr* could have lots of well-trained agents ready for orders. We don't know that they don't—in fact, I'd find it incredible if they didn't. Just because the ones they've sent here in the past were under-trained, doesn't mean they all are." He looked at Martin. "What's your take, Schuller?"

"I think the British have information about something that's about to happen—probably in Europe, and most likely Poland—and they want to cozy up to our government before it happens. That's why they're providing us with information about *Abwehr* agents here, to put us in their debt. To be able to say, 'See we helped you out against the Nazi threat, now you help us.' And conversely, that's why the Germans want to send more agents here now, to stir political sympathies for Germany, and undermine our relationship with their enemies. I think a war is about to start."

"That's a bold assessment," the chief said. "What makes you so sure the Germans are about to provoke a war with the British?"

"Hitler's been ramping up his rants against Poland all summer, and it's coming to a head," Martin said. "We've seen this before, and it usually precedes some sort of aggressive action."

The chief nodded. "Agreed—but so what? Why a war now, and not six months ago when Hitler invaded Czechoslovakia?"

"The British and French have sworn to defend Poland," Martin said.

"They swore Czechoslovakia's safety as well. That didn't happen."

Martin was ready for that. "That was because the *Wehrmacht* was able to march across Czechoslovakia in a day—the British and French didn't have time to do anything about it, and they weren't prepared in any event. The Czechs hadn't had time to rebuild border defenses—the Poles don't have that problem. Plus the British and French are *expecting* Hitler to make a military move against Poland, so they're prepared to do something. Czechoslovakia shocked them, but they won't be caught with their pants down again."

The chief nodded. "Well-reasoned, Schuller. Draft me a memo that I can share with the higher ups. Hansen—draft a communiqué that we can send to our Information officers in Germany. I want to see both drafts on my desk in an hour."

The chief looked back at the files on his desk, and Hansen walked out; Martin stayed standing at the chief's desk.

"Is there something more, Mr. Schuller?" the chief asked without looking up.

"I'd like to discuss something confidential, Chief," Martin said. "May I close the door?"

"Please do. Then have a seat."

Martin closed the office door and sat across from the chief, who continued browsing through papers for another minute before looking up at Martin with a certain amount of impatience on his face.

"You have something you want to talk about? Then let's talk. I'm a busy man."

"I need a leave of absence for a few weeks," Martin said without preamble.

"What for?" the chief asked, his eyes narrowing and his brow furrowing in irritation.

"A family matter," Martin said. After a second's hesitation, he added, "I'm in the middle of a divorce, and it's acrimonious concerning the children. My wife has taken them to Philadelphia, which is where the divorce proceedings are taking place. I need to be there until everything has been sorted through."

It wasn't an outright lie, Martin thought. Everything he'd said was true enough.

"For how long?"

"A few weeks."

"You can't be more specific than that?"

"Ask my wife." Martin let the bitterness show in his tone.

The chief snorted. "Understood. When must you leave?"

"After the end of this week, preferably."

"You haven't given me much notice," the chief grumbled.

"I wish I could have, sir," Martin said. "Circumstances being as they are, though, it wasn't possible. I'll be sure to wrap up everything I'm working on by the end of day on Friday, so there won't be anything for Hansen or anyone else to have to clean up while I'm gone."

"If what you said earlier is true, we're going to be buried in intel reports from the European missions in the next few weeks—and I'll be short an analyst."

"I'll be back as soon as I can, sir. I promise."

The chief released a heavy sigh. "Alright, do what you must. I'm sure there's a form you'll have to fill out for Personnel—I'll have Trudy look into it. Anything else?"

"No sir, thank you."

Martin got up and left the office. He suppressed the tiny bit of guilt he felt about misleading the chief, and concentrated on what he needed to do.

Hutson

27

Monday, August 21, 1939

"Ah, Martin! Welcome. Have a seat."

"Thank you, sir." Martin noticed that Congressman Barbour had not asked permission to use his given name; but now that he was purportedly working for him, he supposed the congressman felt free to do so without permission.

"Glad to have you on board finally," the congressman said with an automatic smile. "I'm looking forward to seeing what we accomplish together."

"Thank you, sir," Martin said. "I'm eager to get started."

"Excellent! That's what I like to hear. You've met John Wiseman, my chief of staff—he'll get you settled in. You'll report directly to him, no intermediaries. I've had John prepare a list of assignments we want you to take over from other members of the staff—things that fit with the duties we discussed, things that will help you get settled in the role. Then by the end of the week, I'll expect you'll be finding and working your own leads."

"Understood, sir."

"Any travel you need to do in order to facilitate our work on behalf of American industry, we're happy to arrange—just be sure to clear it through John for official approval, to make sure it meets legal requirements and budget constraints, that sort of thing. We can't waste the taxpayers' dollars."

"I agree wholeheartedly, sir."

"Good. Now let me see if Louise has your paperwork ready. Excuse me."

While the congressman talked over the telephone with his secretary in the next room, Martin took a moment to look around at the photographs on a nearby shelf, all of the congressman with other members of Congress, cabinet secretaries, and captains of industry.

He'd seen these the first time he was in the congressman's office back in March, but hadn't paid them much attention at the time; now that he'd seen similar photographs at the congressman's home, he studied them a bit.

Martin recognized Edsel Ford from his pictures in the newspapers and on the newsreels. The politicians were recognizable, but most of the other businessmen he couldn't identify.

Then he noticed a photograph on the desk, of the congressman with two much younger men. One was Maximilian Showalter, but the youngest one, standing between Showalter and the congressman, Martin didn't recognize. The three stood in front of a large timbered dwelling surrounded by pine groves, on a snowy hilltop with a view of distant mountains behind them.

Showalter's 'place in the Poconos,' Martin reasoned. What struck him was that, while the congressman wore a nice woolen overcoat, the two younger men both wore ski jackets, the kind you could buy from the LL Bean catalogue, and both held a pair of snow skies in one hand.

Was one of them *Der Skiläufer*? Martin had come to "work" for the congressman precisely because he suspected Barbour was the one mentioned in *Schwarzkiefer*'s communiqué to Berlin in June; he just hadn't expected to see potential evidence of that in his first moments on the job.

Barbour hung up the receiver. "Louise will bring your paperwork to your desk in a few minutes," he said. "I'll buzz for John."

"Thank you, sir," Martin said, rising and shaking the congressman's hand. Then he indicated the photograph on the desk.

"I recognize Mr. Showalter with you in that picture—but who is the other young man between you?"

"That's my son Richard. He's getting ready to start his last year at Brown. That photo was taken last February, at Showalter's cabin in the Poconos."

"That's very nice, sir," Martin said. The large structure behind them seemed to him more of a lodge than a cabin. "Perhaps I'll get to work with Mr. Showalter on a common objective soon. It would be nice to renew our acquaintance."

A hint of smile crept across Barbour's mouth. "I think that sounds like an excellent idea. Feel free to reach out to him."

"I will, sir. Definitely."

Thursday, August 24
Easton, Pennsylvania

Martin smiled at the blonde receptionist at the big desk by the entrance to the office building next door to the Showalter Glassworks. She paused from her typing and looked up at him.

"May I help you, sir?"

"Yes, I'd like to see Mr. Maximilian Showalter, if he's available, please."

The receptionist gave him a doubtful look. "Do you have an appointment? Mr. Showalter's very busy."

Martin gave her his most charming smile. "No, I don't—this is just a courtesy call from Congressman Barbour's office."

Her expression and tone changed immediately, and Martin resisted the urge to chuckle.

"Of course, sir! I'll be happy to give him that message right away. He *is* in a meeting now, however—but I'm sure he can squeeze you into his schedule as soon as he's available. Would you like to wait here? Or you can take a tour of our visitors' center, through those doors over there." She pointed to a pair of glass doors leading into a brightly-lit space with wood paneled walls.

"Thank you. I'll take a look."

"I'll be happy to take your hat, sir."

"Thank you," Martin said, handing her his blue fedora, and then walking through the glass doors.

The visitors' center was a large room, lined with big, framed photographs over plaques with several paragraphs of text. At the far side of the room stood a pair of old Kinetoscopes, appearing shiny and new instead of forty years old.

The first photograph was a sepia-toned portrait of a dark-haired young man with a thick mustache, wearing a Victorian-era suit and necktie. The plaque below had biographical information about Frederick Showalter, founder of the Showalter Glassworks.

Martin skimmed it—born in Salzburg, Austria in July 1874; apprenticed in the famous Salzburg Chrystal factory; came to America in September 1895 with a little capital inherited from a grandfather who was a physician; and founded the Showalter Glassworks in Easton in April, 1896.

Martin browsed past the other photographs—one exterior view of the glassworks, and various scenes from within the factory—skimming the plaques, and made his way to the Kinetoscopes. He fished a nickel out of his pocket and inserted it into the coin slot.

The six-minute film about the triumphs and successes of Showalter Glassworks was narrated in the same voice and frenetic style as a newsreel, and Martin was about to walk out halfway through when the narrator's voice grew suddenly somber, speaking about the death of Frederick Showalter in March 1936, and the passing of the company to his son, Max.

Then the rapid-fire newsreel delivery returned, and Martin's attention was glued to what the narrator said about Max:

"Maximilian Frederick Showalter is a man destined for greatness. His birth on January 1st, 1901—the first day of a shiny new century— marked an auspicious beginning for this enterprising young man, and he has not disappointed the Fates. A successful scholar as well as an athlete, Max Showalter graduated Suma Cum Laude from Columbia University, and went on to earn a place on the U.S. downhill ski team for the first ever Olympic Winter Games in 1924. Here he is at the bottom of the slopes in Chamonix with a pair of teammates.

"Knowing the value of sport in the lives of this country's young men and women, Max Showalter helped to sponsor the U.S. men's and women's downhill ski teams for the Second Olympic Winter Games in 1928. Here he is in St. Moritz, posing for photographs between both teams. A kiss on each cheek from a pair of pretty ski bunnies seems to be a nice reward for his sponsorship, wouldn't you say?

"Not far from his parents' native Salzburg, Max Showalter visited his Austrian relatives after the games, and stayed for months of intensive learning about the famous Salzburg crystal.

"An enthusiastic supporter of science, Max Showalter has single-handedly spearheaded his company's advances in the exciting new field of plastics. Here he is in the lab with some of Showalter Glassworks' award-winning scientists, discussing their latest experiments. But don't worry—their scientific jargon doesn't go over the head of this Company executive!"

The film ended a moment later, and Martin made his way toward the door. He took a seat in the lobby to wait.

As he waited, he was stunned to see Dr. Atherton come out of the heavy mahogany door behind reception, his hat in his hand. His gaze lingered on Martin for a second, registering recognition, and then he leaned down to say something quietly to the receptionist.

He approached Martin with his hand extended. "Good morning, I believe we've met before. I'm Dr. Milton Atherton."

"Yes, Dr. Atherton, it was at the gala for the hospital last spring. I'm Martin Schuller."

"Ah yes, forgive me. My memory for names isn't what it used to be."

"Do you work here now, Dr. Atherton?" Martin kept his voice even with effort.

"Once a fortnight," Atherton said. "I drive up from Philadelphia and hold a clinic here for Mr. Showalter's employees. I'm afraid I've just shut down for lunch, but feel free to come by this afternoon if you need a physician's advice on anything that ails you."

Martin nodded, but said nothing. Atherton put on his hat and walked out the door.

Martin glanced at his watch, and thought it strange that the clinic would close for lunch at eleven AM. He mulled over the exchange while he sat and waited.

Ten minutes later, the heavy mahogany door opened again, and Max Showalter himself stepped through to the lobby. He fixed Martin with a dazzling smile and extended his hand.

"Mr. Schuller, what an unexpected pleasure—both the visit, and the news that you are now working for Congressman Barbour. My congratulations, sir."

"Thank you," Martin said with a nod. "This is really just a courtesy visit, to introduce myself as the Congressman's liaison for business with German-speaking markets, and to see how we might work with you on expanding our state's trade abroad."

"Absolutely," Showalter said, putting his hand on Martin's shoulder and guiding him through the door toward a plush office space bustling with activity. "Come with me, and I'll introduce you to my Director of European markets. I wish I had more time to visit with you myself, but I'm sure Mr. Dendler will take good care of you."

28

Martin was both surprised and not surprised at the same time. He had expected some sort of breakthrough here, but wasn't sure what he'd expected exactly.

"Fritz Dendler" looked exactly as Ketterman had described him: young, tall, athletic build, with wavy blond hair, and startlingly blue eyes—the Nazi ideal indeed. Too young to be a Director of European Markets for a multi-million dollar company, Martin thought—he couldn't be older than twenty-eight or twenty-nine.

"I am happy to acquaint you, Mr. Schuller," Dendler said after Max Showalter made a hasty departure upon introducing them. "You sit?"

"Thank you."

Dendler sat behind his desk and gave Martin a broad smile. "Mr. Showalter met me to Congressman Barbour in June. We spoke business for an hour. We met two times more for business."

His English, while decent, was not quite fluent—another detail that made Martin doubt he'd earned his position on merits—and so Martin answered in German. "I'll take most of those meetings from now on, and I can speak for the Congressman on most matters pertaining to business. You can speak to me as if you were speaking to the Congressman."

Dendler looked surprised. "Ah, you speak *very* good German, Mr. Schuller. I assumed you were American, but you sound like a native speaker—Swiss, perhaps?"

"Perhaps." Martin noted Dendler's clear Austrian accent, but he pretended ignorance. "What part of Germany are you from, Mr. Dendler?"

"Linz," Dendler said, then he caught himself and hastily added, "In Austria, actually."

The fact that it was already natural for Dendler to think of Linz as a German city first, and Austrian second, spoke volumes.

"How long have you been in our country?" Martin asked, feigning interest.

"Since right after the Anschluss," Dendler replied, his words coming out a little stiff, his mouth set a little tighter; to a casual observer that would imply discomfort with the *Anschluss*, but Martin read it as the tell-tale sign of a lie.

Martin nodded, and faked a sympathetic look. "I understand. Is that when you came to work for the Showalter Glassworks?"

"No, I started working here in May of this year. I am new to Pennsylvania."

"Ah, I see." Martin forced a smile. "You'll find many people in Pennsylvania who speak our language, Mr. Dendler. You should feel welcome here."

Dendler's face lit up. "Yes, indeed—there are several here at the glassworks, in fact."

"I'm not surprised," Martin said. He wasn't.

"It has not been difficult to find good food here. Or good beer, either." Dendler's grin looked genuine, stretching from ear to ear.

Martin chuckled and nodded. He took a deep breath and took on a more business-like tone. "Why don't you fill me in on what work you are doing for Mr. Showalter, and elaborate on your past discussions with Congressman Barbour?"

**

246

Martin drove away from the factory an hour later, and turned south on the highway toward Philadelphia. His mind turned over everything from the last few hours.

Finding "Fritz Dendler" had been a remarkable stroke of luck, and confirming all of the known details about *Schwarzkiefer* had been almost too easy. His English was a bit better than Ketterman had described, but Martin supposed it had probably improved after three months in this country.

But what to make of Dr. Atherton's presence at the Showalter Glassworks?

Was it possible that Atherton was *Der Skiläufer* after all?

All of the evidence seemed to imply that possibility, but Martin couldn't believe it. It just didn't *seem* right.

And what did *Schwarzkiefer*'s presence at Showalter Glassworks imply about Max Showalter?

Two little details kept popping into Martin's mind. First, when he asked Dendler to take him to Showalter's office so he could say goodbye, they had passed a large bulletin board; and among the many notifications was a flyer—in English, but printed in big, elaborate German script—announcing a German Festival on Sunday, September 3rd at the Deutschhorst Country Club in Sellersville.

This was the grandiose name for the German American Bund's campground in Pennsylvania.

The second was in Showalter's office, during the ten-minute friendly conversation that Martin and Max shared. Showalter was quite clearly pleased that Martin now worked for Congressman Barbour, and suggested he come up for dinner some time. Then he had opened a desk drawer and handed Martin a photograph.

"I can't display this openly," Showalter had said. "It's classified, of course—but since you work for the Congressman..."

Martin took the photo, and saw Max Showalter standing beside Charles Lindbergh, both men turned slightly toward one another, smiling for the camera, their arms behind each other in a friendly sort of way.

"That was a couple of weeks ago, when Colonel Lindbergh came to inspect our new assembly line in the Plastics Division, where we're manufacturing airplane windshields for the Army Air Corps. Plus other parts that are classified." Showalter looked and sounded quite pleased with himself. "I'll give you advance notice the next time he comes, and you can come up and meet him."

Now Martin had to wonder, what did that all mean? State had kept close tabs on Lindbergh's activities in Europe over the last few years, particularly his visits to Germany, and his ties to the Duke of Windsor—who was also known to have sympathies for Hitler and several of his minions. Now Lindbergh's army commission had been reactivated.

And he had come to Showalter Glassworks this summer.

Where *Schwarzkiefer* was working.

Could it be? Could Charles Lindbergh—an American hero—be *Der Skiläufer*?

No, that wasn't possible—Lindbergh had just returned to the States in April, and they knew that *Der Skiläufer* had been in the country more than a year.

But still, there were an awful lot of coincidences here...so perhaps one of Colonel Lindbergh's associates in the Army Air Corps?

If so, then their mission was far more than just political.

And Martin still didn't know who had helped Dendler when he was in New York. Who was the courier? And who had arranged the safe house? If they remained at large, other agents from Germany were certain to follow the same path.

Martin needed time to figure this out. He hoped he had time.

29

Monday, August 28, 1939
New York

Sloan stared at the stocky man on the other side of the desk with undisguised amusement at his discomfort. This Frederick Weideman, nervous from the beginning, had become increasingly fidgety each time Sloan revealed something that Weideman had said to be untrue.

It was perhaps a touch sadistic to take pleasure in the man's discomfort, but what of it? It was an effective method, and the man was clearly a sleaze.

"Tell me again how you first met Fritz Dendler, Mr. Weideman."

"I told you—he came into a glass store where I was doing some business on behalf of my employer," Weideman said.

"And?"

"And like I said before, he was looking for work and a place to stay. I couldn't help him with the work, but I knew someone who was renting a room for cheap."

"And who was that?" Sloan asked. "The person who was renting the room."

"A neighbor of mine," Weideman said, hesitating. "His name's Jones—Bill Jones."

"But we've established that Fritz Dendler only stayed in New York for a few days," Sloan said. "Your neighbor—this Mr. Jones—he was only renting out the room for a few days?"

What little color remained in Weideman's face seemed to drain away. "I don't know."

"So did Fritz Dendler pay your neighbor—Mr. Jones—for a full month, and then just disappear?" Sloan shook his head. "That doesn't make much sense, now does it, Mr. Weideman?"

"I—I don't know."

"You don't know?"

"He never told me."

"Who never told you?"

"My neighbor—Bill Jones."

"I see." Sloan got up and walked around behind Weideman. He put his hands on the back of Weideman's chair, and spoke down at the top of his head.

"So you expect us to believe that you offered a neighbor's room for rent to a complete stranger that you met in a glass store—a stranger who didn't even speak very good English, or so we've been told by others from your neighborhood—"

Sloan loved the startled way Weideman straightened in the chair at that news.

"—and that this stranger rented a room and only stayed for a few days. Why didn't he get a room in a hotel? Or the YMCA, if he was too poor for a cheap hotel?"

Sloan walked around to the side of the desk, put his hands on the edge and leaned toward Weideman. "Does *any* of that make any sense to you, Mr. Weideman?"

Weideman swallowed hard. "How should I know?"

Sloan walked back to the opposite side of the desk, and took a seat again. He leaned back, crossed his arms, and stared hard at the nervous man across from him. He sat there, staring in silence for almost a minute—until Weideman squirmed and looked away.

"Are you in the habit of referring total strangers to your neighbors for boarding, Mr. Weideman?"

Weideman shrugged. "Not really."

"So why did you do that for this one?"

He shrugged again. "I don't know."

Sloan leaned forward, slapping his palms hard on the desk and making Weideman jump.

"Oh, come on, don't treat me like a fool. Either you can explain why you did that—what motivated you to make the suggestion to this particular stranger at that particular time—or it simply didn't happen that way."

Weideman stiffened, and a deep scowl came to his face.

Sloan briefly wondered if he'd pushed too hard too soon, and now Weideman was going to clam up, but he dismissed that thought almost as soon as he had it. He had more ammunition to use.

He waited a couple of minutes, while they stared at each other without a word. Then he shrugged with indifference, opened a desk drawer and pulled out a manila file. He opened it on the desk, slowly, and took pleasure in the nervous glance that Weideman gave to the papers inside.

Sloan held the pages up so that only he could read them, and then slapped one down hard on the desktop in front of Weideman.

"Recognize that?" he asked, his voice suddenly cold and hard. "That's your signature, I believe?"

"No," Weideman said, trying to look earnest, but his voice trembling. "That's not my signature."

"Isn't it?" Sloan asked, playing along. "I could have sworn it looked just like the signature you made on the inventory of your belongings we took from you when we brought you in." Sloan narrowed his eyes, and his voice grew cold again. "I've seen that inventory, you see, and your signature on it. It's the same signature on that paper in front of you— that lease paper for the apartment on East Eighty-third Street where Fritz Dendler stayed for three days."

Weideman swallowed hard again, and his eyes darted around the room. His hands began to shake, and—too late—he folded his hands together and put them in his lap to try to hide it.

"And this one," Sloan said, slapping another page onto the desk, on top of the first one. "Also your signature, on a lease for another apartment, this one on East Eighty-fourth Street, where a certain young German man going by the name of Jan Hoffman stayed for four days in February—until we arrested him at Madison Square Garden."

Sloan got up from his seat, walked around the side of the desk, and sat on the corner of it next to Weideman and the papers.

"Both leases were for a single month only. Very unusual, wouldn't you agree? And you paid a premium for that privilege—almost double the normal monthly rate of an apartment that size, in that part of New York. And the neighbors we've talked to say you came by a few times, but never stayed there. Do you have any explanation for that, Mr. Weideman? I mean, other than that you were renting them as a temporary safe house for German agents."

Weideman stood rod straight. "I want to talk to a lawyer."

Sloan pretended he hadn't heard that. "Why don't you tell us where you got the money to pay those exorbitant leases? Who was sponsoring you?"

Weideman stared straight ahead. "I'm not saying anything more until I talk to a lawyer."

Damn it! Sloan cursed to himself. "Fine, you can call a lawyer right now. But let me tell you this—we know you hired that kid Greg Spooner to be the courier for your agents, from the safe house to wherever they needed to go. We've got witnesses that saw him at those apartments you rented. We've also got a witness that told us Greg wanted out of the business, that he was scared—and then he ended up dead."

Sloan sat back on the corner of the desk again, leaned down and pointed a finger at Weideman's face. "So you can have your lawyer, but let me tell you—as of right now, you're going down for murder in the state of New York, plus the federal charges of espionage. So if you want to come clean, and let us know who was paying for your little operation, maybe we can cut a deal."

Sloan got up and sauntered toward the door, but turned around as he put his hand on the door knob. "Talk it over with your lawyer, and get back with me."

He turned the knob and walked out.

Tuesday, August 29
U.S. Highway 46, northern New Jersey

Sloan switched off his headlights a moment before pulling off the road in the dark. There was enough moonlight that he could see the park shelter ahead, but he kept in the shadow of the trees, and killed the engine some distance from the shelter. He rolled up the windows in spite of the heat.

He'd chosen the roadside park some thirty miles west of New York City because of its rural surroundings, lessening the risk of being observed. He knew the remote location posed a difficulty for his informant, who didn't own an automobile, but saw little alternative.

A moment after he stopped his car, he saw the shadowy figure of a man, short but solid, emerging from the darkness of the park shelter and hurrying toward him.

The passenger door creaked as it opened, and Otto Schnell cringed as he got in the car.

"You weren't followed?" Sloan asked.

"No."

"How did you get here?"

"Freight car to Trenton, then hitch-hike. I hid in the woods until dark."

"Anyone else on the freight car?"

Schnell nodded. "A few hobos. I jumped off first. The others rode to the railyard."

He seemed nervous, fidgety. Sloan's eyes narrowed. "Did you recognize any of the hobos?"

"No."

Satisfied, Sloan got to the point. "The meeting is still set for Sunday?"

In the dim light, he saw Schnell nod. "Yes, and I got the names."

A thrill ran through Sloan. "Let me have 'em."

Schnell wasn't wearing a jacket, and he leaned back to fish a piece of paper from his front pants pocket, and handed it to Sloan.

Sloan held the paper low, below the steering wheel, and switched on his flashlight long enough to read the seven names and ranks. His pulse quickened.

"You're sure of these?" he whispered after switching off the flashlight. In the sudden darkness, he couldn't see Schnell's face, but detected the motion of his head nodding.

He removed a stack of ten dollar bills from his jacket pocket, counted five of them, and handed them to his informant. *Worth every damn penny.*

"Have you heard anything about that one I asked you to listen for, The Skier?" Sloan asked.

"No, nothing."

Sloan exhaled in frustration, but wasn't really surprised. The Skier had eluded them this far by being very cautious.

Ever since Sloan and his Philadelphia counterpart recruited Schnell four months before to infiltrate local Bund chapters in Pennsylvania, he'd provided valuable information and names that their offices were using in their investigations.

The Philadelphia office was building a case against Fred Dickman, an American in Philly who owned two buildings at the Deutschhorst Country Club near Sellersville. They knew he'd passed along military secrets to the German embassy in Washington, but lacked proof.

If Sloan was right, the list he held in his hands would lead them to that proof.

If they could manage to nab The Skier in the process, it would be a major win.

"Anything else?"

Schnell looked down at his hands. "I want to stop," he said. When Sloan didn't respond, he looked at him, and his eyes pleaded. "I am frightened they will find out I spy on them for you. I have given good information, yes?"

Sloan snorted. That was an understatement, given what he had handed over tonight. And his previous information had focused their attention on two factories in Pennsylvania making parts for the Army—U.S. Gauge in Sellersville, and Showalter Glassworks in Easton—that employed dozens of Bund members.

"You've kept up your end of the bargain, and if this list is real, we won't need your help for a while. If I need you for something in the future, I'll find you."

Schnell kept fidgeting.

"Are you in danger now?" Sloan asked. "Are they onto you?"

Schnell hesitated, nervous. "I don't think so. But after those names, they will know." He nodded at the paper in Sloan's hand. "I must go somewhere else."

"If you leave now, it will only look suspicious." Sloan thought of Gregory Spooner. "You might end up dead. Wait until next week, and then you can disappear."

Schnell nodded, but said nothing.

As he got out of the car, Sloan added, "By the way, we cleared all of your arrest records, as promised. You keep clean, you'll have no trouble with naturalization."

"Thank you," Schnell said, and disappeared into the trees.

Thursday, August 31

"Mr. Hansen, I have a call for Mr. Schuller on the line," Trudy said. "Should I put it through to you? It's that Special Agent Sloan at the FBI."

A brief frown crossed Hansen's face. *He* was the one who had sent the French memo to the FBI on Tuesday, why wouldn't Sloan ask to speak to him? "Yes, please put that through to me."

His phone rang a few seconds later. "This is Joe Hansen."

"Mr. Hansen, this is FBI Special Agent in Charge Reginald Sloan. I'm sure you've heard all about me from Mr. Schuller." Sloan's voice carried a touch of wry amusement.

"Yes, Agent Sloan, what can I do for you?"

"I was calling to speak with Mr. Schuller, but your secretary says he's not in. Can you say when he'll be back?"

Hansen hesitated, not wanting to say that Martin was on a Leave of Absence. He supposed if he were vague, Sloan would assume that Martin was home sick.

"I can't say for certain, but I can help you. Mr. Schuller and I collaborate."

"I'm calling about a memo you fellas received from the American Embassy in Paris, a hot tip from French Intelligence. Your office sent it to us a couple of days ago. You're familiar with it, Mr. Hansen? Or should I wait for Mr. Schuller?"

Hansen's lips pursed. "I was the one who sent that to you, Agent Sloan. I'm the analyst who took that intel."

Hansen hadn't believed the luck when he read through the memo. It wasn't unheard of for their group to get intelligence from the Paris embassy, but unusual enough that it piqued his interest when he saw the packet.

Then when he'd read the memo, his heart had skipped a beat.

Sunday, August 20, 1939
To the Office of the Chief Special Agent
From Frank Dryden, Second Secretary
URGENT, TOP SECRET

One of my trusted contacts in the Deuxième Bureau informed
me last night that a certain Abwehr agent in Paris that they are
monitoring met with a visiting German General and discussed the
state of U.S. fighter plane advancement. The General cited recent
on-the-ground intelligence from an Abwehr agent, code named
Black Pine, who is embedded in the United States. The visiting
General chided his agent for failing to get similar intelligence on
French air corps capabilities.

Signed: Franklin H. Dryden

Copied:
The Honorable William Bullitt, United States Ambassador
Colonel Horace Fuller, U.S. Military Attaché

Hansen rushed into the chief's office to show it to him, breathless.
"Get this off to the FBI right away," the chief had said. "And also
have a courier take a copy to MID. I know their attaché is copied, but
Heaven only knows what sort of mire it's lost in over there."

Now it irritated Hansen that Sloan assumed it came from Martin.

"Then you know what a bombshell this revelation is," Sloan said.

That's an understatement. "Yes, it certainly is." Hansen didn't
mention that until now, State had believed the mission of German
agents in the United States to be primarily political.

"I'm coming to Washington," Sloan said. "As you might expect, my
superiors are on this like glue. I want to meet with you and Mr. Schuller

to get your take on it. You probably know this Second Secretary Dryden and his sources. I could use your insights."

Hansen frowned again. "Mr. Schuller's unavailable right now, but I can meet with you. When do you get into town?"

There was silence on the line for a few seconds. "I'd really like to speak with both of you. When is Mr. Schuller available?"

Hansen didn't bother to hide his irritation. "I really don't know. I'll meet you myself, Agent Sloan. When and where?"

Sloan had the taxi let him off a block from Hansen's building, and told him to wait. As dusk slid into twilight, he noted lights on in Hansen's window. The thought crossed Sloan's mind that the young agent might have one of his, um, *friends* with him. He went inside the building anyway. He didn't have much choice after finding no one home at Martin Schuller's apartment.

He took the stairs two at a time to the third floor, and banged his fist on Hansen's door.

Hansen looked startled when he answered, his eyes widening as he saw Sloan. The young man had removed his necktie, and the collar of his white shirt was open, the sleeves rolled up past the elbows.

"Agent Sloan," he said, sounding rattled. Then his jaw set, and he fixed Sloan with a stern glare. "I thought we were meeting tomorrow morning at ten. What's the meaning of this?"

Sloan enjoyed the momentary advantage of the surprise visit. "We'll talk now." He barged inside, not waiting for an invitation. Hansen meekly stepped aside and closed the door.

"Where is Schuller?" Sloan asked.

Hansen looked rattled again. "He's probably at home." He scowled and crossed his arms. "He has a telephone—have you tried calling?"

"Yes, I have, wise guy. He didn't answer. I already stopped by his place, and he's not home. The neighbor lady said he's been gone a while."

Sloan stepped forward and stood close in front of the younger man. He towered over him by several inches. He gave Hansen the same hard stare that he gave to uncooperative suspects in an interrogation room. "Now, why do you suppose that is?"

Hansen didn't move, kept his arms crossed and his mouth shut.

"He wouldn't be off somewhere playing undercover detective again, would he?"

Hansen still said nothing, and glared up at Sloan.

Sloan pointed his finger at the younger man's nose. "You don't want to make an enemy of the FBI, Mr. Hansen," he said, practically spitting the words out. "I think you'd find Director Hoover to be very persuasive. We'll get your cooperation one way or another. We have a file on you, you know—complete with photographs."

He paused for a few seconds to let the implication sink in. He enjoyed the look of panic that came to Hansen's eyes.

"Have I been under surveillance?" Hansen demanded, squaring his shoulders.

Sloan chuckled. "Since February. You picked up Mr. Schuller when he was released after the Bund rally—you didn't think we'd look into you? You tangle with the FBI, you get investigated, it's as simple as that."

Hansen appeared to be contemplating that. "So, what you're saying is?"

"That we know all about you and your trysts. Not a single dame among them."

Hansen nodded absently, lost somewhere in his own head. Sloan waited.

"You're threatening to expose me if I don't 'cooperate' with you, is that it?"

"Let's hope it doesn't come to that, shall we?" Sloan said. "Put your duty to your country above any loyalty you have to Mr. Schuller, and we'll pretend none of this happened."

Hansen stiffened, and he squared his shoulders again. "I think you should leave, before I call the police."

Sloan was shocked. Then he seethed.

"I wouldn't want your boss to find out what we know about your extracurricular activities, Mr. Hansen," he said through gritted teeth. "I'd hate to ruin a promising career."

Hansen laughed, but it sounded forced. "Go ahead. You think that will matter? The Department of State hires the best men, and they don't ask personal questions."

Sloan considered that. It was true the halls of State were full of more than their fair share of faeries. That was well known at the FBI. He glared at Hansen, but the younger man didn't shrink from it.

"Have it your way, Mr. Hansen—but I suggest you get word to Mr. Schuller right away that I'm onto him, and I'm going to find out what he's up to and haul him back in handcuffs."

He shoved his way past Hansen, knocking his shoulder, and stormed out the door.

Hansen exhaled hard and leaned back against the door as soon as he closed it.

It had been a bluff, but it worked. He honestly had no idea how the chief would react to learning his secret.

He could just imagine how his coworkers would react, though. No doubt about that. He shivered, and wrapped his arms around himself, slipping to the floor.

He wouldn't be fired, of that he was certain. There was a network of well-placed men in the State Department with his same secret, including an Assistant Secretary who had recruited Hansen to State when he was a bright-eyed college graduate.

But his day-to-day would become more difficult if it were widely known. Of that he was also certain. So he had made a big bluff.

And Sloan bought it.

30

Friday, September 1, 1939
Philadelphia

Martin sat on a bench in the marble hallway outside of the courtroom, holding open the morning newspaper.

The German invasion of Poland at 4:45 AM local time dominated the front page. Hitler had gone bold—naval and aerial bombardments, plus infantry and armored divisions dashing across the border from three sides. By eight AM local time, the Polish government had issued a call to the British and French for assistance.

As of print time, the British and French response was unknown.

Martin knew the afternoon papers would have more details when they hit the streets in a few hours.

He wondered how long the British and French would equivocate before declaring war on Germany. They had no alternative this time, but that didn't mean they wouldn't hesitate.

He glanced up at the sound of leather-soled footsteps approaching, and saw Bernard Gold carrying a briefcase and fedora in one hand while extending the other toward Martin. He was dressed in a three-piece navy blue pin-striped suit, and his dark hair was slicked back with Brilliantine.

"We're all ready," he said as he took a seat next to Martin after shaking hands. "I think things will go our way today. And after this, it's just waiting out the clock on the ninety days."

Martin nodded, refusing to acknowledge the sudden butterflies in his stomach.

"You nervous?"

Martin shrugged, but then admitted, "Yeah, a little."

"Of course you are, but don't worry. I have this well in hand. We have William Walsh right where we want him."

Martin hoped that Gold was correct about that. He feared his father-in-law had cards still hidden up his sleeve.

He saw Becky coming up the hall toward him, her father beside her. She wore a smart burgundy suit, the skirt hanging mid-calf, with matching burgundy pumps. Her eyes met Martin's and held them for a second before turning forward and studiously ignoring him.

William Walsh wore a black three-piece suit, and his black shoes shined like mirrors. He nodded to Martin and his attorney in a cold but professional sort of way. "Martin, Mr. Gold."

"Mr. Walsh," Gold said, smiling as he stood and extended his hand toward the opposing counsel.

Walsh appeared uncomfortable as he glanced at Gold's outstretched hand, and Martin was sure he hesitated half a second before shaking it.

Martin stared at Becky while the lawyers exchanged formal pleasantries.

She stared at her burgundy purse, unclasping the hinge and removing a compact. She checked her makeup in the tiny mirror, taking longer than she needed—to avoid looking at him, Martin assumed. Her dark red lipstick was flawless, as was the hint of rouge on her cheeks.

Her makeup was always perfect. She never left the house otherwise. This was for show.

The court clerk opened the door a moment later, and motioned them inside. "He's ready for you."

When the judge entered the courtroom a moment later, Martin's stomach flipped somersaults. He took a deep breath and forced himself to calm down.

"I've reviewed the documents filed by both parties," the judge intoned in a flat, level voice. He was about fifty, with hair more salt than pepper, black-framed glasses resting on the end of a long nose, and a long face that seemed permanently serious. "It seems we are in agreement on most matters. Is that correct, counselors?"

"All except for the matter of the children, your honor," William Walsh said.

The judge looked at Becky. "The petitioner is waiving all right to alimony. Are you certain you wish to do that, Mrs. Schuller?"

"Mrs. Schuller is well set up in her present lodgings, your honor," William Walsh said.

"I'd like to hear from Mrs. Schuller herself, if you don't mind, counselor. Are you sure you want to waive your right to receive alimony from your husband, Mrs. Schuller?"

Becky stared at the judge, and gave him a firm nod. "Yes, your honor, I'm sure."

A slight frown crossed the judge's lips, but he looked down at the papers in front of him. "Very well, the matter is settled. We move on to the custody and maintenance of the three minor children—Martin Alan Schuller, Jr, age eight; Jacqueline Elaine Schuller, age five; and Steven Joseph Schuller, age four. I will entertain arguments, starting with the petitioner. Mr. Walsh?"

Martin braced himself as Walsh stood and straightened his vest.

"If it pleases the court, Mrs. Schuller requests full custody of the minor children. They currently reside with Mrs. Schuller in Philadelphia, and the elder two children are registered for school here, which begins on Tuesday. Since her separation from Mr. Schuller three months ago, the children have seen him only one time. This is unsurprising, given the lack of interest that Mr. Schuller has shown in family life for many years.

Mrs. Schuller and the children have endured frequent prolonged absences on the part of Mr. Schuller, with little explanation, and often little warning. These unexplained absences began four years ago, and have only grown more common as time has passed. Given Mr. Schuller's apparent lack of concern for his family, the petitioner requests that all rights to the children be granted solely to her. Thank you, your honor."

Martin's anger grew with each half-truth his father-in-law spoke, and by the end of the speech his temples throbbed.

The judge's dour face looked their way. "Mr. Gold, does the respondent wish to answer the petitioner's charges?"

Bernard Gold stood. "We do, your honor."

"Proceed, please."

"Mr. Walsh is quite skilled at limiting the facts he brings before the court to those few that will—when taken entirely out of their context— conjure up an image of an uncaring and distant father. This image could not be further from the truth."

Gold stepped out from behind the table and stood next to Martin.

"He tells you that Mr. Schuller is often absent for periods of time, but he does not mention that these are for official government business, Mr. Schuller being employed by the United States Department of State. He tells you that there is little explanation or warning given, but he does not tell you that Mr. Schuller is restricted in what he can say to Mrs. Schuller regarding his government business. Nor does he mention that Mr. Schuller reveals what he can to his wife, and only withholds what he must. And lastly, he fails to describe the affection and involvement that Mr. Schuller displays for his children when he is at home with them."

Gold placed his hand on Martin's shoulder as he continued. "Mr. Walsh states that the children have seen Mr. Schuller only one time since the separation, but he does not disclose that this was for an entire week—an entire week in which Mr. Schuller took the children with him on a trip, during which time he cared for them entirely by himself. The children were well looked after by their father that week, and all enjoyed the closeness they shared. Mr. Schuller requests equal right to the children with Mrs. Schuller. Thank you, your honor."

The judge stared at Bernard Gold as he retook his seat. Then he frowned. "What sort of work does Mr. Schuller do for the State Department that requires frequent absences for 'official government business,' about which he cannot speak with his wife?"

Gold stood. "Mr. Schuller's position at the Department of State is classified, your honor. We can say only that Mr. Schuller does important work on behalf of the country."

The judge's frown remained, but he nodded his head and looked down at the papers on his desk. "This fact has been verified in your filing?"

"It has, your honor," Gold replied. "There is an employment verification letter in our filing from the Personnel office at the Department of State, confirming Mr. Schuller's employment there, and declining to specify his duties."

"Very well," the judge murmured, shifting papers. "Mr. Walsh? Would you care to counter the respondent's argument?"

Walsh stood, and Martin thought from the set of his jaw that his father-in-law looked rattled, less sure of his position.

"Regardless of the reason for Mr. Schuller's absences, or however important his work is while he is away from his family, *away from them he is*. The children are almost entirely dependent upon their mother, who has had to take up the slack left by her oft-absent husband. She has seen to their education, their health and well-being, even their discipline. To grant Mr. Schuller equal right to the children is to reward him for his absence."

He paused, and looked over at Martin with what Martin was certain to be false sadness.

"The fact remains, the children are settled here in Philadelphia with their mother, and Mr. Schuller continues to reside in Washington, D.C.

This physical distance, coupled with the demands of Mr. Schuller's important government work, demonstrate how impractical is the hope that he will spend more time with the children in the future than he has until now."

You slick bastard, Martin seethed. Walsh had taken their own argument—the importance of Martin's work—and turned it around to his advantage. He looked at Becky, who sat watching her father, hands folded in her lap, with no visible reaction, and he hated her for her complicity in this.

The judge looked sharply their direction, lips pursed. "Mr. Gold, how does your client intend to overcome these barriers, should the court grant him equal right to the children?"

Martin felt his heart sink at the sharpness of the judge's tone. His stomach felt like it was tying itself in knots. They couldn't keep him from seeing his children. The just *couldn't*.

Gold stood. "Your honor, Mr. Schuller has revealed to me that his duties have shifted, and the previous absences from home are no longer required for his work. He is unable to reveal more than that, due to the sensitive nature of his work."

The judge looked at Martin. "Will you swear that under oath, Mr. Schuller?"

Martin stood, as Gold had instructed him to do when speaking to the judge. "I will, your honor."

The judge looked down at the court reporter. "Let the record reflect that Mr. Schuller has attested under penalty of perjury that his work no longer requires absences from home."

Gold looked at Martin with a hint of smile and a tiny nod, then stepped around the table again and addressed the judge.

"As for the physical distance, there are frequent trains running between Philadelphia and Washington, several each day, and the trip takes less than two hours. To get back and forth between these two cities is not a hardship in this day and age. Mr. Walsh is inventing a barrier where none exists. Mr. Schuller is both willing and able to see his children any weekend that they are available, and will fully cooperate with Mrs. Schuller to schedule *frequent* visits."

Martin had to smile when his lawyer stressed the word "frequent."

The judge looked back at William Walsh. "Is there any reason Mrs. Schuller would be unable or unwilling to cooperate with Mr. Schuller to schedule these visits, Mr. Walsh?"

Walsh looked shaken by the turn of events, and Martin couldn't stop himself from chuckling.

"Mrs. Schuller will do what is best for the children, and will be happy to cooperate with their father to that end."

Martin felt a weight lift from his shoulders, and his chest suddenly felt less constricted.

He was going to win the right to see his kids.

There was more back and forth for a couple of minutes, but Martin hardly heard any of it. He saw the stiffness in Becky's posture, and knew that she realized it was over as well.

At last, the judge declared that the minor children would live with their mother in Philadelphia, and that their father would have full right to see them at any mutually-agreed time, and banged his gavel.

Martin beamed as he stood and faced his lawyer, who grinned at him and pumped his hand. "Congratulations, Martin!"

The lawyers did a stiff dance that culminated in an uneven handshake, William Walsh's effort far less enthusiastic than Bernard Gold's.

Martin approached Becky, who attempted a half-smile.

"I suppose you'll want to see the kids right away," she said.

He nodded. "I'm in town already. I could take them out tonight."

"Why don't you just keep them for the long weekend," Becky replied. "You can have them back Monday afternoon, so they'll have time to rest and won't be too tired for the start of school on Tuesday."

"Well," Martin began, but stopped himself. He had to go to the German Volksfest on Sunday at the Deutschhorst Country Club in Sellersville. It was his best hope of catching *Schwartzkiefer* and *Der Skiläufer* with their guard down.

Becky must have seen the conflict on his face, for she crossed her arms and pursed her lips. "Did you not just swear to the judge that you'd be available to spend time with your children? And already you aren't so sure about spending a whole weekend with them?"

Martin stopped himself from replying with an angry comeback. "No, it'll be fine." He'd think of something.

His parents—he'd take them to his parents' house on Sunday. Reading wasn't far from Sellersville.

"Fine, I'll have Mrs. Kennedy get them ready for you. You can pick them up at five o'clock." She turned to go, but paused and looked back at him. "Good bye, Martin."

He watched her walk away, no longer his wife, and a profound sadness settled over him.

31

Sunday, September 3, 1939
Sellersville, Pennsylvania

Martin watched the crowd at the festivities with the same sense of anger he had felt when he watched their excitement outside of Madison Square Garden in February. The mix of American and Nazi flags around the grounds made his stomach churn, but he kept a smile on his face the entire time, as if he were as excited as they about their cause.

Today's news that the British and French had declared war on Germany only seemed to enhance the festive mood of the crowd. Martin overheard several excited conversations about it.

The sight of children running around with miniature American and Nazi flags in their little fists made his blood boil. These kids were the same ages as his own kids, and he wanted to punch their parents in the face for exposing them to this sort of vitriol and hatred, hidden behind the façade of ethnic celebration.

He had donned his Augustus Greater disguise this morning—fake mustache and glasses, shabby suit—for the first time since June. Stefan Ketterman had forged the membership card for the German American Bund, which had granted him entrée to this afternoon's festivities at the so-called Deutschhorst Country Club—in reality a glorified field outside of Sellersville, next to an old stone mill beside a swift stream known as Branch Creek.

There were nearly two thousand people in attendance—a large number, Martin thought, considering the rural venue forty miles from

Philadelphia. He looked toward the stage, and saw Fritz Kuhn—their *unser Fuhrer*—talking with a handful of men in the uniforms of the United States Army. On one of the men, Martin recognized the regalia of a Brigadier General, and it almost made him shudder.

A hand-painted sign above the basement door of the mill announced that this was where the rathskeller was. Martin made his way through the crowd toward it. Gray-shirted Storm Troopers moved through the crowd in pairs and trios, their heads high with an air of self-importance and righteous arrogance. He tried to steer clear of them without looking like he was avoiding them.

The kellerbar was crowded, and loud with conversations in both English and German. It took Martin a while to make his way to the bar, and when he arrived there he ordered a stein of the *dunkel*, in English with his parents' Pennsylvania Dutch accent.

"Good choice, they just tapped it," the bartender said. His English was unaccented—a native Pennsylvanian.

While the bartender filled his stein, Martin listened to the crowd. The conversations around him would have shocked polite society— hateful references to negroes and Jews ruining American society, even threatening civilization itself—and they might have shocked him, had he not known he stood amongst Bund members.

Even so, it was startling at first. The free-flowing beer loosened lips and relieved inhibitions that would have normally kept such sentiments to whispers.

Perhaps the most disturbing aspect of the experience was how *normal* all of these folks looked. If one didn't know better, they looked as if they could have been the crowd at any county fair in Pennsylvania. It bothered Martin to think that—although a tiny minority, certainly— these people lived and worked among them undetected, their hatred carefully hidden on the inside and only shown in the safety of the current company.

Or, he thought, *they're not such a tiny minority after all*. He thought of the twenty-two thousand people who had shown up to the big Bund rally at Madison Square Garden in February, and thought again how two thousand attending here seemed much larger than he would have expected for a rural area, even on the edge of a heavily German-American belt.

The bartender handed him his stein of dark *dunkel* beer, and Martin slipped a dollar bill across the bar.

It pained him to know that the dollar was going to profit the German American Bund, but he didn't have much choice. Besides, his was only one of thousands of dollars the bar was going to pull in for the Bund today.

The tables in the kellerbar were all full, and the open area was crowded, so Martin made his way back to the door, aware that he would probably not be able to take the stein outside. But it was worth asking.

He approached a pair of young men conversing next to the door. "Excuse me," he said in English with the Pennsylvania Dutch accent. "Do you know if it is possible to take the beer outside?" He pointed to his stein.

"Yeah, sure," one of the men said, a tall, dark-haired young man with piercing blue eyes. His accent, like that of the bartender, was American.

"You're new here, aren't you?" the other said. He was a shorter man, with wavy light brown hair and brown eyes. "Haven't seen you here before."

"Yes, my first time here," Martin said, giving them a gracious smile. "I am new in Pennsylvania. I lived in New York until recently."

"How did you hear about the festival?" the taller man asked.

Martin thought he detected a hint of suspicion in his deep blue eyes.

"I have a friend who told me to come to Pennsylvania when things turned bad for me in New York," Martin said. "He also belongs to the Bund, and he told me about the gathering today. Maybe you know him—Fritz Dendler?"

The young men shook their heads.

"*Ach*, it is not important. I have not seen him here today, not yet."

"Well, good luck," the shorter one said, and the two turned back toward each other and resumed their conversation.

Martin made his way outside. He was certain Fritz Dendler—*Schwarzkiefer*—would be here today. The question was how difficult it would be to locate him in a crowd of two thousand people.

He'd found *Immergrün* in a crowd of twenty-two thousand at Madison Square Garden only because a rendezvous spot had been predetermined. He had no such focal point today. He was adrift in a sea of American Nazis, looking for one German Nazi hiding in plain sight.

He stayed near the stone mill for a while, drinking down the beer in his stein to the halfway point so it wouldn't slosh all over as he walked across the bumpy ground of the green field. He watched the passersby as he stood beside the stone wall; lots of grins, laughter, and excited conversations.

Even more than the rally at Madison Square Garden, with all of its Nuremburg-esque Nazi pomp and circumstance, this gathering was a party, a celebration. A small part of Martin envied their excitement, even as he condemned their motivations.

He set off across the field, making his way slowly through the crowd. He meandered toward the stage, where seven Army men still stood in their dress uniforms and medals, talking with the leaders of the German American Bund. He thought it was a decent bet that *Schwarzkiefer* would be nearby, either keeping watch on the military men, or waiting to be introduced to them.

Perhaps one of them was *Der Skiläufer*, Martin thought. It was as plausible as any other explanation. He wished he knew more about these seven men—where were they stationed? What were their backgrounds? If nothing else, the answers to these questions could rule them out as candidates for the cell leader.

Not seeing his target anywhere, Martin continued to wander. When a trio of gray-shirted Storm Troopers hurried past, he grew a little bit concerned that he might look suspicious wondering around the grounds by himself, looking around. He could explain that he was looking for someone, but judging from the stern demeanors of the Storm Troopers, he doubted that would make a difference.

On the far side of the field, beside a bend in Branch Creek, stood a makeshift rifle range, with sand bags instead of proper rifle mounts. The *Abwehr* was military intelligence in Germany—so *Schwarzkiefer* might well be drawn to the rifle range to keep his shooting skills sharpened.

"Hey! You there—what are you doing?" one of the rifle range attendants shouted at him. His English was thickly accented—a native German—and he wore a Nazi-style short brown mustache.

"I am sorry," Martin said, in German to let the man know that he belonged here. "I am waiting for a friend to meet me by the rifle range. I am new here, and I do not know anyone except my friend, Mr. Dendler."

The man replied in German, "Ah, very good. Come, shoot a round while you wait," and motioned Martin over.

"How much is it?" Martin asked.

"Twenty-five cents for five shots."

Martin reluctantly pulled a quarter from the pocket of his trousers and handed it over. The man handed him a Mauser K98 rifle—the standard issue rifle for soldiers in the *Wehrmacht*, and Martin wondered how the German American Bund had gotten ahold of these.

Martin knew how to shoot—he'd been taught in high school by the father of a friend from the football team, who used to hunt deer every fall—but the last time he had fired a rifle was during his counterintelligence undercover training four years ago. He trusted it would come back quickly, and he wouldn't look like a fool.

He took a spot along the line of sand bags, positioned himself with his elbows up and the barrel of the gun pointed at his target. The Mauser was a bolt action rifle, with a five-round stripper clip that the attendant loaded.

He sighted down the barrel and pulled the trigger.

The bullet hit the top of the target.

Not too bad, for the first shot in four years, he thought.

He worked the bolt to load the second bullet, adjusted the rear sight, aimed and fired again, and this shot hit slightly closer to center than the first one.

He concentrated harder, aimed carefully, and his third shot hit just above the bulls-eye. The fourth and fifth shots landed all around the center, creating a sort of ring around the bulls-eye.

"Not bad," the attendant said to him in German, giving him a half-smile. "Want to shoot another round? You might hit the center this time."

It was tempting, but Martin shook his head as he stood and handed the rifle back to the attendant. "I should really wait until my friend, Mr. Dendler, arrives. We are supposed to shoot together, and I do not want to spend all of my quarters before he joins me."

"Alright, well, hopefully we won't be too busy when he gets here," the attendant said, and turned to another man who handed him a quarter.

As he was turning away, Martin spotted him. Dendler—*Schwarzkiefer*—was talking with a middle-aged man in a white dress shirt and dark gray necktie.

"Good afternoon, Mr. Dietzman!" the rifle attendant called out in English, waving and beaming. "It is a pleasure to see you, sir."

"Yes, good to see you, too, Hoffman," the man replied. His English was American.

"The youth have finished their target practice for the day," Hoffman said, sounding apologetic. "But you will see them soon, on the stage to begin the presentations."

"Very good," Dietzman said, sounding dismissive, and turned away. He and *Schwarzkiefer* began walking toward the stage.

Martin followed at a discreet distance, and hoped Hoffman wouldn't notice him sneaking away.

A large number of children between the ages of eight and fourteen began filing onto the stage—Martin counted about forty boys in uniforms that resembled the Hitler Youth, and perhaps twenty-five girls in traditional German folk dresses. One boy held the American flag, while a second held the red, white and black Nazi banner.

The crowd grew silent, and all eyes turned toward the stage, where Fritz Kuhn himself mounted the steps and stood behind the children while they began to sing—the Nazi national anthem, in German, Martin realized, and a chill ran up his spine.

After the children had finished singing, to enthusiastic applause from the crowd, Kuhn took the podium, and began a Hitler-esque rant— in English, with a German accent—against the evils of "Jewish Socialism" as espoused by "President F. D. Rosenfeld."

It was the typical Kuhn rant, the type he had made at the Bund rally at Madison Square Garden in February, and many times before and since. Martin concentrated on *Schwarzkiefer* and his companion, Mr. Dietzman, whoever he was. They were conversing in hushed tones, and then moved through the crowd and around the side of the stage toward a thick hedge behind it.

Martin waited a few seconds, and then followed at a discreet distance.

He saw them slip through a narrow opening in the hedge, and he moved that way, looking over his shoulder to see if anyone were watching. Convinced he was unseen, he followed.

275

He saw the two of them standing next to a Rolls Royce limousine, talking with a familiar-looking figure.

Maximilian Showalter himself.

Martin hid in the hedges and watched, cautious lest Showalter see him and recognize him.

A moment later, shouts and blaring police whistles disturbed his concentration. He looked back at the field and saw uniformed police officers moving through the crowd, shouting orders, while plain-clothed officers held up badges.

He recognized FBI agent Anderson some twenty yards away, and a moment later he saw FBI agent Pagliaro a short distance behind him.

Sloan would be nearby. Martin had no doubt this was his operation.

He had to get away.

He looked back at the limousine, only to see Showalter himself behind the wheel, pulling away in a hurry.

"Damn it!" Martin said, cursing his momentary distraction as the limousine sped away.

He looked around for *Schwarzkiefer*—had he left with Showalter? He was nowhere in sight. Neither was Dietzman.

Where would they have gone? To Max Showalter's house? To the Showalter Glassworks? Somewhere different altogether? Martin couldn't be certain.

Hearing the shouts behind the hedge, Martin knew he didn't have time to contemplate it. The FBI had control of the Deutschhorst Country Club, and he had to get away from here.

He began to run in the direction the limousine had gone.

They wouldn't go back to Showalter's house, Martin reasoned. Max Showalter was too smart to leave open the possibility that they might be followed back to his home—that would be too damning. But if he were followed back to the Glassworks, a place where more than a thousand people worked, there was still plausible deniability on his part.

"Stop right there!" he heard a commanding voice shout behind him. For a second, he hesitated in his stride, but didn't stop.

"Stop or I'll shoot!"

Martin stopped, and put his hands up, cursing under his breath.

He felt the barrel of a pistol at his back, and a man's hands began to pat down his pockets, ribs, and legs.

"Why were you running, fella?" the man asked, coming around to face Martin, his gun leveled at Martin's chest.

Martin gave the agent his most commanding tone and expression. "They're getting away. Go tell Special Agent Sloan that Martin Schuller said they're getting away."

The agent's eyes narrowed. "What are you talking about, mister?"

Martin scowled, the way he would scowl at his children when they were misbehaving. "I said go! Find Special Agent Reginald Sloan, and tell him that Martin Schuller said the suspects are getting away—but I know where they're going. Go!"

The agent's face flushed with anger at being ordered around. "You're coming with me," he said, grabbing Martin's arm and thrusting him toward the hedge. "Where's Sloan?" he asked another agent after they ducked through the bushes and back into the field.

"Over by the mill," the other agent said, pointing toward the large group of people gathered on the lawn outside the entrance to the kellerbar.

Martin saw Sloan before he saw them. He was handing out orders to FBI agents, who parsed the crowd into small groups. Sloan's eyes widened briefly when he saw Martin approaching, and then narrowed. He shook his head.

"I might have expected to see you here, Mr. Schuller—or is it Mr. Graeter today?"

"This man was running down the dirt road, other side of that hedge," the agent holding Martin's arm told Sloan. "When I stopped him, he said to find you and tell you the suspects were getting away."

Sloan stared at Martin hard for several seconds. "You made contact with them?"

Martin returned Sloan's hard gaze. "I would have."

Sloan snorted. "So you know who they are, then?"

Martin nodded.

"*Schwarzkiefer*?"

"Yes."

"*Der Skiläufer*, too?"

Martin stared back at him with undisguised pride, and a hint of a smile raised the corners of his mouth. "Yes."

The agent, who had been watching this exchange with a dumbfounded look, recovered his composure. "He said to tell you, sir, that he knows where they're going."

Martin almost chuckled at the man's attempt to stay relevant in the situation. His half-smile grew a little as he watched Sloan's expression.

"Is that true?" Sloan asked.

Martin knew he'd be in real trouble if his hunch didn't pan out. "Yes," he said anyway.

Sloan felt his pulse quicken. He might yet be the one to nab this *Skiläufer*, cell leader and spy master.

This sting at the so-called Deutschhorst Country Club was technically a joint-operation with the Philadelphia office, and months of work by both offices had gone into it—but if what Schuller said was true, Sloan himself might still be the one to bring in *Der Skiläufer*.

He looked at Agent Muldoon, still holding Schuller's arm. "I'll take it from here, agent."

Muldoon looked disappointed for a second, but he said "Yes, sir," and departed.

Sloan looked back at Schuller. "Where?"

Schuller shook his head. "I'm going with you."

Sloan scowled. "You understand this is an FBI operation, Mr. Schuller. You're lucky we don't arrest you on the spot for aiding and abetting."

Schuller's gaze remained level, his green eyes never wavering, and he said nothing.

Sloan exhaled hard. "Fine, have it your way—but I can't guarantee your safety, understand?"

Schuller nodded.

"I'll need to bring some of my men with us."

"Not too many," Schuller said, with a slight shake of the head. "No more than one car, or we'll alert them."

Sloan exhaled again, fighting the exasperation. "I know how to do my job, Mr. Schuller."

Schuller said nothing, just stared back at Sloan, unblinking.

"Ok, let's go. You're coming with me."

Hutson

32

The limousine was parked in front of the office building next to the Showalter Glassworks when they arrived. Martin pointed and identified it to Sloan. The parking lot was otherwise empty, though about twenty cars were parked in front of the factory next-door.

Martin had refused to tell Sloan where they were going, lest Sloan kick him out of the car in the middle of nowhere, and instead just told him where to turn. He spent the forty-minute drive from Sellersville going over everything he'd learned in the last two weeks. When he mentioned Charles Lindbergh, Sloan had interrupted him with a guffaw.

"You know Lindbergh was working for MID all those years he was in Europe, right?" Sloan asked, his tone dripping with condescension. "I know from the files you fellas gave us that State was *very* concerned about all his visits to Germany. What you didn't seem to know was that every time he visited Germany, and all those tours of munitions factories he made with German military brass, he reported everything back to MID in Washington. You boys were on a political witch hunt there."

MID—Military Intelligence Division. Martin's heart sank as he realized they should have suspected that. Lindbergh's antisemitism was well-known long before he left the States in '35, as was his professional admiration for the German military, and his personal admiration for Adolph Hitler—but Martin had to admit there had never been an explicit endorsement of the Nazi regime.

Still, Sloan's tone rankled.

"When did you learn that?"

Sloan was silent a moment. "In June," he finally admitted.

Martin chuckled. "When MID had to start sharing their counter-intelligence files with the FBI."

Sloan ignored him. "Continue with what you found out, Schuller." Martin finished recounting his discoveries. They rode the last ten minutes in tense silence.

And now they were here, as was Showalter's vehicle—Martin breathed a little easier now that he knew he'd been right. Sloan drove past it and pulled his car off on the side of the road about a hundred yards away. A thick hedge hid them from view, and the second car parked behind them.

Sloan opened the trunk and removed a shotgun; Martin noticed this was in addition to the pistol holstered at his hip. Sloan took another pistol from the trunk, and checked the cartridge.

Then he surprised Martin by handing it to him.

"If you're coming in with us, you'd better be armed," he said. Then his eyes narrowed. "I know you're going to follow us in, and I can't guarantee your safety, so you'd better have this. You know how to use it?"

"Of course," Martin said, taking the pistol and checking the safety, then shoving it into the waist of his pants behind his back, under his suit coat.

Sloan pointed a finger at Martin's nose. "Don't make me regret that, Schuller."

Martin didn't respond, and Sloan turned toward the four agents who had emerged from the car behind them.

"They've probably got someone watching the parking lot, and maybe other approaches as well. There's not a whole lot of cover between here and the building, so run low and get to the landscaping along the edge of the building as fast as you can. Mr. Schuller and I will cover you from the end of this hedge. Then we'll make our approach, and you cover us—got it?"

"Got it," they all replied.

"Anderson, Pagliaro—you approach from the north. O'Neal, Muldoon—get yourselves to the other side of the main door, and wait there until Schuller and I join you. Let's go, on my mark."

They crept to the end of the hedge, single file. Martin took up the rear, right behind Sloan. They stood in place for several seconds, pistols drawn, and then Sloan spoke. "Go, go, go!"

The four agents burst around the hedge, running. Sloan and Martin crept up to the end of the bushes, and Martin saw an open stretch of grass about fifty yards wide between them and the building. The four agents ran across it, bent over, guns in front of them.

Then glass shattered, and a loud crack echoed across the parking lot, followed by another, and then another.

Anderson fell backward, a spray of crimson shooting from his back, and he sprawled across the ground.

Muldoon grabbed at his own shoulder, yelling curses, and dropped to the ground, rolling into a ball.

Pagliaro darted to the side, making a full-on sprint to the building in a zig-zag. O'Neal dropped to the ground and lay flat, pointing his gun at the broken window twenty yards in front of him and returning fire.

Sloan's shotgun was already in place. He fired a split second before O'Neal's pistol. The semi-automatic weapons fired over and over, and broken glass flew from the front of the building as every window shattered.

There was a cry from inside the building, and the shots ceased.

Martin's pulse pounded in his ears, which were ringing from the countless gun shots fired so near to him. Otherwise, all was still.

Pagliaro had made it to the building some distance from the door, and stood flat against the wall, looking to Sloan, who stood with his hand raised and head tilted, listening.

O'Neal crept across the grass, keeping flat against the ground.

"Last chance to go back to the car," Sloan whispered to Martin.

Martin shook his head.

"None of us'll think any less of you, Schuller."

Martin shook his head again. "No, I'm in."

He thought he saw a hint of admiration in Sloan's eyes as he nodded. "OK, we go on three, I'll lead. One, two, three."

They ran at full speed, as fast as they could bent over. Martin imitated Sloan and the other FBI agents, every second expecting to hear another gun shot.

But nothing happened, and they reached the door a moment later, and flattened themselves against the wall beside it. O'Neal got up and ran the last few feet to join them, standing on the opposite side of the door.

Martin looked around to see Pagliaro edging toward them from the corner of the building.

"Anderson's dead," Sloan muttered when everyone was near. No one reacted, everyone already knowing it, their faces grim and set with determination and controlled anger.

Sloan appeared calm and collected. Martin hoped he didn't look as shell-shocked as he felt.

"Pagliaro, you stay out here and watch for anyone approaching the building." Sloan's voice was quiet, but as commanding as ever. "O'Neal, secure the entrance."

O'Neal nodded, raised his pistol, and then spun toward the door and kicked it in with one powerful move. Wood splintered and flew, and O'Neal disappeared inside.

Sloan counted to three with raised fingers, then slipped in behind. Martin followed.

The lights were off. It took Martin's eyes a few seconds to adjust to the dimness. The wooden blinds hung in shambles in front of broken windows, and pieces of glass littered the lobby floor. Spent shotgun shells lay scattered about. A body lay sprawled across the floor between two chairs near one of the windows.

After scanning the room, Sloan joined O'Neal beside it, motioning to Martin to join them.

"You recognize him?"

Martin did, though the top of the man's head had disappeared, and a gruesome mix of red and gray lay on the ground above it in a spray pattern, like it had been shot from a fountain. A shotgun lay on the floor some five feet away, as if it had fallen from the table.

"That's the one they called Dietzman," Martin said, fighting the nausea.

"But we don't really know who this Dietzman is—was—is that right?"

"No, we don't." Martin paused, sniffed at the air. Smoke.

"I smell it too," Sloan said. "They've set the damn building on fire, trying to smoke us out so they can escape."

Martin shook his head. "No—they're burning incriminating documents. In Showalter's office, I guarantee it."

"Stay here, I'll handle it. Just tell me where to go."

But Martin was already on his way to the heavy mahogany door behind the reception desk. "Uh-uh. Follow me."

"Fine, you lead the way," Sloan growled. Then Martin heard him mutter, "Go on and get yourself killed, you meddling bastard."

The smell of smoke grew stronger as he hurried toward Showalter's office. He was about ten feet from the door when he tripped over an unseen chord stretched across the hall a few inches above the carpet. He crashed to the floor, and his pistol skidded out of his hand and came to a stop at Showalter's door.

A second later there was a crash of gunfire and splintering wood as a hole blew through Showalter's office door a foot above Martin's head. Then he heard heavy footfalls inside the office, followed by a slamming door.

Martin grabbed his gun and scrambled up, noticing a little blood on the back of his hand where a couple of sharp pieces of wood had pierced his skin. Sloan pushed him out of the way, and O'Neal kicked in the door. Martin wiped his hand on his slacks and followed them in.

Showalter's safe stood open behind his desk. Smoke and flame rose from the trash can beside it. A half-empty bottle of brandy stood uncorked at the edge of the desk.

Sloan and O'Neal were looking in the safe, but Martin hurried toward the side door. "This way!" he called.

He found the door locked, and this time he kicked it in himself, the lock breaking on his third kick.

The door led into a large boardroom, a giant oval table surrounded by tall leather chairs taking up most of the room. Another door on the far end of the room stood open, and Martin ran toward it. Out the window, he spotted Showalter and Dendler running toward the Glassworks factory.

Martin sprinted through the door and down a hallway, hearing Sloan and O'Neal running behind him. He ran through an open door at the end of the hall and emerged into the daylight, with a stretch of tall grass about a hundred yards separating them from the tall blackened brick walls of the factory.

Showalter and Dendler disappeared inside the factory.

Sloan and O'Neal caught up with Martin at the door, and Sloan put his hand on Martin's shoulder to hold him back.

"We need back-up," he said. Then he turned to O'Neal and told him to go back and call the Philadelphia office. "Get as many men out here as they can spare."

O'Neal ran back inside.

"We can't wait," Martin said, swatting away Sloan's arm. "They'll get away."

"We can follow their trail, like we've followed a thousand others," Sloan was saying, but Martin was already running toward the factory.

33

Martin barely heard Sloan. He thought about his children, and pictured them growing up in a world of Showalter and Dendler's making.

And he hadn't hesitated a second longer.

He had to get those bastards before they got away.

He was hardly aware of the seconds that passed as he crossed the open space, focused entirely on the door that Showalter and Dendler had used. It wasn't until he reached the door that he realized he could have been shot on the way.

And ended up like Anderson.

He forced that from his mind, and focused on one thing—catching the spy and his American handler. He threw open the door and dashed inside.

The hum of the factory became an almost deafening noise inside the door, and he took a few seconds to look around and get his bearings.

It was a new-style factory, all light and open, built of steel and concrete. Probably only a few years old.

Two assembly lines were moving, and a handful of men worked each one. Large curved windshields—far too large for an automobile— came off the end of one line. A man there stacked them on pallets. They seemed to flex in his hands as he picked them off the line, pivoted, and set them down on the pallet.

Plastic, Martin realized. These were the airplane parts for the Army Air Corps.

A man in dark slacks, white dress shirt and black necktie marched toward him, a clipboard in his hands. "Can I help you?" he barked, mouth pursed and eyes narrowed in suspicion.

"FBI," Martin heard Sloan's deep voice say behind him, and he turned to see him holding up his badge. "I need for you and your men to shut down the line immediately, and leave in an orderly fashion."

"What's the meaning of this?" the man demanded. "I'm the shift manager, and I'm responsible for producing these units for a deadline."

Sloan kept his badge up in his left hand, and raised his pistol with his right. "Shut it down. Now."

The man swallowed hard, and nodded.

Martin saw him glance at a metal staircase that rose beside a small office before turning to direct the workers to shut everything down.

That was where Showalter and Dendler had gone. The shift manager looked there because he had seen the owner of the company go that way a moment before.

Martin ran there, and took the stairs two at a time.

The staircase led to a catwalk that crossed the roof of the small office, and emerged into a large warehouse area. Several other catwalks branched off from this one, crisscrossing the warehouse twenty-some feet above the concrete floor.

He spotted Showalter and Dendler on the far side of the warehouse, several hundred yards away, heading toward a door in the brick wall at the end of the walk.

Behind him, he heard heavy footsteps on the metal stairs, and hoped it was Sloan.

A forklift loaded with pallets rumbled beneath him as he rushed down the catwalk. It stopped when the shift manager shouted to the driver, and the engine died.

Martin reached the door at the end where Showalter and Dendler had disappeared a moment before, and found it locked. He stepped back to kick it in, and heard Sloan shout his name.

"Schuller! Schuller! Stop, before you get yourself killed!"

Martin ignored him, kicking the door as hard as he could below the lock.

He heard a little crack, but nothing else.

"Stop! You're doing it wrong!" Sloan yelled, not far away now.

Martin stopped the second kick that he was about to give the door, and turned toward Sloan. The older man was out of breath as he reached Martin, but his voice still carried the commanding tone he'd had all day.

"You're kicking upward. You've gotta raise your foot higher and kick straight in. And if you're right in front of it, your enemy might shoot you dead the moment the door flies open."

Sloan shoved Martin out of the way, stood slightly to the side, raised his foot, and kicked hard at the lock. The direct hit sent the door flying open, and Sloan spun out of the way at the same time. He peered around the side, pistol drawn, before dashing through.

Martin both appreciated the lesson, and hated that Sloan had given it. He cursed himself as he hurried after the FBI special agent in charge.

This was the old factory, dark and stuffy, the brick walls blackened with forty-three years' worth of soot, its ceiling high above them. Martin and Sloan were on a long balcony that stretched the length of the building, looking out over the factory floor. Martin saw glassware of every shape and size at various work stations, but no one seemed to be working here today.

Then he spotted Showalter slipping through the shadows on the far side of the floor, heading for the front of the building. Dendler wasn't with him.

He tapped Sloan's shoulder and pointed at Showalter.

Sloan motioned him closer, and said quietly, "You follow him, but keep yourself covered, and I'll go around and cut him off."

Martin nodded, and Sloan ran off to their right.

There was a ladder to the factory floor about twenty feet to his left, and Martin scrambled down. The stuffy heat made sweat run down his face and sting his eyes. He wiped at it with his sleeve as his feet hit the floor.

He spun around to chase after Showalter.

And a fist slammed into his chin.

It was a poorly-aimed blow, but Martin still took an involuntary step backward. He saw another fist start to swing at his face, and he ducked out of the way just in time. He scrambled backward several steps, then planted his feet and raised his gun.

Fritz Dendler stood in front of him. His eyes darted to Martin's gun pointed at his chest.

"Are you going to shoot me, Mr. Schuller?" he asked in German, a mocking grin spreading across his face. Then his face darkened with rage. "Who do you really work for, Mr. Schuller? Are you with the FBI?"

Martin noticed Dendler's right hand slipping backward around his hip.

"Don't try—" he started to say, but Dendler's hand flew back and whipped a pistol from the back of his pants.

Martin pulled the trigger.

Dendler screamed. His gun skittered across the floor. Blood sprayed onto a nearby workstation, coating the glassware. His right arm hung uselessly at his side, half of his upper arm gone below the shoulder, blood dripping from the gaping wound.

"You son of a bitch!" he shouted in German, and lunged at Martin head first.

Martin spun out of the way, and Dendler's head butt only glanced his ribs—still painful, but not debilitating.

Dendler crashed into a wooden stool a few feet behind where Martin had stood, and lay sprawled on the floor. He started to push himself up with his good arm, but Martin brought the butt of his pistol down hard on the top of Dendler's head.

Dendler slumped to the ground and didn't move.

Martin grabbed Dendler's gun where it had come to rest, and took off after Showalter with a gun in each hand.

Sloan crept down an old wooden staircase from the balcony to the factory floor. He was hidden by deep shadows here, but some thirty feet in front of him the floor was bathed in daylight from the front doors.

Showalter was there, talking to the watchman. Sloan couldn't hear what they were saying, but from time to time Showalter would gesture toward the factory floor behind him, and Sloan knew he was telling the watchman there were two "intruders" in the building.

Sloan saw the heavy iron chain across the front doors, held by a massive padlock. A large key-ring hung from the watchman's belt, with at least twenty other keys.

Sloan crept forward, gun drawn, keeping to the shadow along the wall. He was still fifteen feet away when the watchman pulled off his key-ring and began flipping through the keys as he stepped to the doors.

"Stop right there! FBI!" Sloan shouted, stepping from the shadow.

The watchman froze in place, and Sloan realized belatedly that Showalter was half-hidden behind him. In the blink of an eye, Showalter had an arm around the watchman from behind, and a pistol pointed at the man's temple.

"Drop your gun, or I'll kill this man," Showalter said. His voice was cold as ice, his eyes boring into Sloan.

The watchman whimpered, and his big brown eyes pleaded with Sloan.

"I'm not joking, Mr. FBI Agent—drop your gun. Now."

"He's an innocent man, Mr. Showalter," Sloan said, knowing as he said it that Showalter wouldn't be reasoned with.

Showalter cocked the pistol.

The watchman whimpered again, and squeezed his eyes shut.

"I'm going to count to three—one, two—"

"Alright, alright," Sloan said, and slowly crouched down to lay his gun on the floor.

A cruel smile crept across Showalter's face. He shoved the watchman away, and aimed his gun at Sloan's chest.

Martin hurried around the side of the factory floor, seeing Showalter talking with the watchman, and knowing if he were seen he'd be taken for an intruder. He hid behind a large barrel twenty feet from them and crouched low, trying to think of the best way to surprise them.

Then he heard Sloan's voice shout "Stop right there! FBI!"

He saw Showalter pull the pistol from the back of his pants, and was about to shout a warning, but his voice came out as nothing but air. Showalter had grabbed the guard instead, and was threatening to kill him.

Martin breathed a sigh of relief that Showalter hadn't shot Sloan. He began to crawl forward, using his wrists instead of his hands, careful not to make noise on the floor with the pistols he held. His ribs ached with every breath from where Dendler's head had hit them.

It took great effort to keep his breath shallow and slow, so as to stay silent as he worked his way to the cover of the watchman's desk, less than ten feet behind Showalter.

He watched Showalter shove the watchman to the ground in front of the doors, and level is pistol at Sloan.

Martin got his legs underneath him, prepared to spring forward like a panther. He set Dendler's pistol on the floor and held his own in both hands.

"It seems my watchman has caught an intruder trying to steal equipment," Showalter was saying, cool as a mountain stream. "Sadly, they killed each other in a shoot-out."

Martin whipped his right arm up and fired. His bullet ripped into Showalter's shoulder blade. Showalter's right arm flew upward as he fired, sending a bullet somewhere into the dark.

Martin sprang forward as Showalter crumpled to the ground, placing a foot on the small of Showalter's back and aiming his gun at the back of Showalter's neck.

"Don't move, you son of a bitch," he said, teeth gritted.

Sloan laughed. "Don't worry, he won't! He's dead as a door-nail."

Beside them, the watchman pissed his pants, and a puddle of urine spread across the floor and soaked into Showalter's expensive leather shoes.

"You know I could arrest you for what you've done," Sloan said to Martin after several dozen FBI agents arrived a short while later, securing the area and photographing and bagging the evidence. "Interfering with an investigation—again. Killing a man. Tsk, tsk." But the corners of his mouth curled up in a hint of smile.

Martin didn't smile back. "The way I see it, I did you a service. You would have never found *Der Skiläufer* yourselves."

Sloan chuckled. "Don't be so sure—we have an employee of his in custody—Fred Weideman. Sooner or later he would have told us everything."

Martin doubted that—Weideman couldn't point the finger at Showalter without incriminating himself in the process, and he would know that. But Martin didn't argue.

"But you did help us get him sooner, at least," Sloan said, his lips cracking into a little smile. "For that, I guess I won't arrest you."

"Thanks," Martin muttered.

"We should go into town and have a celebratory beer," Sloan said. Then he grew more somber as he added, "And raise a toast to Stu Anderson, one hell of an agent."

Martin shook his head. "Thanks, but I have to get to Reading tonight. I'm spending Labor Day with my kids."

Sloan looked briefly disappointed, but then shrugged in a show of indifference. "Suit yourself. You got a car back at Sellersville?"

Martin nodded.

"I'll have an agent give you a ride back there. Anything else you need, Schuller?"

Not from you, Martin thought. "Thanks, just the ride."

Martin started walking toward the door, when Sloan's voice made him turn back.

"You should call your boss the Congressman," Sloan said with a sly grin. "We found papers in Showalter's safe that document Congressman Barbour met with 'Fritz Dendler' on at least two occasions. Now, there's no evidence the Congressman knew Dendler was a foreign agent—or had ever heard of Black Pine—but if it gets out in the press, his career will be ruined all the same."

Martin wondered what Sloan was getting at, and gave him a questioning look.

"I would just hate for that to happen, wouldn't you?" Sloan said, his grin growing.

Martin chuckled. "I don't really work for the Congressman. He only thinks I do. I'm going to let him know first thing Tuesday morning, and go back to my job at State."

"Good luck with all that, Schuller."

34

Tuesday, September 5, 1939

Martin sat at the conference table in his best suit, across from the chief and the Assistant Secretary of State for Intelligence.

"The entire situation puts us in a very awkward position," the assistant secretary said. "On the one hand, you disobeyed direct orders from your chief, department policy, *and* you falsely filed for a leave of absence." He paused, and seemed reluctant as he added, "On the other hand, you apprehended two extremely dangerous German agents—one of them a cell leader."

"If it were up to me, you'd be fired," the chief said with a deep scowl.

The assistant secretary held up his hand, and the chief fell silent.

"I don't think that will be necessary, given the service you have done for your country," the assistant secretary said. "However, your disobedience cannot be overlooked, or ignored without consequence."

"You're being transferred," the chief said, his voice hard and cold.

The assistant secretary looked uncomfortable, as if he wished the chief would keep quiet and let him talk. "Yes, this is true. A transfer is being arranged through Personnel as we speak."

"What sort of transfer?" Martin asked, concerned. Would he be put into some job he would hate, just to drive him to quit? He couldn't afford to be out of work, not with fifteen percent unemployment.

"We're sending you back out into the field, for the Foreign Service," the assistant secretary said.

Martin breathed a sigh of relief. He had loved his two years in the Foreign Service, and his posting to the U.S. Embassy in Vienna. He wondered where he would be going now—a posting anywhere in the Third Reich would be much less enjoyable these days.

Then he thought about his kids in Philadelphia, and his heart sank.

"We're posting you to our embassy in Buenos Aires, Argentina, where you will serve as an Information Officer."

Martin's mouth fell open. *Buenos Aires*? What were they thinking?

"But I don't speak Spanish."

"That's not a problem," the assistant secretary said. "I mean—you *will* be expected to learn, but you can do that while you're in country. We're sending you there because of the large German community in Argentina, particularly in the area around Buenos Aires. We have reason to believe the Germans are sending agents into Argentina, Chile, and Brazil to infiltrate the German communities in those countries. Especially Argentina."

Martin's heart sank. "For how long?" he asked.

The assistant secretary hooked an eyebrow. "Pardon?"

"How long is the posting?"

"The normal length—two years."

"But my kids—" Martin began, and stopped.

The assistant secretary looked uncomfortable. "Yes, I understand that's delicate—you'll let us know if you refuse the position, of course."

Of course, he thought, *it's this position or the street*. And he knew he could be unemployed for a very long time.

"Can I reapply for my old position after a certain length of time?"

The assistant secretary appeared taken aback by the question. "I—I suppose that would be allowed," he said. "You would have to demonstrate your qualification all over again, and demonstrate your willingness to abide by the rules and operating procedures."

Martin nodded, but said nothing.

The chief snorted. "I would have thought you'd be happy with this," he said, scowling. "You keep your job, and who knows?—maybe you'll get to do some undercover work down there in South America."

That was small comfort to Martin, but even a glimmer of hope was something to latch onto.

"When do I leave?"

"I'm really going to miss you around here," Hansen said as Martin packed up his desk.

"I've been gone for the last two weeks already," Martin said.

Hansen shrugged. "Sure, but that was kind of like when you used to be out in the field, undercover. We knew you'd be back soon. But now..." he let his voice trail off.

"You'll be fine," Martin said, brusque. "I'm the one being sent into exile."

Hansen looked stung briefly, but then he gave Martin a sad sort of smile. He knew it was true.

"Mr. Schuller? Are you available to take a call?" Trudy called over her shoulder. Normally she would have put the call through, and told Martin after he answered who was calling.

Martin was surprised that anyone was calling, and he asked who it was.

"He said he's one of your new colleagues," Trudy said and looked at her notepad. "Reginald Sloan. Isn't he that FBI agent?"

Martin closed his eyes and took a deep breath. *For the love of God, please don't let me be stuck working with Sloan.*

"I'll take the call, Trudy."

"Congratulations on your new position, Schuller," he heard Sloan's voice say over the line.

"Thanks," Martin said, without enthusiasm. He wondered how Sloan knew about it already. Did he have some hand in this?

"I'm in Washington," Sloan said. "Thought you might like to get a beer, anywhere you'd like, and we can talk about our upcoming assignment to Buenos Aires."

"You're going, too?" Martin asked, incredulous.

"That's right," Sloan said. "Bit of a promotion for me, the Bureau's reward for catching *Der Skiläufer*. And besides, I've always wanted to see something of the world. When the Director learned that you were going to be assigned to an overseas posting, he pulled some strings to get you posted where I'm going, so we can work together. We're both pretty dogged in our investigations, and your Secretary agreed with the Director that us working together would produce some nice results."

Martin didn't reply. He seethed in silence.

"Come on, Schuller—even you have to admit that us working together will be a whole lot better than working at cross purposes like we have. We have the same goal—keeping the country safe. Let's work together for that, shall we?"

Martin knew Sloan was right, and he hated him for it.

"I'll work with you. For the sake of the country."

"That's what I wanted to hear!" Sloan said, and Martin could picture his self-important grin. "We've picked one hell of a terrific time to go to South America—it's almost springtime down there. By the time our ship arrives, it *will* be springtime. So for this year, we get to skip fall and winter, and go straight from summer to spring. How about that?"

"It sounds wonderful," Martin said, without enthusiasm.

"Cheer up!" Sloan said. "I hear Buenos Aires is a wonderful city. You can learn the tango, and dance with beautiful Argentine women."

Martin didn't respond.

"So how about that beer?" Sloan said. "I think we should get to know each other on a friendly basis before our ship departs from New York on Saturday. It could be a long trip, otherwise."

Martin knew he was right. He took a deep breath and sighed.

"Alright, Mr. Sloan, I'll meet you for that beer. You're buying."

The End

Thank you for reading Hidden Among Us. If you enjoyed this book, please tell a friend, update your social media, and/or write a review on Amazon, Goodreads, or other forum.

Questions or comments? Feel free to contact me at www.garretthutson.com

Also by Garrett Hutson:

In A Safe Town

The Jade Dragon

About the Author

Garrett Hutson writes upmarket mysteries and historical spy fiction. He lives in Indianapolis with his husband and their three dogs and three cats. He has one grown daughter. You may contact him at his website, www.garretthutson.com.

Afterword

This is a work of fiction, and the characters and events portrayed are fictitious, although I have alluded to some real historical events and persons.

When I have alluded to historical figures in the story, the real people alluded to are **not** portrayed as characters, and are, to the best of my ability, discussed by the characters in their correct historical context. Examples include President Franklin Roosevelt, Secretary of State Cordell Hull, Undersecretary of State Sumner Welles, and FBI Director J. Edgar Hoover; as well as German spies Dr. Ignatz Griebl, Gunther Rumrich, and Mrs. Jessie Jordan.

I have deliberately avoided using the name of the Chief Special Agent, to maintain that fictional element.

I took a few historical liberties with the Office of the Chief Special Agent. For example, while it is true that there were approximately seven special agents in the late 1930s, at least four of them were based in New York rather than Washington D.C., where the Chief Special Agent was based. I have chosen for artistic reasons to depict the office only in Washington.

Also, there is no evidence that the Office of the Chief Special Agent engaged in undercover activities against alleged spy rings in the same manner that the FBI did—but I believe it is completely plausible that they *might* have, and we know that they did travel into the field for investigations. This story is a realistic imagining of hypothetical undercover operations.

I have also found no evidence that the agents specialized in Soviet or German targets—but I believe such specialization was likely, given individual differences in language skills, cultural knowledge, etc.

The inter-agency rivalry I depicted was real, and I have endeavored to depict it realistically. Franklin Roosevelt's order to consolidate domestic counter-espionage under the FBI in June 1939 was real, and was viewed as a strategic loss by the Department of State. This is one reason I believe it plausible that the Office of the Chief Special Agent may have conducted undercover operations of their own prior to June 1939.

The rally of the German American Bund at Madison Square Garden in February 1939 was a real event; as was the festival at the Deutschhorst Country Club in September, the presence of U.S. Army officers there, and the FBI raid on that festival. All other events in this story are fictional.

Amerikadeutscher Bund (German American Bund)

The German American Bund was founded in 1936, with the aim of promoting German culture in the United States, and favorable relations with Germany. In addition to its cultural activities, the Bund took an openly political stance that was right-wing and anti-Semitic. Fritz Kuhn was the real-life *Bundesfuhrer* of the German American Bund, and I have made every attempt to depict his activities accurately.

While it must be stressed that not everyone who belonged to the German American Bund at this time was a Nazi sympathizer, it should also be stressed that they belonged to an organization that unabashedly supported Germany during a period when Germany was unambiguously Nazi. Between 1937 and 1941, the Bund ran several youth camps across the country that were modeled on the Hitler Youth camps in Germany, and taught Nazi doctrine to the children and grandchildren of German immigrants.

Draw your own conclusion, but if it waddles like a duck and quacks like a duck... I believe that my portrayal of the Bund as an American Nazi organization is accurate.

Gay culture in 1939

While it seems incredible now, Washington D.C. in the interwar years of the 1920s and '30s had a thriving, semi-open gay and lesbian community. The New Deal expansion of the federal bureaucracy after 1933 brought tens of thousands of young people to Washington to work in the government. For many, this was their first taste of freedom, and the gay men and lesbians among them were naturally drawn together.

Finding a community, the more effeminate gay men often felt free to be themselves for the first time in their lives. They were openly referred to as "faeries" by others, and sometimes referred to themselves as the "fine sisters." Others, of course, would have been less obvious to those outside the gay community. I believe my depictions in this book reflect the reality of Washington in 1939.

For multiple reasons, the State Department attracted more than the average share of gay men. After World War II, this would arouse the suspicions of the House Un-American Activities Committee, not to mention Senator Joe McCarthy; but in the time of this story, the State Department was a relatively safe place to work if you were a not-entirely-closeted gay man.

The population of the District of Columbia expanded by 36% during the 1930s, a growth of nearly 200,000 people. Most of the new young government workers in Washington lived in tight quarters downtown, sharing small apartments with multiple roommates. Privacy was hard to come by, so the wooded areas of Lafayette Park and the National Mall became well-known among gay men as places to cruise for sex with other men. George Chauncey has noted that "privacy could only be had in public." And as in many east coast cities, the YMCA became a gathering place for young gay men.

There were three gay bars operating in Washington in the 1930s. The Horseshoe and The Showboat were located within blocks of the

White House and Lafayette Park, sported entertainment, and catered to both gay men and lesbians. Carroll's—which features in a scene in this novel—was located amid the burlesque halls and tattoo parlors of Ninth Street, and catered to "rough trade." It was known to attract soldiers, sailors, and marines on shore leave. As I have depicted it in this story, it was run by an elderly bartender, while two waitresses kept watch over the customers.

For more information, check out *The Lavender Scare* by David K. Johnson, especially pages 41 to 51.

Much has been written about the contributions of gay men and lesbians to the Harlem Renaissance, and the presence of gay men and lesbians among the bohemian population of early 20th century Greenwich Village, so I will not belabor that point beyond saying that I believe my characterizations of Gregory Spooner and Alan Carmody to be realistic for New York City at that time.

As always, I have done my best to be as historically accurate as possible, except where noted above. Any errors are mine alone.

Acknowledgments

I started work on this story in July 2016, at a bar in Muncie, Indiana. The idea had been swirling in my head for years, as a prequel to a manuscript I wrote between 2010 and 2012 about Martin Schuller in Switzerland in 1941. I loved the character, and wanted to dive deeper into his background. I'd even had the opening sequence in mind for a while, but hadn't done anything with it. But with the political turmoil our country saw that summer, the echoes seemed very real to me, and as I sat at the bar the first evening of Midwest Writers Workshop, waiting for friends to arrive, I started writing.

Many people contributed to the development of this book in ways big and small. As always, many thanks to my awesome partners in the IndyScribes critique group—Laura VanArendonk Baugh, Stephanie Cain, Stephanie Ferguson, Marcia Kelly, Peggy Larkin, Jim Meeks-Johnson, and Jim Thompson—who patiently read and critiqued many sections of the first draft, and provided excellent feedback. You all are the best!

I owe a debt of gratitude to the wonderful people at Midwest Writers Workshop for making me the writer that I am today. Even with the difficulties they have had this year, I firmly believe that there is no better writers conference than MWW, and I hope they come back in 2019 better and stronger than ever.

My sincerest thanks to Brenda Havens, Stephanie Cain, Lisa Wheeler, and Ann Griffin, who took the time to read the entire manuscript and provide valuable insights and feedback. You are all amazing, and you helped bring out the best in this story. It is definitely better for your comments. Steph, your productivity as a writer amazes and inspires me. Lisa, you are a wizard.

Thank you to Ann R. Carey from the U.S. Department of State's Office of the Historian. The documents you provided saved me from numerous historical errors, and helped me bring the setting and the characters to more vibrant life. Thank you also to Heather Davis from the Sellersville Museum (Sellersville, PA) for the nuggets of information you provided.

Thanks to Steven Novak for the amazing cover.

And lastly, most importantly, my deepest gratitude and devotion to my husband David Lee, for letting me live the crazy, frustrating, wonderful life of a writer, and always being supportive through all of its myriad ups and downs. I love you more than you can know.

-Garrett B. Hutson, May 2018

Made in the USA
Monee, IL
09 March 2020